# The ANIMALS of FARTHING WOOD

## COLIN DANN

Illustrations by Jacqueline Tettmar

MODERN
CLASSICS

**MODERN CLASSICS**

### *For Janet*

First published in Great Britain 1979 by William Heinemann Ltd
This edition published 2016 by Egmont UK Limited
The Yellow Building, 1 Nicholas Road, London W11 4AN

Text Copyright © 1979 Colin Dann
Illustrations copyright © 1979 Jacqueline Tettmar
Cover illustration copyright © 2016 Sam Usher

The moral rights of the author, illustrator and cover illustrator have been asserted

ISBN 978 1 4052 8180 5

www.egmont.co.uk

A CIP catalogue record for this title is available from the British Library

Printed and bound in Great Britain by the CPI Group

63305/1

Rabbit: Pim/Shutterstock.com
Fox: Juli Gin/Shutterstock.com

MIX
Paper
FSC FSC® C018306

# CONTENTS

PART ONE: ESCAPE FROM DANGER

| I | Drought | 3 |
|---|---|---|
| II | The Assembly | 11 |
| III | Toad's Story | 22 |
| IV | Preparations | 34 |
| V | Farewell to Farthing Wood | 41 |
| VI | The Long Drink | 50 |
| VII | Two Narrow Escapes | 57 |
| VIII | First Camp | 66 |
| IX | Fire! | 84 |
| X | Confrontation | 96 |
| XI | The Storm | 112 |
| XII | Trapped! | 122 |
| XIII | Pursued | 134 |
| XIV | The Copse | 143 |
| XV | The River | 153 |
| XVI | A New Leader | 167 |
| XVII | Which Way? | 178 |
| XVIII | The Butcher Bird | 186 |

PART TWO: JOURNEY TO WHITE DEER PARK

| XIX | Fox Alone | 199 |
| XX | The Vixen | 211 |
| XXI | Vixen Decides | 222 |
| XXII | The Hunt | 230 |
| XXIII | Fox to the Rescue | 242 |
| XXIV | Reunited | 256 |
| XXV | The Celebration | 272 |
| XXVI | The Motorway | 282 |
| XXVII | Some Comforting Words | 303 |
| XXVIII | The Deathly Hush | 309 |
| XXIX | The Naturalist | 320 |
| XXX | The Church | 332 |
| XXXI | The Final Lap | 352 |
| | Epilogue: In The Park | 366 |

# PART ONE

## Escape from Danger

# I

# DROUGHT

For most of the animals of Farthing Wood a new day was beginning. The sun had set, and the hot, moistureless air was at last cooling a little. It was dusk, and for Badger, time for activity.

Leaving his comfortable underground sleeping chamber, lined with dry leaves and grass, he ambled along the connecting tunnel to the exit and paused, snuffling the air warily. Moving his head in all directions, his powerful sense of smell soon told him no danger was present, and he emerged from the hole. Badger's set was on a sloping piece of ground in a clearing of the wood, and the earth here was now as hard as biscuit. No rain had fallen on Farthing Wood for nearly four weeks.

Badger noticed Tawny Owl perched on a low branch of a

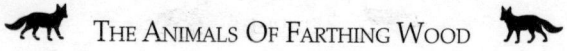 

beech tree a few yards away, so he trotted over for a few words while he sharpened his claws on the trunk. 'Still no rain,' he remarked unnecessarily, as he stretched upward and raked the bark. 'I think it's been hotter than ever today.'

Tawny Owl opened one eye and ruffled his feathers a little. 'They've filled in the pond,' he said bluntly.

Badger stopped scratching and dropped to all fours. His striped face took on a look of alarm. 'I could hear the bulldozer moving around in the distance, all day long,' he said. 'But this is serious. Very serious.' He shook his head. 'I really don't know where we'll go to drink now.'

Tawny Owl did not reply. His head had swivelled, and he was looking intently under the trees behind him. Presently Badger's snout began snuffling again as he caught the scent of Fox, who was approaching them.

Fox's brush started to wag in greeting as he spotted his friends. He could guess from Badger's worried expression that he had heard the news.

'I've just been over there to look,' he called as he ran up. 'Not a drop of water left. You wouldn't know there had ever been a pond.'

'What can they be doing?' asked Badger.

'Levelling the earth, I suppose,' said Fox. 'They've cut some more of the trees down as well.'

Badger shook his head again. 'How long before . . .?' he began.

'Before they reach us?' interrupted Tawny Owl. 'Could be this summer. Human destruction moves swiftly.'

'What do you think, Fox?'

'Tawny Owl's right. In another year all of this could be concrete and brick. In five years they've dug up all the grassland, and cut down three-quarters of the wood. There are human dwellings on either side of us. We've been driven back and driven back, so that we're like a bunch of rabbits cowering in the last stalks of corn in the middle of a cornfield, listening to the approach of the harvester, and knowing we've very soon got to run.'

'And now they've taken our last proper water-hole,' groaned Badger. 'What can we do?'

'We still have the stream at the foot of the hill,' said Fox.

'It must be just a muddy trickle by now,' retorted Badger. 'With all the animals in the wood using it, it'll be dry in a few days.'

Tawny Owl rustled his wings impatiently. 'Why don't you go and look?' he suggested. 'There are sure to be others there. Perhaps someone will have an idea.'

Without another word he jumped off the branch, flapped into flight and disappeared.

The last faint rays of daylight were gone as Badger and Fox descended the slope into the depths of the wood. Everywhere the ground was baked hard, and even the quivering leaves on the trees sounded brittle and dusty. Only the darkness around them was any comfort: that familiar, noiseless darkness that enfolded the timid animals of Farthing Wood in a cloak of security.

Badger and Fox trotted along, shoulder to shoulder, each wondering what they would find at the stream. Neither animal spoke. Eventually they could see some movement ahead. A number of creatures were jostling together on the banks of the stream, milling about in a rather purposeless, disconcerted manner. There was a family of fieldmice, and about half a dozen rabbits, all of whom scuttled away when they saw Fox approaching.

A number of hedgehogs remained. Some of them stood their ground, but the majority quickly rolled themselves up, projecting their spines in a precautionary way against the two most powerful inhabitants of the wood.

'Tut, tut. Don't be alarmed,' Badger reassured them. 'Fox and I have merely come to examine the stream. It's the only piece of water left to us now, you know.' He smiled kindly. 'We're all in this together – big and small alike. There must be no . . . er . . . er . . .' He broke off, unable to find the right words.

'Differences of opinion?' suggested Fox, with just the beginnings of a grin.

'Er . . . quite,' replied Badger. 'How diplomatic.' He peered forward over the bank, his weak eyes straining in the darkness. 'Oh dear!' he exclaimed. 'Oh dear, oh dear!'

At this point the rolled-up hedgehogs unrolled themselves,

and the young ones began to squeak excitedly: 'It's dried up!
All dried up!'

From under the trees, and from the entrance to their
burrows, the rabbits edged forward again, wondering what the
clever Fox and experienced Badger would decide to do. One by
one they seated themselves, still a little nervously, on the bank,
keeping in a group as they watched Fox and Badger discussing
the situation.

The fieldmice returned too, and pretty soon their noses,
like the rabbits', were all twitching expectantly.

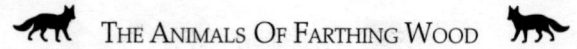 

'There will have to be an Assembly,' Fox was saying. 'Everyone must attend. We ought to discuss this problem together, so that everyone will be able to put forward their ideas.'

Badger nodded. 'Yes. It must be held without delay,' he said. 'The situation is critical. Our lives are in danger.' He looked earnestly at Fox. 'I suggest no later than tomorrow night – at twelve,' he said.

Fox was agreeable. 'Will you chair the meeting?' he asked.

'Certainly. Unless Tawny Owl . . .'

'Oh, Owl! He probably won't even come. You know what he's like. Can't bear anyone else to arrange anything,' grumbled Fox.

'He *must* come,' insisted Badger. 'I'll tell him so myself. When an Assembly is called, the whole of Farthing Wood has to attend. Five years ago, my father chaired the Assembly that was called when the humans first started to build here. There were more of us then, of course. Farthing Wood was almost a forest in those days, with a large stretch of grassland all round it, and also . . .'

'Yes, yes,' Fox cut in, a little impatiently. He knew Badger loved to talk about 'The Old Days', but once he started it was sometimes very difficult to divert him. 'We know what it used to be like,' he said. 'But *we're* concerned about what it's like at present. *My* father,' he added, in case Badger was offended, 'was at that Assembly. But no good came of it. What could

mere animals do?'

'So true,' mumbled Badger sadly. 'But this time, unless we're all to die of thirst, something has *got* to be done.'

He turned towards the group of onlookers. 'Fox and I are agreed that an Assembly of the animals of Farthing Wood must be called,' he announced. 'You should all arrive at my set by twelve o'clock tomorrow night.' He began to digress again. 'There's plenty of room for everyone. Once upon a time many families of badgers lived there, but now I'm the sole survivor . . .' He sighed reminiscently. 'The last of a long line of Farthing Wood badgers, going back for centuries.'

'We must spread the word to the others,' Fox cut in quickly. 'You rabbits must find Hare and his family, and, fieldmice, you can pass the word to the voles. Badger knows where to find Weasel, and I myself will look out for Adder and the lizards. Any of you who are about during the daytime can tell the squirrels about it.'

'What about the birds?' asked one of the hedgehogs.

'We'll leave them to Tawny Owl,' replied Fox. 'Badger was right – he must play his part.'

'I'll tell him when I get back home,' said Badger. 'Now don't forget, all of you. Twelve o'clock tomorrow night.'

The smaller animals scurried away, the younger ones chattering excitedly and feeling important because of the duties entrusted to them.

Badger turned to Fox. 'You'd better impress on Adder,' he

warned, 'that we haven't arranged this meeting to provide him with a wonderful opportunity to gorge himself. Remind him that every creature attending an Assembly is strictly bound by the Oath of Common Safety.'

'Your father introduced that, I believe?' Fox queried.

'He did,' replied Badger seriously. 'It was very necessary, to prevent the possibility of bullying or fighting. Do you think Adder will listen to you?'

'As much as he ever does,' Fox replied evasively. He shrugged. 'But I think even Adder respects the rules of the Assembly.'

They stood a little longer; then Badger turned to go. Fox called him back. 'What about Mole?' he asked.

'Oh, don't worry about him,' Badger managed to laugh. 'Once he hears all the feet running overhead, he'll soon surface to discover what all the commotion is about.'

Fox grinned. 'Till tomorrow then,' he said.

'Till tomorrow,' said Badger.

## II

# THE ASSEMBLY

By eleven o'clock Badger felt that everything was ready. Since he had risen, he had been busy enlarging one of the unoccupied chambers of his set to a size which would accommodate everyone who was likely to attend the Assembly. Even with his powerful digging claws, it had been exceptionally hard work. The soil was dry and hard, and he had to remove all the loose earth into one of the unused corridors. Then, outside, he had gathered together several mounds of dry leaves, and dragged them down, backwards, into the chamber, spreading them evenly over the floor.

When he had finished, he had sallied out again, this time to the borders of the wood. Underneath the hedgerows he gathered together a number of glow-worms, which he tucked into the thickest parts of his fur, in order to transport them back in bulk. Back at the set, he stowed the little insects at intervals along the entrance corridor, and with those he had left over he illuminated the Assembly Chamber, placing them in tiny clusters, just as he had watched his father do before him.

At length, satisfied with his evening's work, he left his set again to dig up a few roots and bulbs for his supper, which, garnished with a number of beetles, made a welcome meal. It was now eleven-thirty, and Badger decided to take a short nap before the other animals started to arrive.

He did not seem to have been dozing in his sleeping-chamber for more than a few minutes when he heard the old church clock strike twelve in the distance, and simultaneously he heard voices outside. He jumped up and wriggled his way quickly to the exit. It was Weasel, who had arrived with Fox.

'Go straight down the corridor on your left, Weasel,' said Badger. 'After a little way it turns to the right. Take the first turning left after that bend into the Assembly Chamber, and make yourself comfortable. I'll join you in a moment.'

Weasel followed his directions and the glow-worm lights, and had only just disappeared from view when more voices could be heard approaching. They belonged to the rabbits and Hare and his family. Just behind them came the fieldmice.

'Fox, will you go down and keep Weasel company?' Badger asked. 'I'd better stay here to direct the others.'

'Of course,' said Fox and, bowing his head, he eased

himself into the tunnel.

'This way, everyone!' called Badger. 'Straight in there.' He used his snout to indicate the entrance. 'Just follow the little lights.'

The rabbits, in their particularly timid manner, were unable to decide on who should be the first one down the hole, and they began quarrelling until Hare, with some impatience, said, 'I'll lead.' He nudged his mate encouragingly. 'Come on dear. And you, children! Our cousins and the fieldmice will be right behind us.'

The lizards were next on the scene, though Badger did not notice them until they were darting around him like individual threads of quick-silver. After the squirrels, hedgehogs and voles had arrived, only Adder and the birds were missing.

The latter arrived together, led by Tawny Owl. He had rounded up Pheasant and his mate, and even Kestrel, who spent most of his time hovering high in the air above Farthing Wood, had agreed to attend.

'I didn't deign to invite the other birds,' explained Tawny Owl. 'Blackbirds, starlings, pigeons, thrushes – they're all half-domesticated. They thrive when humans are around. The more humans there are, the better they like it. No purpose in them coming. They don't really represent Farthing Wood at all.'

'Do we have to go in there?' Pheasant asked Badger in some alarm. 'Soiling our feathers with all that dirt?'

'My set is quite spotless!' Badger retorted. 'I've spent all evening getting it ready.'

'We haven't come here to admire each other's plumage,' Tawny Owl said shortly. 'If you haven't anything more to offer the Assembly ~~than that,~~ you might as well not have come.'

'I didn't say anything about not attending the Assembly,' said Pheasant in a small voice, and without further ado he walked into the hole with his mate, followed by Kestrel.

'Vain as a peacock,' muttered Tawny Owl, and Badger shook his head.

'You go in, Owl,' he said presently. 'I'm only waiting for Adder, and then we're complete.'

Just then Fox's head reappeared at the opening. 'Mole's just dropped in,' he announced with a grin. 'He came direct. Dug a long passage from his tunnel straight into the Assembly Chamber.'

Badger laughed. 'I'd forgotten Mole,' he admitted. 'Hallo, here's Adder.'

'Good evening, gentlemen,' Adder whispered, as he slid to a halt. His forked tongue flickered all around. 'I trust I'm not late?'

'I suppose someone had to be last,' remarked Fox pointedly. 'Well, after you, Badger.'

Inside the Assembly Chamber, the expectant faces of the young animals contrasted strangely with the solemnity of their seniors in the faint greenish glow. Badger took his place in the centre of the room, flanked by Fox and Tawny Owl as his self-

appointed committee. The other animals spread themselves evenly round the Chamber against the hard earth walls. Most of the fieldmice and voles and rabbits took care not to sit anywhere near Adder or Weasel.

Without ceremony, Badger opened the meeting. 'This is only the second Assembly called in my lifetime,' he began, 'and for most of you it will be the first you've attended. My father called the last Assembly five years ago, when the humans first moved in to lay waste to our homes. In those days there was a Farthing Heath, as well as Farthing Wood. I don't have to tell anybody what happened to the heath that once surrounded the whole of our wood.'

'Gone. All gone,' hissed Adder from the corner where he had carefully coiled himself up, and was resting his head on the topmost coil.

'All gone!' echoed the voles.

'But the humans weren't content with that,' Badger went on bitterly. 'They began to fell our trees. They continued to do so, at regular destructive intervals, until what was once a large wood had been cut back to the present sad remnant, not much larger than a copse.'

'What do you think will happen, Badger?' asked one of the rabbits timidly.

'Happen?' Badger echoed. 'Why, the same thing that has *been* happening. They will cut down *more* trees, and build *more* houses, and *shops*, probably a school, and offices and roads, and ghastly concrete posts and signs everywhere, faster and faster and faster still, until eventually . . .' He broke off with a despairing shake of his head.

'Until eventually we are destroyed with the wood.' Tawny Owl finished the sentence with determined pessimism.

'And all this – how long will it take?' asked Hare.

'The very question I myself asked yesterday,' nodded Badger. 'Though all the time I suppose I knew the answer. We animals can never accurately forecast what the humans will do; we only know what they are capable of doing. And they're capable of cutting down the remainder of Farthing Wood in twelve months, perhaps less.'

There was a stunned silence for a moment, then one or two animals coughed nervously. Kestrel began to preen his wings. His livelihood was not as completely threatened as the others' by the advancing destruction.

'And on top of all this,' Badger said in pained tones, 'comes a drought.'

'The very last straw,' said Mole.

'Merely accelerating the end,' Tawny Owl muttered, more to himself than to anyone else.

'Friends, we are up against a brick wall,' Badger intoned with deadly seriousness. 'Leaving aside the threat of our extermination, if we don't, in the next couple of days, find a safe, secluded place where we can all go to drink, we're going to find ourselves in the worst kind of distress.' He coughed huskily, already feeling his throat to be unusually dry. 'This is why I've asked all of you to join me tonight. The greater the gathering, the better the chance we have of finding a solution to end our immediate danger. So I entreat you all: don't be afraid to speak up. Size and strength have no bearing on anyone's importance at an Assembly. The only important fact is that all of us live in Farthing Wood, and so we all need each other's help.'

The smaller animals seemed to receive some encouragement from Badger's remarks, and began to murmur to each other and shake their heads in bewilderment. But none of them seemed to have any definite ideas.

Badger looked at Tawny Owl, and then at Fox, but they were both scanning the circle of faces to see who was going to be the first to make a suggestion.

'Surely you birds can help us?' prompted Weasel. 'You cover a wider stretch of country than we ground dwellers. Can any of you say where the nearest water is to be found outside our boundaries?'

Pheasant's dowdy mate shifted uncomfortably, as she felt many pairs of eyes turning towards her. 'Say something, Pheasant,' she whispered to him.

'My mate and I don't really venture outside the wood,' he said hurriedly. 'Being game birds, there is always the danger of being shot at.' He thrust out his gaudy breast. 'I'm told we're considered to be a great culinary delicacy by all well-bred humans,' he added, almost smugly.

'Kestrel, can you offer a more worthwhile piece of information?' Badger enquired, directing a withering glance at Pheasant. 'Of all the birds present, you spend more time than any outside the wood.'

Kestrel stopped preening and looked up with his habitual piercing glare. 'Yes, I can,' he said evenly. 'But I doubt if it will be of any real use. There's a sort of marshy pond on the enclosed army land on the other side of the trunk road. I haven't hunted over there for some weeks – it's never very rewarding at the best of times – and for all I know that, too, could have dried up. Apart from that, the most secluded expanse of water is a goldfish pond in a garden near the old church.'

'But that's in the old village, well over a mile away!' exclaimed Badger. 'Is there *nowhere* else?'

'Oh yes,' Kestrel replied without concern. 'There's a swimming-pool in one of the gardens on the new estate.'

'How close?'

'I suppose, for you, about fifteen minutes' travelling.'

'There'd be no cover: no cover at all,' Fox warned.

'I know,' Badger answered worriedly. 'But it's nearer. The smaller animals could never walk as far as the church and then back again, all in one night.'

'We could try!' piped up one of the fieldmice.

'Of course you could, and you would be very brave to do so,' said Badger kindly. 'But that would only be one journey. If this drought continues we'll all have to make several journeys to drink what we need.'

'The only suggestion I can make,' said Hare, 'is for the larger animals to carry the smaller – as many as we can manage.'

'Yesss,' drawled Adder. 'I could carry several little mice and voles in my jaws, and I should be so gentle, they wouldn't feel a thing.' His tongue flickered excitedly. 'I should so enjoy carrying the plump ones,' he went on dreamily. 'And Owl could manage a young rabbit or two in his talons, couldn't you, Owl?'

'You're not looking at the situation in at all the right frame of mind, Adder,' admonished Badger, looking with some sympathy at the smaller animals, who were huddling together as far away from Adder as they could manage without actually bolting into the tunnel. 'You're merely thinking, as usual,' he went on, 'of a way in which you can benefit personally from it. I know what you're thinking, and it won't do. It won't do at all. We're a community, facing a dangerous crisis. You know the Oath.'

'Just a suggestion,' hissed Adder, with a scarcely disguised leer. He was quite undismayed by the effect his words had had on the fieldmice and voles.

'Now calm down, mice,' soothed Badger. 'Calm down, rabbits. You'll come to no harm in my set.'

When the Assembly appeared to be more relaxed again, one of the squirrels said, 'Couldn't we dig for water?'

Badger looked towards Mole. The latter shook his black velvet head. 'No, I don't think it's really possible,' he said. 'We'd only be wasting our energy, I'm afraid.'

There was silence then, while every animal cudgelled his brains for a way out of the difficulty. The seconds ticked past.

Suddenly, a voice was heard calling from the passage outside. 'Hallo! Who's there? Who's there?'

Weasel ran to the tunnel. 'I can see something moving,' he said. Then he called out, 'This is Weasel! The other animals are here, too . . . Good Heavens, it's Toad!' he exclaimed.

'I've been looking all over the place for everyone,' said the newcomer, as he stumbled into the Chamber. 'I've been so worried: I thought you'd all deserted the wood. Then I heard voices.' He sat down to regain his breath. 'And I noticed the lights.'

'Toad, whatever happened to you?' Badger cried, as all the animals gathered round him. 'We'd given you up for lost. Wherever have you been? We haven't seen you since last spring. And you're so thin! My dear chap, tell us what has happened.'

'I . . . I've been on a long journey,' Toad said. 'I'll tell you all about it when I've got my breath back.'

'Have you had anything to eat recently?' Badger asked with concern.

'Oh yes – I'm not hungry,' he replied. 'Just tired.'

The heaving of his speckled chest gradually quietened as he recovered from his exertions. The other animals waited patiently for him to begin. He looked wearily round his audience.

'I was captured, you know,' he explained. 'It happened last spring, at the pond. They . . . they took me a long way away – oh, miles away! I thought I would never see any of you again.'

He paused, and some of the animals made soothing, sympathetic noises.

'Eventually, though, I managed to escape,' Toad went on. 'I was lucky. Of course, I knew I had to make my way back here – to the pond where I was born. So I started out that very day. And ever since, except during the winter months, I've managed to get a little nearer: little by little, mile by mile, covering as much ground as I was able to each day.'

Fox looked at Badger, and Badger nodded sadly.

'Toad, old fellow, I . . . I'm afraid there's bad news for you,' Fox said with difficulty. 'Very bad news.'

Toad looked up quickly. 'What . . . what is it?' he faltered.

'Your pond has gone. They've filled it in!'

## III

# Toad's Story

Toad looked at Fox with an expression of disbelieving horror. 'But . . . but . . . they couldn't!' he whispered. 'I was born there. My parents were born there . . . and all my relatives, and acquaintances. And every spring we have a reunion. Toads all around leave their land homes and make for their birthplace. They couldn't take that away from us!' He looked pathetically from one sad face to another, almost compelling someone to deny this awful piece of information; but he received no answer.

'Filled *all* of it in? Is it . . . quite gone?' Toad's voice shook.

'I'm afraid so,' Badger mumbled. 'But, you know, there was very little left of it really. With this drought the water had nearly all dried up anyway.' He knew his words were of no comfort.

'What about the other toads?' Toad asked hoarsely.

'I think they had probably left the pond before this happened,' Fox said encouragingly. 'After all, it is May now . . .'

'Yes, yes,' Toad agreed morosely. 'I'm late. It's not spring any more, really. Not what we toads call spring.'

'This drought,' Badger rejoined, 'is a danger for all of us. That's why I called this Assembly. There's *no* water left, Toad. None anywhere in Farthing Wood. We just don't know what to do.'

Toad did not reply. His downcast face took on a new expression. He looked considerably more hopeful. 'I've got it!' he exclaimed excitedly. 'We'll leave! All of us! If I could do it, so can all of you!'

'Leave Farthing Wood?' Badger queried with some alarm. 'How could we? What do you mean?'

'Yes, yes! Let me explain.' Toad stood up in his excitement. 'I know the very place to go to. Oh, it's miles away, of course. But I'm sure we could manage it, together!'

The other animals began to chatter all at once, and Badger completely failed to quieten them.

'We must face the facts!' Toad cried. 'What you've just told me about the pond has brought our danger home to me with a jolt. Farthing Wood is finished; in another couple of years it won't even exist. We must all find a *new* home. Now – before it's too late!'

The other voices broke off. Toad's voice dropped to a whisper. 'The Nature Reserve,' he announced dramatically.

'We shall all go to the Nature Reserve, where we can live in peace again. And *I* shall be your guide.' He looked round triumphantly.

'Dear, dear! I don't know.' Badger shook his striped head. 'You'd better tell us all about it, Toad. I don't know if it's a good idea. If it's so far . . .'

'Go on, Toad,' Fox broke in. 'Tell us about your adventure, right from the beginning.'

Toad sank back into his accustomed comfortable squat, and cleared his throat.

'You'll recall how last spring was very warm – in March particularly,' he began. 'Well, one weekend there were a tremendous number of humans at the pond; young ones with their horrible nets and glass jars – and a lot of them had brought their parents along. Everything in the pond was in a panic; there seemed to be no escape anywhere. The young humans were even wading out nearly to the middle of the pond in their eagerness to capture us. I remember I dived underwater and tried to hide in the mud on the bottom. So did a lot of others. But it was no use. They found me; and I was prodded into a jam-jar and carried away.'

'How awful for you,' one of the lizards commiserated. 'They come after us, too, with those stifling glass jars that are made specially slippery, so that you can hardly grip the bottom.'

'Ghastly things,' muttered Toad. 'I must have been kept in it for three or four hours, I should think. I was submitted to

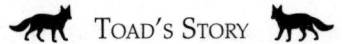 

the indignity of watching my captors eat their food by the side of *my* pond, while I was left out in the sun, trying frustratedly to scale the sides of the jar, without so much as a leaf to protect me. If the weather had been any hotter, I'm sure I would have dried up.'

'I *like* to sunbathe, myself,' said Adder. 'But, of course, you amphibians have never really learnt to live comfortably on dry land.'

'Just the same as you reptiles can't adapt to swimming and diving!' retorted Toad.

'I can swim when I have to,' Adder returned.

'Well, well,' nodded Badger. 'What happened next, Toad?'

'They took me away,' he said. 'I don't know for sure how far, because I took the opportunity of having a nap during the journey. They put me in the back of their car, and the next thing I knew I was being tipped into a glass box in their garden.'

'How long did they keep you in this glass box?' asked Fox.

'I suppose about four weeks,' replied Toad. 'They put some netting on the top as a lid, and one day their wretched cat, who was always prowling around trying to get at me, knocked it off. So I leapt as high as I could, and I managed to jump out of the box and hide behind a shed. That very night I started my journey home.

'I hadn't got very far before I decided I ought to strengthen myself with a good meal. All the humans had ever given me was mealworms; tasty enough, but so boring without some change to relieve the diet. I still think you can't beat a juicy earthworm, fresh and moist from its burrow.'

'Hear, hear!' cried Mole feelingly. 'Nothing like them! I could eat them till I burst. Never tire of 'em.'

'It's a wonder there are any left at all, with your appetite,' remarked Tawny Owl.

'Oh, nonsense, there are plenty for everyone,' Mole justified himself a little shamefacedly. 'Though during this dry weather I have my work cut out finding them. They do go down so deep, you know.'

'Yes, of course,' said Toad. 'Anyway, when I had eaten my fill, my first problem was to get out of that garden. The great difficulty lay in getting round the wall. There was no wooden fence with convenient gaps in it – just a stone wall all round the garden. However, I was determined not to be disheartened, and there was one thing in my favour. The wall had bits of pebble and flint stuck into it – for decoration perhaps, I don't know – and I knew I could use these projecting pieces to climb up.

'It took so long, however, that I was sure daylight would break before I had reached the top, particularly as I fell off about four times, and had to start again. But I knew I had to get up that wall, even to have a chance of setting out for Farthing Wood.

'Well, I got to the top eventually, and walked along to the end of the wall. By that time it was just starting to get light, and I knew I would have to jump for it. I looked all round for a plant or something to break my fall, but there was nothing; only

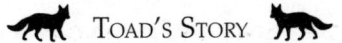 

concrete all around. Of course, I couldn't possibly risk jumping on to that, so I had to lower my legs over the edge, and climb down the pebbles again. Fortunately, it didn't take as long as going up, and I was just thinking I could probably jump the last few inches when that horrible cat came out of the house. I pressed myself close to the wall and froze.'

Toad broke off, and contemplated his enthralled audience. The room was completely, utterly silent, so that you could have heard a pine needle drop. The young squirrels had wrapped themselves cosily in their mothers' thick tails, and the fieldmice and voles were now all bunched together in a large, furry mass, which was animated only by a score or so of quivering pink noses. Every animal gave Toad his rapt attention. Only Adder appeared to be taking no further interest in the proceedings. He had allowed his head to drop forward, but whether he was asleep or not would have been difficult to say.

'Would you believe me,' Toad went on quietly, 'if I told you I stayed in that spot all day, trying to look like another pebble? I couldn't risk climbing down any further because there was nowhere to hide, and if the cat had seen me it would have been the end of me.

'Fortunately, the day was reasonably cool, and as soon as it was safely dark, I let myself drop the rest of the way to the ground, and then crawled and hopped as far as I could away from the house. There were only one or two other houses nearby, and once I'd got past them I began to feel much freer. My sense of direction told me what course to take, and I kept on down to the end of the road. This was sealed off by a sort of ditch, and behind that a fence. I knew I was on the right route, and those two things didn't present much of a barrier to me. I hadn't gone far on the other side when I realized I must be in some sort of private park, because the fence stretched as far as I could see in both directions.

'Now I don't know exactly why it was, but the more I looked at that fence, the safer I felt. I suppose it was because I knew I was on the right side of it.

'It was very quiet and peaceful in there, and a lovely bright moon was shining as I made my way along, flicking up a few insects on the way. I decided to make my bed under some trees, so I scooped out a little hole in the earth, and pulled some dry leaves round me. I slept quite well during the day because, apart from the birds, no one seemed to be about.

'When it was dusk I emerged again, and continued forward. After a while, the trees gave way to some open land, and ahead of me I could sense water. You can't imagine how excited I became at that, after all those weeks without a dip. It was another bright, moonlit night, and eventually I could see a pool ahead, where the moon was reflected perfectly. As I approached I thought I could hear one or two croaks coming from the water. I realized I had not been mistaken, when the whole party of the pool's inhabitants started croaking in unison, making a tremendous racket. It was a call I couldn't place, unlike any I had heard before. They were obviously frogs – but what sort of frogs?

'As I didn't know if they were likely to be friendly, I approached the water's edge cautiously, and just watched them for a while. There seemed to be quite a number of them splashing about in the centre of the pool, and some were just floating, with their heads out of the water. These were the ones making the noise. They were blowing out their cheeks like two bubbles in their efforts to croak the loudest.

'After I had been there for a little while, they stopped croaking, and seemed to decide amongst themselves that it was time to leave the water. They began to make for the shore, some swimming in my direction. I stood my ground. As they clambered out, one of them called, "We've got a visitor. A toad."

'They all came up to have a look, remarking that they hadn't seen me before, and that the toads who shared their pond in the spring had all been gone a week or more to make their homes on land. They made quite a fuss of me when I told them my story. They explained to me that they had just left the pond to feed, and invited me to join them.

'There was no shortage of food, and we were all able to eat our fill. Although it was night-time, I was able to discover that these unusual frogs were a definite shade of green, with darker spots, and a stripe of a paler colour down the centre of the back. When we had finished eating, they asked me to join them in a swim, and I was glad to accept.

'We swam out to the centre, and rested amongst the water-weed, and I took the opportunity of asking them about the park. Their spokesman was an old, fat male who seemed to be a sort of patriarch of their society. He told me the park was called White Deer Park, and it was a Nature Reserve.'

Toad paused for effect, and there were obliging murmurs of, 'Ah' and 'Of course – the Nature Reserve.'

'We have heard of these Nature Reserves,' said Badger. 'Do they, in fact, reserve nature?'

'Exactly as the name implies,' Toad answered emphatically. 'My friends the frogs told me all about it. A Nature Reserve is a piece of land – or water – of exceptional value and interest because of the rare animals or plants – or both – in it. There is a certain breed of human called a Naturalist, who, unlike most ordinary humans, spends his time learning about, and caring for, animals and plants. Their prime consideration is our well-being and safety. The frogs told me these Naturalists usually work in groups, and it was one of these groups that decided that *their* homeland, White Deer Park, was too valuable to be left unprotected. So, about three years ago, it was sealed off, designated a Reserve, and now no humans are permitted entry to it without a special pass. Even then, they may not remove any animal or plant from the Reserve whatsoever.'

'It sounds wonderful,' said Hare's mate. 'Peace and security all the time. No hiding. No running away. No guns!'

'And that's not all,' Toad went on. 'The Reserve is under

the permanent care of one of the Naturalists, who is called a Warden. The animals' health and safety is in his keeping, and he patrols the Reserve to ensure their protection.

'Apparently, in the frogs' park there is a herd of albino deer which is unique. They themselves are a colony of rare frogs, called Edible Frogs by the humans, although luckily nobody is allowed to eat them. There is also an unusual type of water-plant in their pond, and they believe one or two rare butterflies feed in the Park. But they assured me that there is also a good representation of the commoner animals, like ourselves, who live there and benefit from the protection.'

'Why, it sounds like Paradise,' breathed Badger. 'I can't think why you wanted to leave it.' Fox looked at him meaningfully, and Badger went on quickly, 'That is, of course, I understand why you did. But . . . but . . . tell me, Toad, how far is it? It's taken you months to get here.'

'It's certainly a long way,' agreed Toad. 'I wouldn't deny it. I spent a week with the frogs, and then explained to them that I had to go on. Of course, they understood perfectly.'

'Is it a large park?' asked Fox.

'One of the frogs told me that he'd heard it was about five hundred acres, which, as you can imagine, would more than hold all of Farthing Wood! And I mean the old wood – as it used to be.

'Anyway, it took about another week to cross the park completely. Then, every day after that, I pressed on, never staying in one place more than a day. I travelled mostly in the dark hours, finding a convenient hiding-place during the day-time. I ate what I could on the move . . . and so the weeks went on. I must tell you that I was constantly buoyed up by the thought that every day, every step or hop, brought me nearer to my friends.'

'Good old Toad,' said Badger under his breath.

'When I noticed the weather was beginning to get colder I tried to hurry. I could sense there wasn't a tremendous distance left, and I wanted to get home before the winter really arrived. But I knew if I didn't eat properly, and the winter overtook me, I would die. So I compromised, I kept on going, but at a more leisurely pace, eating as much as I could find every night. Finally, I knew it was time to hibernate. The other frogs and toads, and lizards too, that I had encountered during the previous week or so, had been looking for a comfortable roost, and I found one on some farm land.

'I chose a grassy bank, by a ditch where there was plenty of cover. Food was becoming scarce by now, and I spent all day picking up what I could. Then, as night was approaching, I dug myself a nice hole under a large stone, and settled into that. It was really quite cold by then, and I felt so sleepy that I went out like a light as soon as I closed my eyes.

'Well, there I stayed until the warm spell at the beginning of March woke me up, and then I had a good meal at an ants' nest, and set off again. And . . . the rest you know, really.'

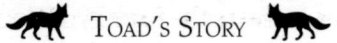 

'A brave fellow indeed,' remarked Badger warmly.

'Very courageous,' agreed Weasel.

'What tremendous perseverance!' commented Fox. 'I have always admired you toads for that. Once started on something, you just won't be diverted!'

'I'd do it again, gladly, if you'd all come with me,' said Toad stoutly.

'That's fighting talk!' cried Badger. 'How about it, everyone? Shall Toad be our guide to a new home?'

'And a fresh start for everybody,' Toad added, 'away from the threat we've been living under here for so long?'

There was a deafening chorus of agreement.

'Then it's farewell to Farthing Wood?'

There were more shouts of approval. The animals were excited now.

'Better to say, "Welcome to White Deer Park",' said Mole.

'Now Mole, don't get carried away,' said Badger kindly. 'We haven't even taken our first step yet, you know.'

Mole grinned contritely. Badger looked around the chamber.

'Are there any dissenters?' he asked formally, and studied every individual face. There was no reply.

'Then I take it as unanimous. We go to White Deer Park!'

# IV

# PREPARATIONS

There was a tremendous hubbub as all the animals started chattering at once, and the young animals ran around chanting: 'White Deer Park! White Deer Park!' in their shrill voices, as if they had already forgotten the existence of Farthing Wood. Even Adder evinced enough interest to uncoil himself and slither towards Toad to ask him for more details about the colony of frogs. He had decided these must be particularly succulent if even the humans considered them edible.

'Really, Adder, can't you forget your stomach for one minute?' asked Toad testily. 'Besides, you must promise not to hunt the frogs. They're very rare and important. We don't want to be accused of harbouring a viper in our midst, you know.'

Adder scowled, his red eyes turned to a deeper hue by the

pale, greenish light in the Chamber. The pun did not amuse him.

'Quite right, Toad. We must have no ideas of that sort in our minds as we set out,' Badger agreed. 'As their prospective guests, we should be determined to be on our best behaviour. But enough of this! We have a very dangerous, harrowing journey ahead of us. We must plan! Quiet, everyone! Quiet PLEASE!

'Now, er . . . Fox, how shall we begin? I'm rather a sedentary animal. I'm afraid I haven't any real experience of this sort of thing. But you go further afield.'

'I suggest we begin by asking Toad what sort of terrain we shall have to cover on the journey,' said Tawny Owl drily.

'H'm!' Badger cleared his throat. 'Yes, of course . . . I was just coming to that. Toad?'

'To be absolutely truthful,' said Toad, 'because I don't want you to have any illusions, I can't offer you much comfort. The country we have to cross is almost all hostile. We begin by going through the housing estate, thus skirting the army land . . .'

'Hold on,' interrupted Badger. 'That's a bit risky, isn't it?'

'Well, of course we should travel at night,' said Toad.

'But supposing there were cats about? Or dogs? There might be dogs loose.'

'*I* came that way,' said Toad, a little offended. 'The army land is more dangerous. They have shooting practice – and bombs.'

'I think I must appeal to you birds,' Badger said. 'None of you, I know, is obliged to join us land animals. But we shall need you for reconnaissance. You can fly on ahead – spy out the land, as it were – and tell us if it's safe to proceed. What do you say?'

'I can't see in the dark!' retorted Pheasant.

'I'll scout for you during the day,' said Kestrel, 'but only Tawny Owl can help you at night.'

'Will you help, Owl?' asked Badger.

'Of course I will,' said Tawny Owl, very much on his dignity. 'How could you think otherwise? I brought the birds to the Assembly, didn't I?'

'Thank you, my feathered friends,' said Badger, looking so pointedly at Pheasant that he turned away and pretended to be passing a remark to his mate.

'If we're all to travel together,' said Fox, 'we shall have to do so at a speed that *everyone* will be able to maintain comfortably, from the largest to the smallest.'

'From the swiftest to the slowest,' corrected Badger. 'Who is the slowest of us?'

'Mole!' a dozen voices shouted accusingly.

'I can walk as fast as Toad,' Mole said, a little hurt.

'Not overland,' said Toad. 'We shan't be digging tunnels, you know.'

'Never mind, Mole,' said Badger sympathetically. 'We're all made in different ways. It's not your fault. None of us can dig as fast as you can.'

'We don't seem to be getting very far,' Tawny Owl broke in impatiently. 'We haven't got beyond Farthing Wood yet.'

'I think we should go through the estate, as Toad says,' remarked Fox. 'We shall all need to drink our fill where we can. Kestrel will have to direct us to the swimming-pool he mentioned.'

'Very well,' Badger conceded. 'Then that is our first objective. But we must aim to be well clear of the estate by daylight.'

'How are *we* to manage?' asked Pheasant. 'We're not nocturnal like Owl and most of you animals. We can't fly at night.'

'You'll have to follow me,' said Tawny Owl. 'You'll be able to see *me*, I suppose?'

'But how will Kestrel find his way to the swimming-pool?'

'I shall manage,' said Kestrel. 'Don't forget the estate is well lit. I shall fly slowly, ahead of the main party, and stop at the pool, where I shall hover as a signal, until the rest arrive.'

'Excellent,' said Badger. 'Now, Toad, would you care to continue?'

'Well, once we've left the estate behind,' Toad went on, 'and, remember, we have to cross the trunk road on the way – we have a long stretch of farmland to pass through; lots of fields and orchards. That shouldn't be too difficult at night. After that we come to the river. If the drought holds, that won't be much of an obstacle. Then it gets more difficult. But I can tell you more about what's ahead as we go on.'

'Yes, that's the best plan,' agreed Badger. 'We'll cross our bridges as we come to them.'

'Well, let's hope we come to one when we reach the river,' Hare said jocularly. 'I'm no water lover.'

Everyone laughed at this, and when the laughter had died down, one of the voles piped up: 'When do we start?'

'At once,' replied Badger. 'That is, tomorrow night. We all need a good rest first, so that we can start refreshed.'

Some of the animals started to edge towards the door, feeling that the meeting was over. 'We haven't quite finished yet,' Badger called to them. 'There are various officers to appoint. We've decided Toad is to be our guide. Kestrel and Owl will go ahead as scouts. But we need a leader; someone who is courageous, and able to make quick decisions. I can't think of anyone better than you, Fox.'

Fox showed his appreciation by wagging his tail. 'I, in turn,' he replied, 'should like to nominate you as quartermaster, Badger. With your good sense applied to food, I'm sure we shall all have enough to eat every day.'

'I'm most obliged to you, Fox,' he said. 'But I beseech all of you to fill your stomachs well tomorrow, before we meet. We can't know for sure when we shall eat next. Now are there any other points we haven't discussed, anyone?'

'Yes,' squeaked one of the fieldmice. 'For the benefit of the

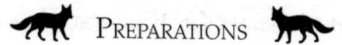 

smaller animals, I'd like to ask that we all renew the Oath tonight, in full company. I'm sure we'd feel more comfortable with the knowledge that everyone is bound by solemn oath to help all the others.'

'A worthy thought,' agreed Badger. 'We shall call this new oath, the Oath of Mutual Protection. We must all swear that, for the duration of our journey, our first consideration is for the safety of the party; in other words, the safety of each individual. Adder, I think it might be appropriate if you were the first to swear.'

'I swear,' said Adder with resignation, while actually still thinking about the Edible Frogs.

One by one the animals and birds of Farthing Wood adopted the Oath, and even the young repeated the words as their parents had done, feeling proud of the fact that they were not excluded from the solemn procedure.

'I think it would be as well,' said Badger afterwards, 'if each *group* of animals chooses a leader, who will be able to represent them at any discussions we need to have for planning our journey. They can report to Fox tomorrow, when we meet for a last talk before we leave.'

'When the village clock strikes twelve tomorrow night,' said Fox, 'I shall be under the Great Beech by the hedgerow. Meet me there.'

Badger looked all round again. No one had anything further to say. 'I now close the second Assembly of Farthing

Wood,' he intoned.

The animals filed slowly out along the tunnel to the open air. Adder brought up the rear and, feeling hungry, doused the insect lights as he went.

## V

# FAREWELL TO FARTHING WOOD

All day the bulldozers crashed forward on their path of destruction. Shrubs, young trees and undergrowth fell before the cruel onslaught of the monsters' greedy steel jaws. Old trees, stately and dignified with age, were mercilessly machined down by vicious saws. Yard by yard the forest fell back before the human despoilers; and, crouching in their burrows and tunnels, or huddled in the remaining tree-tops, or cowering under the bracken, the animals of Farthing Wood listened, shuddering, and longed for darkness.

Badger, in his cool set, heard the roaring and crashing grow nearer and nearer, but dared not stir. Fox, in his earth at the foot of the slope, panted in the heat, and waited for the chime of five

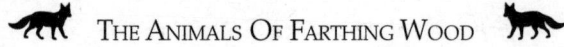 

from the village clock which, he had learnt, signalled the end of the noise, and the departure of the men.

The squirrels leapt from tree to tree, watching old homes uprooted in their wake, and Mole dug deeper and deeper down into the earth, trying to reach a point where he could no longer feel the terrible vibrations.

Under the hedgerows the hedgehogs lay among the leaves like a set of pin-cushions, while Toad and the lizards kept out of sight in the undergrowth.

Tawny Owl, in the highest branch of his favourite elm, ruffled his feathers and closed his large round eyes to the sunlight, while Pheasant and his mate squatted in the thick ground-ivy in the densest part of the wood, and kept as quiet as the fieldmice.

Adder had draped himself over a birch-stump to enjoy the sun, but when the machines had approached he had vanished in a flash into the thick bracken.

Only Kestrel, soaring high above the wood, was free to watch the advance of the humans and their machines. As he watched, he knew he had been right to join the animals' party, for pretty soon everything below would be desolation; and after that followed the brick and concrete.

So the dreadful hours passed, and only when evening came, bringing silence, was it possible for Farthing Wood, in the last few snatched hours, to sleep.

Shortly before midnight, Badger awoke and looked sorrowfully around. Never again would he sleep in his own chamber in this beloved set, where he had fond memories of his young days in the care of his parents, and which had been used by his ancestors for centuries.

For the last time, he shuffled along the corridors and paused at the exit, sniffing all round warily. He wondered if there were badgers in White Deer Park, and, if he should ever reach it, where he would construct his new set. It was hard that, at his age, he should be driven out from his birth-place and ancestral home by callous humans, who seemed to ignore the very existence of their weaker brother creatures.

He trotted out into the open and down the slope, glancing back every so often, and telling himself each time he was a sentimental fool, and that he must forget all about the old life now. He had new responsibilities, and these were more important. After all, the journey ahead was an exciting challenge; a chance for animals to match their wits against the clever and cunning humans. But it was difficult not to feel sad about leaving his old home.

A grey shape fluttered down from a tree in front of him. 'Oh, there you are, Owl!' he exclaimed with a slight jump. 'I'm just taking a last look round.'

'Doesn't do to be too sentimental, Badger,' commented Tawny Owl. 'Yet I must admit I'm glad I shall never witness the final end of the old place. At least we shall be spared that.'

At that moment the clock chimed twelve. 'There it goes!' cried Badger. 'Come on!' He set off briskly, half trotting, half ambling, through the trees. Tawny Owl flapped along almost at his side, sensing his need for company.

At the Great Beech they found Fox and Weasel, Toad and the lizards, and the rabbits. Kestrel was perched on the lowest bough, staring piercingly ahead like a sentinel. Pheasant and his mate had arrived at the meeting-place at dusk, and were dozing at the foot of the tree.

The elected leaders of the lizards and rabbits, in both cases the oldest and most experienced members of their communities, took up their positions alongside Fox and Weasel as Badger and Tawny Owl arrived.

'It's a fine night,' Fox remarked. 'But the moonlight is a

little too bright for my liking.'

'Should we postpone it?' asked Badger.

'No. I don't think that would be a good idea. The humans are too close now for safety.'

Badger nodded. 'It was a frightening day, today,' he agreed.

'I had to run for it,' squeaked Weasel. 'They came right on top of my burrow.'

The other animals were not long in arriving, but when Fox took the count he found Mole was missing.

'Confound it! Where is he?' demanded Fox with annoyance. 'We've no time to lose.'

'It's just as well, really,' remarked Adder spitefully. 'He was going to slow us all up as it was.'

Badger rounded on him angrily. 'He'd be better company than you, at any rate,' he snapped. 'We're not leaving without Mole. How could we leave him alone?'

Harsh words never bothered Adder. 'There's no need to get your fur in a bristle,' he said quietly. 'I was merely thinking of the safety of the others.'

'We'll give him until the next stroke of the clock,' Fox said. 'After that . . . well, we can't wait for ever, Badger, old fellow.'

'Give me a little time,' said Badger. 'I think I know where to find him.'

'All right. But do be quick!' warned Fox.

Badger trotted quickly off in the direction of his set, looking all round as he went for any sign of his friend.

He reached his old home again, and entered it, taking the passage leading to the Assembly Chamber. Once in there he went up to the hole through which Mole had emerged on the previous day, when he had tunnelled his way to the meeting.

'Mole!' called Badger loudly down the tunnel. 'Are you there?'

No answer.

'Mole, wake up and come out quickly! It's Badger! We're all waiting for you!'

Still no sound.

'Oh dear,' said Badger. 'Where *can* he be?' He decided to make one final attempt. Pushing his striped head right inside the tunnel, he took a deep breath and yelled, 'M-O-O-O-L-E' as loudly as he could manage. It made him cough a bit, and he realized again how thirsty he was. Then he thought he heard a faint scuffling noise.

'H-A-L-L-O-O-O!' he called again.

'Is . . . is that you, Badger?' came a timid voice.

'Yes,' said Badger. 'For goodness' sake come out, Mole. What are you doing in there?'

'I'm . . . I'm not coming,' said Mole faintly.

'Not coming? Whatever do you mean? Of course you're coming. Now, hurry up! The others are all waiting.'

'No,' said Mole. 'It's no good, Badger. It's kind of you to come and look for me . . .' His voice broke off in a sob. 'But . . . but . . . I'd be no good to you. I'm . . . too . . . slow.'

'Oh, Mole! What nonsense,' said Badger. 'We can't bear to leave you here. How could we? Please come out.'

'They . . . said . . . I was . . . too slow,' Mole said jerkily, in between his sobs.

'Never mind what anybody said,' Badger replied consolingly. 'We're all going together. *Nobody* is to be left behind. Think how sad the others would be if you didn't come. They'd never forgive themselves.'

There were more scuffling noises.

'I'll tell you what,' Badger went on, convinced Mole was now making his way down the passage. 'You can climb up on to my back, and I'll carry you. I won't notice a thing.'

'Will you, Badger? Will you really?' Mole's voice sounded closer now; and presently Badger could see him, moving along the passage using a rowing motion of his front paws to pull himself through the dry soil.

Badger withdrew his head, and presented his back to the hole. 'Jump on!' he said kindly. Once he felt Mole's claws holding firmly on to his fur, he quickly made for the exit.

'I'm sorry to be so silly,' said Mole. 'You are . . . so kind to me, Badger.'

'Say no more about it,' answered Badger, as they left the set. He trotted hurriedly back towards the Great Beech. 'We'll just be in time,' he muttered to himself.

The village clock chimed the half-hour as they joined the waiting animals. Fox wagged his tail as he saw Mole on

Badger's back, but kindly passed no remark.

'Right, Kestrel, when you're ready,' he called. 'The party's complete.'

Without answering, the small hawk leapt from his perch, and swooped gracefully over the hedgerow. Tawny Owl flew at his side in case of any difficulty in the dark, and the pheasants behind them. The land animals set off in a bunch, Fox leading with Weasel, and Toad hopping alongside. Behind them were the rabbits, hares and hedgehogs; and the smaller creatures – voles, fieldmice, lizards and squirrels, followed close behind them. Badger and Mole brought up the rear, with Adder slithering as swiftly as he was able next to them.

Through gaps in the hedgerow the column of animals passed, all moving as quickly as they could. They stepped on to the vast expanse of dry, hard, pitted earth that had once been woodland, and where now the silent bulldozers stood like monsters regathering their strength for the next day's plunder.

Fox kept his eyes on Tawny Owl, who was flapping and gliding slowly along, about twelve feet above the ground. Ahead of them, all the animals could see scattered lights from houses on the fringe of the estate, where the occupants were still wakeful.

Fox saw Tawny Owl suddenly wheel and come flapping towards him. 'Kestrel says the street lights are out,' he called softly. 'We're in luck!' He flew off again, without waiting for an answer.

The animals watched the remaining house lights go out, one by one, as they drew nearer. Occasionally they turned their heads towards their old home, but Farthing Wood had become just a dark mass, which grew smaller and smaller against the starlit sky.

# VI

# THE LONG DRINK

At Number 25, Magnolia Avenue, the owner of the swimming-pool, Mr Burton, was standing by his bedroom window. Although he had felt very tired and had gone to bed at his usual hour of eleven o'clock, the bright moonlight shining into the room had prevented him from sleeping. So he had wearily slipped out of bed, taking care not to disturb his wife, and had gone downstairs to pour himself a consoling drink. He was gratefully sipping this now, as he stood looking out at his garden.

Mr Burton was proud of his garden. He had nurtured it carefully over four years from a patch of bare earth and weeds to something of colour and beauty. He looked down at his green, sloping lawn and his well-tended flower beds, and at his hedge of mixed shrubs. At the end of the garden, reached by a few steps, lay his new swimming-pool. Blue-painted, with imitation marble surrounds, it had been filled for only a couple of weeks, and although nobody had swum in it yet, Mr Burton felt sure it was the envy of his neighbours. Now he looked down with considerable satisfaction at the gleaming water which reflected the moonlight.

Mr Burton's eyes started to grow heavy with tiredness. Suddenly he saw a variety of shapes moving round the sides of the pool; and ripples appeared on the previously unruffled surface of the water. He wondered if he had perhaps been a little too generous when pouring out his nightcap, and he rubbed his eyes. Sure enough, there *was* some movement down there. Could it be cats?

He was just considering whether to go and investigate when his wife called impatiently to him to stop sleep-walking. Feeling a little guilty at being discovered with a glass in his hand, Mr Burton contritely returned to bed. So the animals, quite unaware that their presence had been detected, remained undisturbed.

Following Fox silently through a gap in the hedge, the little band of animals had arrived at the pool's edge only to discover that the water was too far down for the smaller of them to reach. No matter how far over the sides they leant, it was impossible.

'Dear, dear,' said Badger. 'Now what are we to do?'

'Leave it to me,' said Fox, quite unruffled. 'Let the larger animals drink first, and then they can help the smaller.'

It turned out that only Fox and Badger were able to drink from the pool unassisted, and even they found it an awkward task. All the other animals watched them with concern, except Adder who persuaded Weasel to hold his tail in his teeth, while he slithered the front half of his body directly into the water.

The marble surrounds were shiny, and Fox's and Badger's claws slipped on the surface, putting them in grave danger of tumbling in as they leant over the edge thirstily lapping their first water for three days. However, no such accident occurred, and it was some time before their tremendous thirst was quenched. Finally, they raised themselves and sat back on their heels, licking their chops.

'I never knew water could taste so fine,' said Fox.

'I feel fit for anything now,' remarked Badger.

'Don't forget us,' said Mole, who had dismounted from Badger's back on their arrival.

'Of course we won't,' answered Fox. 'Now, over there are some steps leading down into the pool. The water just covers the top of the second one, so if I lie down on that, you smaller animals can climb on to my back and drink from there.' Without more ado, he jumped down and lay flat on the second step, with his head on his paws. The distance down to the first step was still too great for the short legs of the voles, the fieldmice and the lizards, and so Badger got on to that and lay down too. The smallest animals were then able to jump on to Badger's back, and from there on to Fox.

'Cling on tight,' Fox called. 'We don't want any accidents.'

The voles were the first to drink, and three or four of them were able to jump down at a time. They were followed by the lizards and fieldmice, who all drank their fill without any mishap.

Indeed, Hare's youngsters, the hedgehogs, squirrels and Mole, had all satisfied their thirst, when Toad, who had been casting longing glances at the water all through the proceedings, could withstand the temptation no longer. He took a flying leap and landed with a resounding plop about a yard out. This action, on its own, would have been no disaster, for after all, Toad was more at home in the water than on land, and he began to swim delightedly up and down. But the young rabbits, who had been getting more and more excited as the time approached for their turn to drink, took Toad's leap as a signal to themselves, and all together, in a bunch, they jumped over the edge, landing on top of Fox and knocking him into the water.

The mother rabbits, seeing their babies in the pool, followed them without a thought, and Weasel, who all this time had been on the other side holding Adder's tail in his teeth, opened his mouth to cry out a warning; whereupon Adder shot like a dropped anchor straight down to the bottom.

In a trice the swimming-pool was a mêlée of bobbing heads and thrashing feet, while the animals remaining on the edge ran hither and thither in anguish.

At this moment Kestrel, who had remained patiently hovering over the pool since his arrival, spotted the figure at the bedroom window of the house. 'We're being watched!' he called down. This increased the pandemonium in the water, as each animal struggled to reach the steps out of the pool. None of them was in any danger of drowning, as, in common with almost every land creature, they were all able to swim in their own particular way. The problem was, how to get out of the water?

Adder had swiftly surfaced after his surprise dip, but was only able to undulate up and down the pool quite helplessly. Fox managed to clamber up on to his step, where he vigorously shook his coat all over Badger.

Kestrel swooped down and perched on the hand-rail by the steps. 'All clear again now,' he said reassuringly.

Badger and Fox took up their old positions again, and one by one the rabbits were able to scramble out on to Fox's back.

It only remained now for the father rabbits, Hare and his mate, and Weasel to drink, and then their journey could continue. While this was accomplished, Adder continued to swim up and down in a tremendous bad humour, vilifying Weasel with the most insulting names he could remember.

'Don't worry, Adder,' said Fox. 'We'll get you out, once the water's had a cooling effect on your temper!'

The birds, who did not drink much anyway, were able to wet their throats with the water that had been splashed up on to the marble when the rabbits had dived in together.

'Anyone else?' asked Badger. There was no reply. He and Fox then climbed back up, leaving only Toad and Adder in the pool.

Fox began to run up and down the garden, examining the flower-beds. Finally, he seemed to find what he wanted. After tugging vigorously at a clump of delphiniums, he ran back to his friends carrying a long, thin cane in his teeth.

'What's that for, Fox?' asked Mole.

'It's for Adder, of course,' Fox answered, dropping the cane at the side of the pool. 'Now then, Adder!' he called. 'I'm going to hold this stick by one end in my teeth. When I lower it over the side, you grip the other end in your jaws, and I'll pull you out.'

Adder agreed to this proposal, rather sullenly, and the cane was pushed into the water. 'Come on, Adder!' called all the other animals, and the snake turned in the water and swam towards the stick with his jaws open so wide that they all thought he intended to swallow it. His razor-sharp fangs sank into the end of the stick with a violence that nearly pulled it into the pool, with Fox clinging to the end.

'I think he was imagining the stick to be my tail,' Weasel whispered to Badger.

Fox slowly backed away from the pool, drawing Adder out of the water. Once on dry land again, Adder relaxed his grip on the stick, and slithered irritably up to the apprehensive Weasel.

Fox turned his attention to the pool again. 'Toad, old chap, I think you've had long enough in there now,' he remonstrated. (Toad was still splashing around merrily.) 'We've got to get on, and we need you,' Fox reminded him.

'I'm coming,' cried Toad, cheerfully blowing bubbles in the water. 'Just drop the stick over again, and I'll hang on.'

Fox lowered the cane into the water again, and Toad, clinging tightly to the end with his special grasping pads, was hauled clear.

'No time to lose,' said Fox. 'Is everyone ready?'

'We make for the trunk road now,' said Toad. 'At this hour it should be almost deserted. But we must hurry.'

'We'll meet you there,' said Tawny Owl, as he and Kestrel led the other birds away.

'Lead on, Toad,' said Fox. 'On to White Deer Park!'

The next morning Mr Burton looked with dismay at the grimy water in his previously gleaming pool. There were grubby footprints all over the imitation marble, and his clump of delphiniums was sagging. He knew that his beloved garden had indeed received visitors the previous night. Looking at the assorted footprints, he realized they had been left by a number of wild creatures, but whence they had come, or whither they were heading, he, like all the other human inhabitants of the estate, never knew.

# VII

# TWO NARROW ESCAPES

Swiftly out of the garden and into the unlit road went the group of animals, Badger once more carrying Mole. Toad led the way, hopping more than crawling, and leaving Fox and the larger animals to adjust themselves to a slow pace so that they would all keep together.

The animals chose the parts of the roads where it seemed to be darkest, and their luck held as Toad proudly led them through the maze of turnings towards the trunk road. They heard nothing and saw nothing to alarm them. There were no late cars driving home, and no dogs or cats in evidence.

As time wore on, the danger of discovery gradually lessened. The animals, all of whom had maintained complete silence since they left the garden, felt themselves to be safer and began to whisper to each other.

'Tawny Owl will be getting impatient,' Badger remarked. 'He must have been waiting a good hour and more. I've just heard the church clock chime three.'

'It's . . . not . . . much further,' panted Toad, who was beginning to tire. 'Once we get round the next corner . . .'

'Please, Badger, shall I walk for a bit?' asked Mole. 'I'm sure I'm too heavy for you.'

'Nonsense. Can't feel a thing,' Badger reassured him. 'Once we've got the trunk road behind us, we'll be able to rest.'

The animals' pace had slackened, owing to Toad's increasing tiredness. He was no longer able to hop, but could only manage a weary crawl. 'Can't you hurry up a bit at the front?' Adder hissed from his position as rearguard. 'At this rate, dawn will break and we'll still be on the estate.'

'Toad's doing his best,' said Hare. 'We've come a long way. The small animals are all very tired.'

'I'm not exactly feeling as fresh as a daisy myself,' replied Adder, 'but we've slowed almost to a halt.'

Fox, at the front with Toad, turned his head. 'Do stop complaining, Adder,' he said. 'Remember the rule we made about our travelling pace.'

'I'm sorry,' Toad said wearily. 'Of course . . . I didn't . . . do such long stages as . . . this when I . . . was alone.'

'I do feel guilty, riding like this,' wailed Mole. 'Everybody else is tired out, and I'm not helping at all. Oh dear!'

'You're helping more by staying up there than you would by trying to keep up with us walking,' Badger informed him.

'But I could keep up, Badger, you know, now you've slowed down.'

'If Mole wants to walk so much, I'll change places with him any time,' Adder murmured to Weasel. 'I'm sure I shall rub all my scales off, if there's much more of this hard road.'

'Don't be ridiculous, Adder. How could you hold on?' said Weasel.

'I could coil myself round his neck,' Adder replied with a hint of malice.

'Don't be so unpleasant,' retorted Hare, who had overheard. 'I really can't see what benefit to our party you are at all.'

Adder merely bared his fangs at this rejoinder, and Hare accelerated his family a little further up the column.

At length the animals turned the last corner. Ahead of them, about a hundred yards distant, lay the trunk road, and

beyond that the last few yards of the fenced-off army land which they had to skirt before they reached the first open fields.

Very slowly now, they advanced along the last road on the estate. Houses still posed a threat on either side, but now it was only a matter of minutes rather than hours duration. As they proceeded, four o'clock struck.

Halfway down the road they could hear Tawny Owl hooting to them; soon they could see him flying towards them.

'Thank goodness,' he said, landing beside Fox. 'I thought you'd got lost.'

'Oh no. Nothing like that,' Fox answered. 'Toad knew all the right turnings. He's been marvellous. But this walking on hard roads is terribly tiring.'

'The other birds have all found roosts and gone to sleep,' Tawny Owl told him. 'You'd better find somewhere quickly, where you can hide up during the day. It'll be light in a couple of hours.'

'Any ideas?' asked Fox. 'You've had a chance to look round.'

'There's a big gorse thicket just inside the railings of the army land,' Tawny Owl answered. 'I'd recommend that. There's plenty of room for everyone. And no humans ever come down to that far corner. I'll go ahead now and keep an eye open for traffic. See you in a minute.'

He launched himself into flight and disappeared swiftly into the blackness ahead.

The last few yards of the road took the longest of any to

cover, but the animals finally arrived together at the trunk road, where they rested on the pavement. Tawny Owl was perched on the railings on the other side of the road.

'There's no traffic,' he called across.

'Right-o, Owl,' Fox answered him. 'We'll get the youngsters across first. Hare, you can manage your family, and the hedgehogs and rabbits too. Owl will show you where to go.'

Hare put himself in charge of the first party, and under his direction they scuttled quickly across the wide road, and then followed Tawny Owl through the railings to the haven of the gorse patch.

Fox stood on the edge of the pavement, scanning the road in both directions for headlights. It was still clear.

'Come along, voles and fieldmice,' he called. 'Weasel, will you take them across? Quickly as you can.'

The second party took a little longer to cross, but reached the other side without mishap. Tawny Owl, who had returned to his perch on the topmost bar of the railings, repeated his task of guiding the animals to the gorse. They found that many of the young rabbits and hedgehogs had already dropped asleep.

'Good. Not many of us left now. Adder, you'll take the lizards across, please,' Fox ordered. Adder leered his consent. He was too tired to answer.

Everybody in this third party travelled so close to the ground that, in the darkness, the anxious Fox lost them from sight when they had covered only half the distance. He continued to scan the road in both directions. To his horror, in the far distance to his left, he saw a gleam of light. This rapidly increased in size.

'Adder, are you over yet?' he called urgently. 'There's a car approaching.'

'Nearly there,' Adder rasped. 'Come on, come on, quickly.' Fox could hear him hurrying the lizards.

Tawny Owl flew to the roadside to see if he could be of assistance. Adder and the lizards still had a couple of yards to cross, and the lights were very close now. The lizards put on a final spurt, and darted towards Tawny Owl. But Adder, with no projections on the flat surface to ease his passage, could only continue to wriggle across the road in an ungainly fashion. In the next second the lizards, who were just mounting the pavement, Tawny Owl and Adder were all caught in the beam of the car's headlamps.

'He'll never do it,' Fox whispered in horror to Badger. 'He's going to be hit!'

Then, miraculously, the beam of light swung slightly to the right, towards the animals still waiting to cross. The car was manoeuvring to turn into the estate road, and actually passed right by the struggling snake. Adder was safe.

The lizards had turned on the pavement to watch the fate of their large reptile cousin. As his head, with its sinister red eyes, appeared over the kerb, they cheered in excitement.

'A trifle close for comfort,' drawled Adder, as he slithered towards Tawny Owl.

'You're very lucky,' Tawny Owl said unfeelingly. 'Now quickly, this way. We're being investigated.' They disappeared through the railings.

The driver had stopped his car just inside the estate road down which the animals had travelled. He had first seen, in his headlights, Adder and Tawny Owl; the lizards were too small to distinguish. Then, as he turned the car, the lights had swept the opposite pavement, taking in Fox, Badger and Mole, Toad and the squirrels. In amazement, he hurriedly stopped and got out to look.

'Quick, make a dash for it!' Fox urged them, and with the squirrels and Badger right behind him, he raced across the road just as the car driver arrived on the scene.

Safely on the other side, Fox looked round in dismay. 'Where's Toad?' the animals all cried together. 'We've forgotten Toad!'

Sure enough, at that very moment as they looked back, they saw the man bend down to examine something on the pavement. Then he looked all around for some moments. They held their breath. The man bent down again, and prodded the pavement with his shoe.

Toad, who at the best of times would not have been fast enough to escape pursuit, was so tired he could hardly move at all. As he felt the toe of the man's shoe touch him, he shuffled a mere couple of inches towards the road. His friends were all on the safe side of the road and he felt completely abandoned. The man's shoe started to move towards him again. The next thing he knew, there was a flurry of wings above him, followed by a sharp cry of pain.

Then Fox was by his side. 'Fast as you can, up my tail,' he whispered. Toad grasped Fox's thick brush, and clutching tightly with his front feet, pulled himself slowly up. Fox did not stop more than a moment. Once he was sure Toad was off the ground, he raced back across the road again, with Toad hanging grimly on behind.

Tawny Owl had stretched out his talons and skimmed the man's head, raking through his hair. The man's arms flailed wildly upwards and caught the bird a glancing blow on the back, but Tawny Owl, seeing that Fox and Toad were out of danger, flew steadily upwards in a wide arc until the man could no longer see him. Then he flew back over the road, and over the railings, landing by the gorse patch. The moment of danger had passed.

Tawny Owl looked through the thick, interlocking strands of gorse. Most of the animals seemed to be silent, and in the dimness he could make out various shapes huddled together.

'Thanks, Owl,' he heard Fox whisper. 'All safe now. Everyone's exhausted – no wish to talk at the moment . . .' he broke off to yawn. 'We're well hidden here . . . oh, I'm so tired . . . I think I'm the only one still awake. Toad's asleep already.'

'Goodnight, Fox,' whispered Tawny Owl.

'Goodnight, Owl,' he whispered back. 'See you in the evening.'

Tawny Owl flew slowly away to join the other birds before it grew light. The first stage of the journey was completed.

# VIII

# First Camp

Mole, who had obviously been the least tired at the end of the journey through the estate, was the first to wake the next evening. It was still daylight. He looked all round at his companions, to see if there was anyone awake that he could talk to. But they all continued to sleep, their bodies rising and falling rhythmically; a gentle rhythm that had been undisturbed by the daytime traffic noise, or by passing pedestrians.

Again there had been no rain, and the air Mole sniffed inquisitively was moistureless and still. He was acutely hungry, and wondered if he should begin to dig for worms. Perhaps Badger had other ideas. When they woke, everyone would want to eat.

They had all been too exhausted even to consider food the

previous night, but it had been many hours since any of them had eaten, and their stomachs would all feel uncomfortably empty. Mole looked at each of his companions again, but there were still no signs of life. He thought to himself that, after all, there would not be any harm in digging up just one or two worms – even three – to help pass the time until his friends woke.

He pulled himself out of the gorse thicket. 'Well, goodness gracious me!' he exclaimed. 'Wherever did they come from?'

A few inches away a large shallow hole had been scooped out of the ground. Inside it was a squirming mass of insects, worms and fat, juicy grubs. The temptation was too much for the famished Mole. He made a rush towards the feast.

'Oh, there you are!' he heard a voice above him. He looked up, and saw Kestrel and Tawny Owl perched side by side on a holly branch.

'I . . . I was just going to sample the dish,' Mole explained a little guiltily.

'Of course. Tuck in!' said Tawny Owl. 'We've collected it together while you were sleeping. Even Pheasant helped.'

'Of course I did,' said Pheasant from underneath the tree, where he and his mate were preening themselves. 'I unearthed most of those grubs, you know, Mole.'

'Oh. Thank you, Pheasant,' said Mole politely. 'Can I start then?'

'Go ahead,' Tawny Owl said. 'But where are the others?'

'Still sleeping,' answered Mole, as he selected an earthworm.

However, their voices seemed to have roused some of the sleepers. There were rustling noises in the gorse thicket and, after a moment or two, Badger's snout appeared through the prickles. According to his usual careful habit, he sniffed all round warily for any strange scents. Then he ventured into the open.

'Hallo, Badger!' Mole cried. 'Come and try these earthworms – they're magnificent! I can't remember ever eating such succulent ones before . . .'

'Hold on, hold on,' Badger scolded good-humouredly. 'Don't eat them all, Mole. I know your taste for worms!'

'I said to start on the food,' remarked Tawny Owl. 'Mole looked ravenous.'

'I was,' agreed Mole with his mouth full.

'Very kind of you, Owl, to get this together for us,' Badger remarked. 'I think perhaps I ought to wake the others, though, so that we can divide the food fairly.'

Mole stopped chewing, and looked guilty again. 'I say, Badger,' he said with embarrassment, 'I hope I haven't taken too much.'

Badger looked down at the pile of worms that Mole had scraped from the hollow into a heap in front of him. 'No, no,' he said kindly. 'There's plenty for all.' He lumbered off back into the gorse thicket, and presently there was a chorus of voices.

The other animals began to spill out through gaps in the bushes, uttering glad cries at the sight of food. Toad was last out, crawling rather stiffly. 'I'm still tired, but hunger comes first,' he remarked. 'Owl, I don't know how to thank you for saving me last night! I didn't get a chance to say so before – we were all so exhausted – but I'm very grateful. If it hadn't been for you and Fox . . .'

'Oh, nonsense,' Tawny Owl said, shuffling his feet on the branch uncomfortably. 'That is what our Oath is all about.'

'Nevertheless, I thought I was lost!' Toad said. 'When I felt that boot touch me, and I knew I couldn't run, I at once thought: if I'm done for, *they're* done for. It was an awful moment.'

'Well, well,' Tawny Owl nodded. 'I'm glad I could help. Now come on, Toad, eat your fill!'

Under Badger's direction, most of the animals were able to satisfy their appetites, with food to spare. But Hare and his family, the rabbits and the squirrels, and the little fieldmice were unable to join in, as their diet did not include insects or worms. Since they were equally as hungry as the other animals, they had to set off at once in search of their own food.

Before they left, however, Badger consulted Fox, and it was decided that, on their return, there should be a council of the leading animals. This would be for the purpose of deciding what they should do in future about food, as, to a certain extent, they all had differing tastes.

Eventually, only Mole was left eating, while the rest of

the animals lay down, replete, to await the return of the plant-eating group. The little creature was in raptures. With a blissful expression on his pointed face, he munched his way through his stock of worms, and then looked round to see what the others had left.

Finally he looked up. 'Owl, wherever did you manage to dig up such worms?' he asked. 'I pride myself on being a connoisseur, you know, and I've never tasted their equal.'

'Oh, Pheasant and Kestrel found a lot of them, I think,' Tawny Owl replied, without much interest.

'They weren't difficult to find,' said Kestrel. 'We went to the marshy ground – plenty of 'em there. Though, if there isn't some rain pretty soon, all that marsh will just dry up. A lot of it is dry already.'

A greedy expression came over Mole's face, which he quickly hid. 'Is . . . er . . . is it far to the marshy place?' he asked softly, trying very hard to appear nonchalant.

'Not for us,' replied Kestrel. 'But I couldn't say how long you'd take to get there.'

Mole's face dropped; then he looked quickly at Badger. Badger caught his eye. 'We shan't have time for that sort of thing,' he said. 'We've got to keep on the move.'

'Couldn't we . . . just have a quick look?' the disappointed Mole said beseechingly.

'We'll see,' Badger said. 'I don't think Fox will agree.'

Fox was drowsing in the last of the sun's rays, oblivious

to all around him. He remained so, until the missing party returned.

On their arrival back at the camp, as dusk was falling, Fox hastily organized a meeting inside the gorse thicket.

'Well, everyone,' Badger began, 'it certainly seems that our original idea of my acting as quartermaster, and directing the collection of food for the whole party, will have to be abandoned.'

'I'm afraid it will, Badger,' said the elected leader of the rabbits, whose new position of importance had rather gone to his head. 'It's all right for you meat- and insect-eaters, you know. But we vegetarians find worms and other creepy-crawlies most unpalatable.'

'We squirrels prefer nuts and things,' said their spokesman. 'In any case, we're not used to eating – or sleeping – on the ground. We really only feel at home when we're up a tree, out of harm's way.'

'Your own individual habits may often have to be sacrificed for the benefit, even the survival, of the party,' Badger warned him. 'We decided all this before we left Farthing Wood. We shall not succeed in reaching our destination in one piece unless we conform.'

'Perhaps then, Badger, we could all eat grass for the duration of the journey?' suggested Rabbit. 'There's always plenty available. We never have to search far. It seems to me the simplest answer.'

'No, no,' Badger shook his striped head with some annoyance. 'It would play havoc with my digestion, and that of the other meat-eaters. Anyway, I wasn't referring to food just now. I was really thinking of how we travel, and where we rest. We must stick together. Safety in numbers, you see.'

'I'm afraid there seems to be only one solution to the food problem,' said Fox. 'For reasons of health and comfort we must all ensure that we eat the food we're used to – the food we like. Otherwise there's no knowing how many will fall by the wayside.'

'What do you suggest, Fox?' asked Badger.

'I suggest this. When we stop at the end of each day's journey, we go out in parties to obtain what food we need. The plant-eating animals would form one party, for instance; the squirrels another. We meat-eaters could hunt together, or individually. The birds can please themselves. But there is one point it will be necessary to agree upon: that is, the length of time allowed for searching for food. It should be the same for all, and we can decide on the amount of time we can spare at the end of each day. That way everyone will arrive back at the chosen resting-place at approximately the same time.'

The animals all agreed that that was the best plan.

'There's a second very important point to discuss,' said Toad. 'That is, the rate and distance we travel each day.'

'Surely we can't really forecast that?' Badger asked with a puzzled look.

'No, of course not. I've raised the point because our resolution to travel at a pace that would be comfortable even for the slowest of us doesn't really work in practice.'

At this remark, Mole looked most uncomfortable, as if he were quite sure Toad was alluding to his privileged position as a passenger. But he was relieved to discover that this was not so.

'The reason that we were all so tired after crossing through the housing estate last night,' Toad went on, 'was because for the slower animals, like myself and the lizards, the journey was too much for one day. Also, for the larger, quicker ones among us – like Fox, and Hare, and Weasel – the dreadfully slow pace at which they had to travel so that we all kept together, was fatiguing in the extreme. We'll have to remedy this.'

'I can give some help in that way,' said the leader of the lizards. 'We lizards have decided that it would be best, for ourselves, and for all of you, if we stay here on the army land.'

Toad nodded his agreement. But the other animals showed their amazement. 'This is silly,' said Badger quietly. 'We'll find a way round the problem. We can't just go off and leave you here. After all, you're really no slower than Adder. *He's* going on, aren't you, Adder?'

'Oh yes,' lisped Adder, who was still thinking very much about the Edible Frogs, but had no intention of mentioning it. 'In for a penny, in for a pound, I suppose,' he said.

'The truth is,' Lizard went on, 'the distance might well prove too great for us. After last night, we don't look forward to many weeks – or even months – of such hard going. And we know we'd be a burden to the rest of you.'

'I think you're very wise, Lizard,' said Toad. 'There's really nothing at White Deer Park you wouldn't be able to find here. Kestrel will be able to tell you that no humans use this corner of the army land. You're as safe here as in a Nature Reserve. They can't build here.'

'Exactly,' said Lizard. He turned to Badger, who looked as if he were about to try to persuade him to change his mind. 'You're very kind, Badger,' Lizard said. 'But I know, in your heart of hearts, you can see the sense in our decision.'

Badger dropped his head and nodded weakly. 'Well, I suppose you're right,' he conceded. 'But I hope no one else is going to stay behind?'

None of the other animals appeared in the least disposed to call a halt to their journey.

'That's good,' said Fox. 'Now, I suggest that to recover fully from the first stage of our journey, we remain here for another day. Then, when we're completely rested, we can decide, with Toad's advice, where to make for on our next stage. Any disagreement?'

No voices were raised on this point, and the meeting ended. Lizard's intervention had prevented any definite plan on the animals' future travelling pace from being formulated.

The animals stayed in the gorse thicket until it was completely dark. Then some of them began to ask Kestrel and Tawny Owl about the water-hole in the marshy ground, and it was eventually decided that, after they had all taken another nap, Tawny Owl would show them the way.

Pheasant and his mate and Kestrel returned to their roosts, while the animals found comfortable sleeping-places. Mole decided to dig himself a short way into the earth, where he said he would sleep better, while the squirrels climbed up into a small oak tree.

Tawny Owl, who really came to life at night, and who was completely relaxed in the darkness, went and perched on a railing. Fox and Badger, who also spent most of their waking hours in the dark, elected to join him for a time, as they had too much on their minds to be able to sleep.

They sat down at the foot of one of the metal posts. Fully occupied with their thoughts, none of the three spoke for some time. Finally, Fox broke the silence. He seemed to air the thoughts of all of them when he said, 'I wonder just what chance we've got of going through with this thing?'

'Well,' said Badger, 'if we're careful, you know . . .'

'I'm worried about Toad, you see,' Fox went on, as a light breeze began to blow soothingly through his fur. 'Everything depends on him really, and he's completely exhausted himself on the very first stage.'

'He made the journey before,' Badger pointed out.

'That's the whole point.' Fox gave his head a shake. 'Perhaps two journeys of such length will be too much for him. I was really thinking of *him* when I suggested staying on here another day.'

'He mustn't walk any more,' said Badger. 'He'll just have to ride, like Mole.'

'I've had the same thought,' said Fox. 'I'd carry him willingly. But, apart from that, when he made the journey before, he only had himself to think about. He travelled at his own pace, within his own limits. *We've* got far greater responsibilities.'

'Oh come, Fox, it's early days yet,' put in Tawny Owl. 'It's not like you to be pessimistic.'

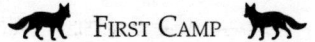 

'I'm trying to be *realistic*,' returned Fox, a little brusquely. 'But you're right, Owl,' he added, 'we must look on the bright side and . . . well, go carefully.'

For some minutes longer, they sat there, eagerly breathing in the coolness of the breeze. Then Fox and Badger rejoined the other animals.

Tawny Owl spent a considerable time skimming noiselessly from tree to tree, enjoying the freedom of solitude and darkness. Occasionally, he hooted with all his old confidence, as he had done in the times when Farthing Wood had been intact. Eventually, deciding that the animals had napped long enough, he swooped swiftly in a graceful curve from a lofty elm branch and landed by the gorse thicket. Here he hooted again. 'If anyone wants a drink, now is the time,' he announced.

Almost at once he felt that he was standing on a small earthquake. The ground underneath him began to shake, and the earth definitely began to give way. Tawny Owl flapped upwards in alarm, and then noticed Mole's snout appearing through a hole in the ground, near where he had been standing.

'Good evening, Tawny Owl,' said Mole. 'I've had a wonderful sleep. I've quite slept off all those worms I ate.'

'You must have a *wonderful* stomach,' Tawny Owl remarked a little coldly. He was feeling peeved about showing alarm in front of Mole, an animal he felt to be distinctly inferior to himself.

'Oh yes,' said Mole cheerfully. 'I could quite easily start all over again now, and eat twice as many. Oh, I can't wait to get to that marsh. Where's Badger?'

'Behind you,' Tawny Owl said drily.

Mole gave a little jump. 'H . . . hallo . . . Badger,' he said.

'Now, Mole, Tawny Owl's taking us to the water. We're not searching for any more worms,' said Badger.

Mole looked very crestfallen. 'I didn't know you'd been listening,' he said in a small voice.

The kindly Badger relented a little. 'Well, perhaps there will be time for one or two,' he said. Then, turning, he called out, 'Come on, everyone! Tawny Owl's waiting.'

The animals began to assemble, talking amongst themselves about the drought, and the problem of finding water during their journey. Toad was still too tired to join them, and Adder's experience with water the previous day rendered him quite unwilling to make one of the party.

So this time the animals were able to set a smarter pace, and with Tawny Owl at their head, flapping like a grey ghost through the air, they moved off through the dry bracken and grass.

Every blade of grass, every fern-frond, seemed to be drooping for want of moisture. The grass stalks were dry and brittle, looking like so much straw, and everything, including the lower leaves on the scattered trees, was grimed with dust, and panting for air.

## FIRST CAMP

Mole, grimly clutching the brindled hairs on Badger's back, thought only of the second feast he intended to have when they reached the marsh.

Under the animals' feet the ground felt bone hard, and it seemed to have retained a lot of the heat from the daytime sun, despite the slight breeze that blew. But after they had walked in silence for some time, the ground grew softer. It had a spongy feel to it; and from the clumps of dry reeds that abounded, the animals knew that they had reached the outskirts of the marsh, a part that had dried up. They began to tread carefully.

Fox, who was leading, saw Tawny Owl fly further ahead and then perch awkwardly on a reed tussock, there being no trees within easy distance. When the animals came up to him, he said, 'I can't go any further now. The water's just ahead. Watch how you go. The ground's very damp here.'

Fox nodded and went forward slowly, picking up his paws carefully, and gingerly testing the ground in front of him at each step. At this pace, the party went forward another twenty yards. Then Fox called back, 'I can see the water now. Everyone stay here, and I'll go forward and find a safe path.'

The animals held their breath as the chestnut body of their leader went further on, one slow pace at a time. After about thirty paces, they saw him stop and bend his head. Then he turned round. 'It's all right,' he called back. 'Just come straight forward, in single file, and don't run. You'll be quite safe. The water's cold, but very bitter,' he added.

One by one the animals went forward, treading carefully along the path Fox had taken. Mole slipped from Badger's back, and sportingly volunteered to be last in the queue.

Once behind the other animals, without Fox's or Badger's eye on him, Mole felt free to follow his own pursuits. His own short-sighted eyes could just make out Fox at the waterside, supervising the drinking. Badger was queuing along with the rest. Mole retreated a few paces and felt the ground under his feet to be promisingly spongy. Swiftly he began to dig, his voracious appetite demanding satisfaction.

Worms! Plump, juicy worms were in Mole's mind as he dug, and nothing else. He paid no attention to the muddy water that was seeping into the hole in little trickles as he dug deeper. In his excitement he forgot he was on dangerous ground.

The other animals eventually finished drinking, and collected on drier ground. All of them felt much refreshed. Fox looked all round to see if everyone was present.

'Are we all here?' Badger asked him.

'No,' replied Fox with a serious expression. 'Mole isn't. I bet he's gone off after those worms.'

'He has. I saw him tunnelling.' Tawny Owl swooped in.

'You might have told us,' Fox said shortly. 'We shall have an awful job getting him up now.'

'Since Badger gave him permission, I saw no reason to tell anyone,' Tawny Owl replied in his most dignified manner.

Fox looked at Badger in surprise.

'Well, before we set out I did just say to Mole there might be time for him to catch a couple of worms,' Badger explained. 'But, of course, he should have waited for the appropriate time. I didn't know this would happen.'

Fox shook his head. 'You're too kind-hearted by half, Badger,' he said. 'He'd eaten more than enough already.'

'I'm sorry,' said Badger, 'But, Fox, you know how Mole can sound so plaintive.'

'Yes, yes,' Fox nodded wearily. 'I'm as fond of him as you. But this is plain greediness on his part. However, don't let's waste any more time talking. Where was he tunnelling, Tawny Owl?'

Tawny Owl flew to the spot and pointed to it by extending his legs downwards over the hole, while he flapped his large wings furiously to maintain his position.

'Weasel, will you take the others back?' Fox asked. 'Badger and I will follow behind with Mole as soon as he appears again. It would teach him a lesson if we all went off and left him to get back to camp on his own, but then we'd probably never see him again.'

Weasel obliged by leading the party off in the direction of the animals' first camp.

'There doesn't appear to be anything in this hole except water,' said Fox, looking closely at the ground. 'Are you sure this is the right place, Owl?'

'Positive. Distinctly saw him go down there.'

'Well, good heavens, he'll drown!' Fox said with alarm. 'Quick, Badger, we'd better dig another hole next to this and see if we can reach him.'

The two animals furiously raked back the spongy soil, but as soon as they got about six inches down more water quickly filled up the hole. They tried three more holes, each time with the same result.

'It's no good,' Fox said, not daring to look at Badger's face. 'He must be drowned already.'

'Oh no! Surely not!' Tawny Owl exclaimed, feeling very guilty. 'He's probably branched off through a tunnel somewhere. I'm sure he'll surface again in a moment.'

At that moment their attention was taken up by what appeared to be a red glow through the trees. 'Whatever's that?' Badger muttered, and looking down, began digging again.

'Should we call him, do you think?' asked Tawny Owl, who had perched on a reed tussock.

'No point,' said Fox. 'He's more likely to feel our vibrations on the ground than to hear our voices. I'm afraid I'm not very hopeful. I'm sure that if he could, he would have surfaced by now.'

'Perhaps he's still eating?' Badger said hopelessly. 'His appetite, you know . . .'

'SSSh,' hissed Fox. 'Listen!'

In the distance they could hear voices, a lot of voices, beginning as a whisper and rapidly becoming louder. They

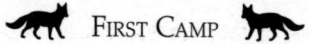 

exchanged glances of alarm, their bodies frozen into stillness. The red glow they had noticed seemed to waver, then glow all anew.

Suddenly they saw Weasel rushing towards them, and close behind him were the hares and rabbits.

'Fire!' he yelled. 'Run for your lives! FIRE! FIRE!'

## IX

# FIRE!

Fox's first instinct was to turn and run, for, like all animals, he was terrified of fire. He knew with what swiftness it could engulf the homes of defenceless wild creatures like himself, burning everything in its path. He also knew that where there was fire there would soon be large numbers of humans, trampling everywhere with strange, frightening machines and awful noise. But Fox did not run. His sense of responsibility returned to him, and he courageously resisted this first impulse.

As Weasel dashed past him in panic, he called out, in a voice ringing with authority, 'Stop! You're running straight into the marsh!'

Weasel's headlong flight was checked, and he dutifully

turned back towards his leader. The rabbits and Hare and his family followed.

'I'm sorry, Fox,' said the sobered Weasel. 'We just panicked.'

'Where are the others?' snapped Fox, one eye on the flickering glow in the distance. 'We've no time to lose!'

'They're following,' said Weasel. 'We were nearly back at the camp when we saw the flames. Adder and Toad were coming towards us, moving as fast they could, and they called out to us to go back the way we'd come.'

'Toad!' Fox exclaimed. 'He'll never be fast enough to get away. The grass is so dry the flames will just roar along. Trees, shrubs, everything will go up. He'll be overtaken in no time. I must go back – before it's too late.'

At that moment Kestrel and the pheasants alighted on the ground by Tawny Owl. 'The other animals are nearly here,' said Kestrel. 'The squirrels and hedgehogs are well ahead of the flames, and the mice are not far behind.'

'What about Toad?' Fox barked.

'He's doing his best. Adder tried to help him, but he told him to go on and save himself. I'm afraid without help . . .'

'I'm going back for him,' Fox said grimly. 'Badger, I'm leaving you in charge. You're to take the party right round the edge of the marsh. If we can get to the other side we might be safe. The damp ground here may check the flames. Anyway, it's our only chance. Wait for the other animals to reach you here; then all go together. Toad and I will join you as soon as we can. Owl, I'm relying on you to guide them clear of the water. Badger, you lead the way, and tread carefully – the ground's dangerous here. But go as fast as you can. Ah! The squirrels and hedgehogs are coming now. Good luck!'

Fox raced off in the direction of the flames. The other animals bunched nervously round Badger and Tawny Owl. The hedgehogs and squirrels joined them.

'How far behind are the fieldmice and voles?' asked Badger.

'They'll be here any minute,' panted the senior hedgehog.

'Have you seen Adder or Toad?'

'No.'

'We must wait for Adder,' Badger said. 'Fox has gone for Toad.'

'I don't think we should wait,' said Tawny Owl. 'We can't jeopardize all the animals' safety for one member of the party. We don't know how far away he is.'

'We'll ask the mice when they get here,' Badger insisted.

The glow through the trees was brighter now, and the animals could hear the noise of the flames. Against the black sky, the trees in the distance flickered redly.

A moment later, the furry mass of mice and voles spilled into the foreground, squeaking in alarm. They reported no sign of Adder.

'We can't wait,' Tawny Owl said again.

'We'll give him as long as it takes for two hundred beats of the heart,' said Badger.

Two hundred heartbeats, while under threat of being overtaken by fire, were obviously several times as fast as usual. Badger listened to his pounding heart and realized the impossibility of counting. But he forced himself to stay still just a little longer, in the midst of all the restless, milling animals. None of them dared to bolt, for the dangers of the marsh were directly ahead, and they felt themselves trapped between that existing danger and the approaching one.

The few agonizing moments paid off. Adder's red eyes, baleful in the darkness, were spotted by Kestrel. In a trice he had joined the ranks.

'At once now, Tawny Owl,' Badger commanded, and Tawny Owl led the birds into the air, while the animals set off at top speed behind Badger.

'Round the marsh,' he called to the birds. 'Kestrel knows the way.'

As the animals raced on, Tawny Owl called down directions to them from his position twelve feet above the ground. Without

answering, Badger religiously obeyed them, leading his party in diversions around marshy ground, avoiding holes and bunches of reeds that screened treacherous mud. With every step and every gasping breath, the animals knew they were putting the flames further behind them. Every so often Badger and the larger animals stopped to allow Adder and the voles and fieldmice to catch up; then they raced on. Weasel dropped back to take up position as rearguard, encouraging the slow ones, and keeping an eye open for Fox.

After half an hour they reached the end of one side of the marsh, and began to turn the long corner to reach the other side – what Fox had hoped would be the safe side. The younger animals were exhausted, and all of them, adults and young alike, ached in every limb.

'Owl!' Badger called up. 'We'll stop for just a very short rest. The youngsters are gasping.'

The birds landed, and the animals sank to the ground, bodies heaving violently, their throats parched and their eyes streaming. They gulped in the air with hoarse, shuddering breaths.

In the far distance they could still see the fire. They were now on slightly higher ground, and they could see the movement of the flames. Even as they watched the fire seemed to come nearer.

'Father, will we ever see Fox again?' asked one of the leverets.

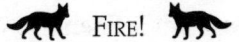 FIRE!

Hare smiled down at him. 'Of course we will, my dear,' he said gently. 'He'll soon be back. You'll see.'

As he sped back towards the camp in the gorse thicket, and in the direction of the flames, Fox resolutely put every fearsome thought from his mind. He told himself to think only of Toad, and how he must save him to save the others. Without Toad they were indeed lost.

The fire grew brighter and noisier ahead of him, and soon the air smelt, and felt, hot and scorched. The heat increased continually. There was no sign of Toad.

Fox began to call him. 'Toad! Toad! Where are you?' Then, raising his voice above the noise of the burning, he shouted as loudly as he could: 'TOAD!'

Fox dared not look directly at the terrifying sight that he was swiftly approaching. He knew that to do so would mean an instantaneous loss of nerve. But he could hear the crashing of blazing boughs – sometimes whole saplings. The roar of the greedy flames was hideous, and at last he could go no further. His courage failed him, and he felt all he could do was turn and run back to safety and companionship.

Then he heard a desperate croak. 'Fox! Have you come back? Here I am!'

Toad was sitting under a gorse bush, making no attempt to move.

'What are you doing there?' Fox whispered through his

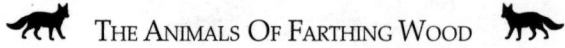 

parched lips. 'Come quickly. The flames are almost on us.'

'I thought I was lost,' Toad answered. 'I knew my poor speed could never get me to safety, so I resigned myself to wait here for my . . . end.'

Even as he spoke, the first flames burst upon them with a tremendous roar. Fanned by a slight breeze, the fire had accelerated, and was sweeping its greedy fingers through the undergrowth. Toad made a mighty leap as the gorse bush went up like a bonfire. The night was lit up around them, as bright as daylight, but more fitful, by the flames.

Now they heard sirens in the distance, traffic, and human voices. Fox bent his head and gently took Toad in his jaws. Then, turning, he galloped away, back through the dry undergrowth towards his friends.

He paused only once, to release Toad and allow him to climb on to his back. Then, with the hateful roar still dinning in their ears, they raced for the marsh.

While his friends had fled for their lives, the unfortunate Mole remained completely oblivious of the existence of the oncoming fire. His insatiable appetite drew him down, deeper and deeper into the earth. Worms were plentiful in that marshy soil, and Mole ate as he delved. He only became aware of the presence of water when his feet began to get wet, and eventually he felt his fur to be wet too. Mole realized the hole he had dug was filling up, and he knew that to turn back would be to drown. So he

went no further down, but continued to dig a path in a straight line, and after about another twelve inches, he clawed his way upwards.

The surface seemed to be a long, long way away. Mole had no idea that, in his hunger, he had tunnelled so far downward. As he climbed upwards he felt warmer and warmer, and he decided this must be due to his exertions in reaching for the surface. But he grew hotter and hotter, and hotter, and even the soil began to feel hot. Soon it was too hot for him to bear: his paws could no longer touch the earth without being burnt. Mole recoiled, and slipped back a few inches. He was trapped between the heat above him and the water below.

When Badger's party had rested for some minutes, and all had got their breath back, Badger and Tawny Owl led them on again at a steady pace. The distance was shorter this time, and they were not long in finally reaching the other side of the marsh.

They looked across the marsh at the fire. They seemed to be far enough away from it now to be safe. The muddy water reflected the flames and seemed to flicker.

'Look, look, the water's on fire!' squeaked one of the young fieldmice.

'It's just the reflection,' his mother answered him, soothingly.

'Water fights fire,' Badger pointed out kindly. 'It's an enemy to fire. Humans use it, you know, to kill flames. We're quite safe. Fox was wise.'

'What will happen then, Badger, when the fire reaches the water?' asked a young squirrel.

'It will burn itself out,' Badger answered. 'It will be quenched by the water, just like you quench a thirst.'

The animals relaxed. Badger, whom they held in almost as high esteem as Fox, was confident that they were safe. They lay down, the young ones snuggling up to their mothers.

Badger called to Tawny Owl, who had perched on a low branch. 'Why don't you fly across the marsh and see if you can spot Fox and Toad?' he asked. 'I can't rest till I know they're all right.' There was some nervousness in his voice.

'I shouldn't worry, Badger,' Tawny Owl reassured him. 'Fox can look after himself.'

'Yes, but what if he couldn't get to Toad in time?'

'Very well, if it will put your mind at rest . . .' Tawny Owl flapped off the branch and flew away over the water. Badger watched him until he was too small to distinguish against the darkness.

He felt someone brush against his fur. It was Hare.

'If he *was* too late to save Toad . . . what then?' he asked.

'I don't know,' said Badger. 'We can't go back. No doubt Fox would think of something.'

Tawny Owl was not long gone. They were still gazing across the marsh when they noticed his grey shape returning.

'They're all right!' Tawny Owl called, and hooted in his

pleasure. 'They're both all right!'

Badger heaved a sigh of relief. 'Thanks, Owl, for going,' he said.

'Believe me, I'm as relieved as you are,' said Tawny Owl. 'Fox is terribly tired, but he's coming as fast as he can. He's just started turning the corner towards this side. He was too tired to talk, but Toad called out to warn everyone to look out for the humans. There are lots of them coming.'

'Toad was on Fox's back?' Badger assumed.

Tawny Owl nodded, and Hare was struck by a thought.

'I wonder what happened to poor old Mole?' he said.

While his friends were wondering about him, Mole, of course, was thinking of them, and bitterly regretting the greediness which had brought him to his present danger.

'Why didn't I answer when I heard them calling?' he wailed to himself in his uncomfortable tunnel. 'Oh, Badger, if I ever get out of here, I'll never again run away because of my awful appetite! I promise. Oh dear, will I ever see him again? And Fox?' The more he thought about his friends, the more miserable and helpless Mole felt himself to be.

He knew there must be some danger on the surface, although he had no idea what it could be. He wondered if Fox and Badger, and all the others, had escaped it, and, as he wondered, the thought came to him that they might now be miles away, having given him up for lost. He was all on his own, deserted! Whatever would become of him? He began to sob violently. He was very frightened. Finally, in his misery, Mole cried himself to sleep.

He had no idea how long he slept, but he was woken by the vibration of heavy footsteps overhead. There were many of them, and they were not animal footsteps. He shuddered afresh at this new danger, for the crashing above told him humans were about.

Eventually the din passed over and the vibrations became fainter. Mole decided it was high time to move if he were ever again to rejoin his friends. He inched timidly upwards. The soil still felt warm to his paws, but he continued. He soon felt sure he had passed the spot where he had previously had to retreat. After a few more moments the soil began to feel damp, and cooler. He pulled himself upwards more quickly, and experienced a new sensation. His snout detected a smell of burning, an acrid, charred smell. Then his claws pierced the surface and he wriggled up to peer out. He could scarcely believe his eyes.

Dawn had broken. Mole found a scene of desolation around him. Everything was a uniform, hideous black. Earth, grass, rushes and shrubs had been burnt to cinders. Stunted saplings with charcoal for trunks, bald of leaves and shoots, stood like skeletons. Some of the larger trees had escaped with a severe scorching, losing only the branches and leaves close to the ground. Even those looked as if they had been severely wounded and would bear the scars for ever. The black ground

was thoroughly wet, and was still smoking in places.

Mole knew that there had been a terrible fire, and that the humans had come with water to quench it. He felt certain that all his friends must have been killed, as they could not possibly have survived such a disaster.

'Oh, I wish I were dead, too!' he howled. 'I'm no good on my own. Where can I go? Oh, poor Badger!' And he laid himself down on the ashes, with his head on his paws, and wept bitterly.

Mole's poor eyesight had been too weak to notice that in the distance, along the sides of the marsh, the fire was still burning, despite the efforts of the humans with their water and their beaters. At that moment the other animals, now rejoined by Fox and Toad, were, while far from dead, in even graver danger than before.

# X

# CONFRONTATION

As Mole lay in despair, his little velvet-covered body shaken by sobs, he was unaware that he was being watched. One of the beaters had remained behind to ensure that no further fires would break out from the glowing embers. Now he had reached the spot where Mole had earlier gone hunting, and was amazed to find any wildlife remaining in the wake of the flames. He bent over the little creature to see if he was still alive, and could see evidence of Mole's breathing. When he saw the hole from which the animal had recently emerged, the beater understood how he had managed to escape being burnt to death. Cautiously he lowered a hand, and found that the animal had no wish to run away. He lifted him up and looked at him more closely. Mole did not even wriggle.

The beater was in a quandary, for he had nowhere to put the creature. At the same time he was unwilling to abandon something he was pleased to think he might have just saved, for he felt sure Mole's docility resulted from the fact that he had been injured. In the end he deposited him in one of the large side pockets of his firefighter's jacket, mopped his forehead, and went slowly on in the direction of the marsh.

After the initial excitement at the reappearance of Fox and Toad had somewhat abated, Toad was able to tell his friends just how the fire had started.

'I had finished with sleeping,' he began, 'and I was simply squatting restfully in the comfortable little hollow in the ground that I'd made for myself. I was alone, because Adder had slid off somewhere.'

'Just went to have a hunt round,' Adder told them with a glint in his red eyes. 'Never know what you might find . . .'

'Anyway, I remember hearing a sizzling noise,' Toad went on, 'and it seemed to get louder.' He paused for effect, looking round at the other animals, who were clustering in small groups among the grass tussocks and reeds. 'I went to have a look. The grass beyond the railings was burning. It must have been a cigarette that started it, thrown out of a passing car. The flames were advancing rapidly, and I could see that in a very short time they would reach inside the army land. I hastened off to tell Adder.

'As the flames got nearer, and I watched the gorse thicket swallowed up, I knew I could never escape the fire, being so slow. I told Adder not to wait for me – to get away, if he could. But, thanks to our brave leader, I'm still here with you.'

'If it weren't for Mole,' said the exhausted Fox, who was lying full length on the ground, 'the party would be complete.' He told Toad about the disappearance of Mole, and all the animals fell silent, thinking about their lost companion whom they presumed drowned, or burnt by the fire.

Dawn approached, and across the marsh the flames seemed to pale as the sky became lighter. But the fire did not stop.

Rabbit expressed the concern of the smaller, more timid animals. 'It's coming on! It's still coming!' he cried to Fox, as if blaming him for its continuance.

'Yes, I see that it is,' Fox replied wearily.

'But didn't you say it would stop at the marshy ground?' Rabbit persisted.

'I said that I *hoped* it would,' answered Fox.

'What if the marsh doesn't stop it?' asked Vole, and his question was repeated in alarm by his brethren.

'Fox will think of something, don't worry,' Weasel said confidently.

'At any rate,' Toad put in, 'the humans have arrived with their machines and ideas. *They'll* soon stop it. Fire is just as much their enemy as ours, you see.'

Fox drifted off into an uneasy sleep, while Badger tried to calm the growing fears of more and more animals in the party. When it was broad daylight Kestrel flew off to see what was happening.

The fire continued to roar on, and began to spread round the sides of the marsh. 'Surely we shouldn't stay here?' Pheasant protested.

'Where do you suggest, then?' Tawny Owl asked sharply.

'Well, er . . . I . . . *we* don't have to stay. We birds aren't in danger.'

'You're free to leave at any time you want,' Tawny Owl said meaningfully.

Pheasant's mate gave him a nudge with her wing, and he looked a little embarrassed.

Kestrel returned at that moment, and attention was diverted from the discomfited Pheasant. 'They're making progress,' the hawk announced. 'But I think the fire won't be mastered for a while yet. We'd better decide what to do. The flames are creeping round both sides of the water, so that there are now in effect, two fires, and, at the moment, we're between them.'

All the animals looked towards Fox, who was still sleeping.

'We'll have to wake him,' Badger decided. He went up close to his friend and gave him a shake with one paw.

Fox looked up at once. 'I was only dozing,' he said.

Badger told him of the advance of the fire.

'Then it looks as if our lives are once again at the mercy of humans,' he said with resignation. 'Only they can save us now.'

The animals looked very alarmed at these words from their leader.

'Are we helpless?' asked Hare.

'Not quite,' said Kestrel. 'From the air I could detect a sort of causeway of land, just a narrow strip, running under the surface of the water, but connected to the ground we're on now. It leads to a small island some way out in the marsh. I think you could all walk on it. Once on the island, there's no question of the flames reaching you.'

Fox was immediately alert again. 'Where is the causeway, Kestrel?' he asked. 'Let me have a look at it.'

He left Badger in charge of the party, and followed Kestrel's flight for a short distance.

'Can you see it?' Kestrel called down.

'I think so,' Fox answered, peering out over the water's edge. 'Yes! Yes, I can.'

Kestrel, hovering expertly above, watched Fox put one foot gingerly into the water, and test the firmness of the sunken ground. He seemed satisfied, and walked a little further in until his whole weight was pressing on it.

'It seems strong enough,' he called. 'Better go and round up the others.'

When the rest of the party arrived, they saw Fox standing in the water. It reached up to just below his knees.

'I'm going to walk out to the island,' Fox told them. 'Badger, will you follow behind me? We need to know how much weight it will bear.'

Slowly, with about a yard between them, the two animals moved forward along the causeway. The water reached to the top of Badger's legs.

'We can't go across there!' squealed Vole as he watched. 'We voles and fieldmice, and the squirrels and hedgehogs too, would be under the water.'

'I'm sure that won't have escaped Fox's notice,' remarked Tawny Owl.

Fox and Badger reached the island without mishap, and remained there a little while in discussion, looking out towards where the flames were now noticeably beginning to encircle the marsh. Then they ran quickly back across the causeway, with the dark water splashing up against their sides.

'We haven't got long,' Fox told them. 'We could see the humans at work on the flames, but I don't think they can stop it in time for our safety. Badger and I will have to carry the smaller of you across in shifts. The larger animals, like Hare, the rabbits and Weasel should be able to keep their heads above water. Kestrel, will you get airborne and keep Badger and myself informed as to the progress of the fire? Now then, fieldmice, up on my back.'

In the urgency of the moment, the excitable little mice, always rather highly strung, all made for Fox's bushy tail, expecting to climb up. But there were too many of them. They got in each other's way, bumping and pushing in their scramble to be the first up.

'Ow! Stop this!' yelled Fox, who felt as if his brush would soon be pulled off. 'Calm down, and climb up one at a time.' He looked across at Badger, who had lain himself down, the better to enable the voles to climb up his sides.

'Now, wait, all of you,' said Fox, and followed Badger's example. The fieldmice scurried up on to his back, and, with Badger ahead of him, Fox stepped down again on to the causeway.

Having deposited the tiny creatures safely on the island, Fox and Badger ran quickly back for the second load. Already the awful roar and crackle of the fire could be heard again, and the animals were able to smell the scorched, ashy air wafting towards them.

'Now, squirrels!' cried Fox. 'Badger and I can manage you all between us. Rabbits, Weasel, follow us. Hare, you must bring your family. Quickly!'

The animals leapt on to the spit of land, Fox and Badger carrying their furry burdens like two grey cloaks that had suddenly been invested with life. Hare followed, with his mate behind him, each carrying one of their babies. The water completely covered their bodies, leaving only their heads and necks above the surface, and the leverets, hanging on to their parents' neck fur by their teeth, were all but submerged.

The rabbits, with their shorter legs, sank even further down in the water, and while the adults were just able to keep their noses, eyes and ears in the dry, Rabbit had to tell the youngsters to stay behind for Fox and Badger to collect them, leaving them in the care of Hedgehog.

'Hurry up, Fox!' Kestrel called, as he hovered above them, his eyes turned towards the fire. 'The flames are racing this way! Quickly, quickly!'

Weasel, having watched the plight of the rabbits, knew that the water would completely cover his low-slung body if he endeavoured to walk across. So, with grim determination, he entered the dark water and began to swim towards the island.

Toad and Adder were quick to join him, and, keeping their various pairs of eyes fixed firmly on the little island where their friends were cheering them on, they struck out bravely.

Adder undulated swiftly through the water, only his small head above the surface, and as he neared land, Fox and Badger were running back across the causeway for their third load.

While Badger carried the young rabbits, Fox managed the small hedgehogs. As they stepped towards the brink again, the fire was roaring at them from both directions.

'You'll have to swim for it too!' Fox panted to Hedgehog and the other adults. 'No time to come back again.' As he and Badger raced for safety, the flames burst upon the hedgehogs, who leapt in one bunch for the water.

Kestrel dropped from the sky like a bullet, while Tawny Owl

and the pheasants had long ago flown to join their companions.

Adder and Toad, both of whom were excellent swimmers, had soon reached dry land again. All of the animals were now safe from the fire, although some were still struggling in the water.

The hedgehogs, and Weasel too, were good swimmers, but their feet were continually becoming entangled in the weeds and reedy water-plants. This made the crossing doubly tiring, but they helped each other and shouted encouragement, as did all the animals already on the island, until finally, the last dripping body emerged from the water on to dry land.

With a quite unconscious movement, all the animals clustered closely together as they watched the dancing flames across the water. Standing in a tightly-knit group, each individual experienced a comforting feeling of security and mutual affection.

Fox voiced their common feelings. 'In the face of danger,' he said, 'we have managed to forge a community. We are all members of one unit and we can never be divided.'

Although he spoke the words quietly, there was some emotion evident in his voice which communicated itself to all of them. Every animal and bird felt that, whatever else might happen to them on their journey, this particular moment would always retain a vivid significance.

Then they heard the voices. They were human voices, calling directions and advice to each other as they fought the fire. They saw tall dark shapes, in helmets and thick coats, wielding huge pipes, which gushed water at the flames. Other men were beating the ground with stout staves to which were fixed heavy fireproof cloths.

'The humans will soon win this battle,' Tawny Owl declared knowingly. 'You can already see the flames receding.'

'All this damage and horror was caused by one foolish human,' said Toad. 'And all of it has to be put right by these others of his kind who had no hand in it.'

'They're certainly a strange species,' agreed Badger. 'I never pretended to understand them.'

As the animals watched the flames gradually diminishing under the efforts of the firefighters, many of them felt, for perhaps the first time, an unusual kinship with the humans who shared their desire to see the fire, their mutual enemy, quenched. Yet this kinship, they each understood, was to be short-lived. For as soon as the fire was finally overcome, the very presence of the humans at such close quarters posed a new problem for their freedom. As long as the men remained on the other side of the causeway, the animals' safest escape route was blocked.

Fox turned towards Badger, and found his eyes on him. He saw they reflected his own thoughts. Fox beckoned his friend aside, and motioned to Tawny Owl and Kestrel to join them.

'I think we shall all have to swim for it,' Fox said.

'Not quite all of us, of course,' Tawny Owl corrected him needlessly. 'But I see your point. The humans are far too close for comfort.'

'We still have one advantage,' Badger pointed out. 'They haven't spotted us yet.'

'Don't rely on that,' the pessimistic Owl warned him. 'At the moment they're too intent on their work to look about them. I don't think we should fool ourselves. There's virtually no cover of any value on the island. As soon as they've mastered that fire, we shall be noticed.'

'Tawny Owl's right,' Fox agreed, grimly nodding his chestnut head. 'As I see it, we've two alternatives. We can swim across to another side of the marsh, or we can wait until the fire is put out, and then make a dash for it back across the causeway.'

'Right under their noses?' Kestrel asked in amazement.

'The element of surprise could give us just the few minutes we need to get clear,' Fox answered.

'Better still,' suggested Badger, 'the birds could create some diversion – I don't exactly know how – that might enable us to slip past without even being spotted.'

'I'm afraid you're forgetting two very important points,' Tawny Owl said somewhat pompously. 'First of all, it will take several trips across that causeway before you're all back on the mainland again; just as when you were coming on to the island. Secondly, even when the fire is out, the ground will remain red-hot for some time. None of you animals could possibly set foot on it, and as for Adder – why, he'd be roasted alive.'

'Of course,' muttered Fox. 'I must say, Owl,' he added after a moment, 'your judgement is of the greatest value.'

Tawny Owl passed off the compliment with the words, 'I merely wish to help,' but he was not entirely successful in disguising an expression that was a little smug.

'What do *you* advise?' Fox asked him.

'If all of you were powerful swimmers, and if there were no juveniles, I shouldn't hesitate to advise you to swim for it straight away,' Tawny Owl replied. 'But even the fully grown hedgehogs, and Weasel, had the utmost difficulty in swimming to the island. So I think there's only one course open to you. You will simply have to stay put, and trust in the good nature of the humans, or in the likelihood of their being too exhausted, after their efforts, to bother about a handful of wildlife.'

Badger and Fox knew there was nothing they could say to refute Tawny Owl's statement.

'However,' Kestrel added, 'although I'm sure you've correctly summed up the situation, Owl, there's still a possibility of we birds diverting the humans' attention, as Badger suggested.'

'Only for a few minutes, surely,' argued Tawny Owl.

'Unless we can attract their attention, and make them follow us far enough, and for long enough, to leave the coast clear for the animals to get away.'

'Sounds like a very long shot to me.' Tawny Owl shrugged his wings.

'It's worth a try,' Kestrel said pointedly, and with some

irritation.

While the four of them were debating the point, a gleeful shout, repeated by all the other animals, reached their ears. 'There's Mole! There's Mole!'

They broke off their conversation, and Fox and Badger looked at each other in astonishment. They hastily rejoined the others, who were all craning their necks over the water, and standing on the very edge of the island, completely disregarding the danger of their toppling in.

On the edge of the marsh there were now only one or two isolated pockets of flames. One of the firefighters, who appeared to have only recently come on to the scene, had removed his jacket and was mopping his brow. He had quite carelessly dropped the coat in a bundle on to the ashy ground, and from one of the deep pockets Mole had half emerged, and was peering short-sightedly all around.

The man had fortunately not heard the animals' cries of excitement, which to him would merely have sounded like a chorus of yelps and squeaks, but Fox at once told everyone to remain silent.

The animals suffered unbearable tension as Mole, not seeming to be in too much of a hurry, pulled himself right out of the pocket, and stepped off the jacket.

'He'll burn himself!' said Tawny Owl.

But Mole seemed to feel no ill effects, and began to wander aimlessly around over the ashy ground.

'Quick, Kestrel, and Owl, I beg you, go up in the air and catch that man's eye,' said Fox urgently. 'I'll try to reach Mole myself.'

The birds glanced at one another for an instant, and then together swooped into the air, uttering their loudest cries.

'Hoo-hoo-hooooo,' called Tawny Owl.

'Kew-kew-kee-kee-kee,' screeched Kestrel, soaring like an arrow way up into the sky, and then diving downwards again, as straight as a javelin.

The man, still holding his handkerchief in one hand, looked up at the cloudless sky. Kestrel and Tawny Owl began to loop round and round each other like two giant gnats, still hooting and screeching as loud as they could.

With one eye on the man, Fox stepped down on to the causeway and streaked towards the shore. The two birds continued to make such a racket that the noise of Fox's splashing was quite unnoticeable.

He reached the other side safely, and realized at once why Mole had appeared to walk quite comfortably over the burnt ground. The gallons of water squirted from the pumps had cooled the surface tremendously, and though it still felt warm, the soft ashy deposit was extremely comfortable to the feet. This encouraged Fox a great deal, and in a few bounds he had reached Mole.

At the suddenness of Fox's approach Mole began to make little twittering noises of alarm. The two animals exchanged not a word as Mole quickly climbed on to Fox's back, and Fox at once turned back for the causeway.

At this moment the man, who had been staring up at the two birds, found his eyes beginning to water, and was obliged to look down again. Out of the corner of one eye he saw a blurred shape dash past, and turning round, saw Fox, with his passenger, jump into the water and run back towards the island.

'Well, I'll be . . .!' he muttered, walking quickly to the water's edge to look more closely. He saw at once the promontory of land running underneath the water, and, looking along its length, soon spotted the little collection of creatures on the island.

'Good – ness gra – cious!' he exclaimed loudly, and began to call his colleagues. 'Quick, lads, come and look at this! There's a regular zoo over there! Just look at them!'

Most of the other men joined him at once, leaving only two beaters at work on the remnants of the flames. Standing in a line by the waterside, they stared pop-eyed at the animals gathered on the island. Even as they stood, unable to speak, Tawny Owl and Kestrel dropped from the blue and landed amongst their friends.

'It's . . . it's uncanny,' one of the men whispered. 'Where have they come from?'

The animals, with their party once again complete, faced the humans with a feeling of solidarity. Behind the men, now joined by the last two beaters, stood the huge scarlet engine, like a dormant monster, in an expanse of black and ash-grey. The fire was out.

And so the two groups confronted each other: human faces staring at animal faces, and animal faces staring back, both wondering who would move first.

## XI

# THE STORM

While the animals and the men had all been absorbed in watching or fighting the progress of the fire, they had not noticed a dark formation of cloud moving slowly towards them. Only Kestrel, sporting with Tawny Owl in the sky, had seen this bank of cloud, but the significance of its approach had not really impressed itself upon him. Now, as the party of animals on their little island stood wondering if they were once again in danger, the first rumblings of thunder could be heard.

The men looked at each other questioningly, and then upwards, noting for the first time the gathering clouds. The slight breeze that had prevailed had blown up into a strong wind, and so the clouds came on apace. The end of the long drought was at hand.

It was only a matter of minutes, while the two groups still stood somewhat uncertainly facing each other, before the first heavy spots of rain fell on the scorched ground. The reverberations of thunder became louder and louder, and it grew steadily darker. The sun was blotted out. Finally lightning began to flicker across the dark sky, and the rain started to fall in real earnest.

The animals felt the welcome wetness on their bodies, and Toad, who always enjoyed really wet weather, leapt joyfully off the bank into the water, and paddled up and down croaking happily.

The men, who only minutes earlier would have rejoiced at the rain, now instinctively behaved as all members of the human race do in such a situation. They dispersed to find shelter from the downpour.

This was the very chance Fox had been hoping for. He hastily called Toad out of the water and on to his back, while he bid Mole take up his usual position on the back of Badger.

'Now, follow me!' said Fox in urgent tones, 'as swiftly as you can!'

On to the causeway he jumped, with the larger animals following close behind.

Three trips Fox and Badger made through the heavy rain before all of the animals were safely on land again.

'Which way do we take?' Fox asked the passenger Toad.

'Straight ahead,' he replied. 'That will bring us to the fence on the other side of the army land. Then we're into the farmland. We'll have to go carefully, but there will be plenty of shelter.'

Water pouring from their drenched fur, and their heads bent beneath its fury, the animals slunk through the downpour. Only Toad and Adder, who had no fur to worry about, seemed to enjoy the feel of the rain. Toad tried to croak a little tune to cheer up the others, but the deafening noise of the peals of thunder unfortunately smothered his good intentions.

Tawny Owl and the other birds had been flying on ahead for short distances, and then waiting for the rest of the party to catch them up.

'This is most unfortunate,' the soaked Badger remarked to Tawny Owl as he passed him again. 'First the fire, now a torrent of water. We really couldn't have been more unlucky.'

'You should remember, Badger, that it afforded us just the diversion we needed,' Tawny Owl pointed out.

'Yes, I suppose we should be grateful that we've come this far and are still all together.'

'I'm the luckiest of all,' said Mole. 'I was given up for dead.'

'You would have had only your own greed to thank for that,' Tawny Owl said sternly.

'Oh well now, Owl,' Badger said, 'I'm sure he's learnt his lesson.'

'Thank you, Badger,' Mole said timidly.

Tawny Owl flew on ahead again, and the animals remained silent for some time.

Suddenly, Mole said, 'But we're *not* all still together.'

'The lizards?' asked Fox quietly.

'Yes.'

'I was rather hoping no one would mention them,' Fox said.

'If only I could have persuaded them to have stayed on the journey,' Badger said miserably. 'I knew they were taking the wrong decision. And now . . .' he broke off, unable to finish the sentence.

'They *may* have escaped,' Fox said with false heartiness, but he knew it was no comfort to Badger, who refused to be consoled.

Presently they crossed beyond the limit of the burnt ground which marked the extent of the fire in this direction, and after that the soil became increasingly spongy and soggy. The small animals, with their lighter weight, were able to run over the surface fairly easily, but the heavier animals began to slow down considerably.

The rain continued to pour down, and soon Fox, Badger, and the hares and rabbits, found that their paws were sinking into the softening ground. As they trudged on, the situation worsened. They sank up to their ankles in mud.

'We'll have to keep on.' Fox barely turned his head to call behind him. 'There's no shelter here, and this mud will only get worse.'

Toad had long since ceased his singing, and was peering ahead through the rain. 'Yes, there it is!' he suddenly cried. 'I can see it! I can see the railings! Not much further!'

Heartened by the news, the line of animals put on a little spurt. Soon they could all see the line of metal posts and rails which was the boundary of the army land.

Beyond the fence was a thick hedgerow of shrubbery and thorn trees, where Kestrel, Tawny Owl and the pheasants were already sheltering, while they preened their drenched feathers. They watched the animals threading their way underneath the rails. They looked a sorry sight, with their fur plastered down, and streams of water dripping from their sides.

Fox led them into a thick mass of holly shrubbery, where

the closely packed leaves had kept the ground underneath comparatively dry. They sank down with dejected faces and empty stomachs.

The mother rabbits and mice had to quieten their hungry children. There was no possibility of looking for food until the storm abated.

Their shelter was periodically lit by a dazzling brightness as the lightning flashed directly overhead. Some of the animals endeavoured to sleep.

Toad wanted Adder to join him in a foraging expedition, but the snake declined. 'I'm too tired,' he drawled. 'I haven't been riding all the way like you.'

'Please yourself.' Toad shrugged, and wandered off into the teeming rain to look for slugs and worms.

The other animals looked at each other miserably. They felt very wet and very uncomfortable.

Badger thought of his old, dry, comfortable set and wondered what had become of it. 'It'll be many long weeks before I can build another one,' he thought to himself.

Weasel and the voles, and Fox and the rabbits, also wished they were in their snug underground homes. Mole wondered if he dare dig a tunnel for comfort, but feared Badger's disapproval.

So the merciless rain lashed down. Toad, returning from his hunting foray, found the animals' makeshift shelter was getting damper and damper. Eventually they were as wet as if they had remained in the open.

'It's no use,' said Fox wearily. 'We'll have to move and look for a drier spot.'

'If I remember correctly,' said Toad, 'there's a barn not far away.'

Fox wanted to know how far.

'I can't be exactly sure,' replied Toad. 'It's so difficult to see anything at the moment, except the rain.'

'But do you know in what direction it is?' asked Fox.

Toad pondered for a minute. 'I'm sure I could find it,' he said at length.

'Then we put ourselves in your hands,' said Fox. He shrugged his shoulders. 'In any case, we can't stay here.'

So the animals wearily formed another line in the rain, their still wet bodies taking a second soaking, and Fox led them off, at Toad's instigation, across the field that lay before them.

In one corner of this field they encountered a stile, which they were all easily able to circumvent, and it gave on to a narrow path which ran between the fields beyond. In one of these a herd of black and white Friesian cows, with a number of calves, were doing their best to shelter under a large oak tree.

Toad advised Fox to continue along the path, so, after satisfying himself that no humans were near, he led the animals slowly down it, keeping well in to the side by the hedgerow border.

They found that the path led into an orchard, where pear and plum trees had recently finished blossoming. At the far end

was a long, low wooden building with small windows.

'Is that the barn?' whispered Fox.

'It's not the one I saw before, but it looks as if it will suit our needs,' Toad answered.

The animals lost no time in running over to it, and for once they were lucky. It was open.

'It's a storehouse,' remarked Fox. But at that time of year there was no fruit to store. There were a few empty boxes lying around on the floor, and a few odds and ends on a shelf that ran the length of one side. At one end there were the remains of a bale of straw that must have been used for packing. Apart from this the storehouse was quite empty.

The straw and the floor were dry. 'This is marvellous,' said Hedgehog. 'We'll be snug and dry in no time.'

The rodents had already begun to pull lumps of straw from the bale. Fox stood irresolute, his head down. His fur dripped continuously, and a little puddle of water had formed at his feet.

'What's troubling you, Fox?' asked Badger, who was fashioning himself a comfortable nest of straw in one corner.

'I don't like the idea of that open door,' Fox said. 'Why should it be open if the storehouse is not in use?'

'I can't say,' said Badger. 'But if it had been closed it would have been no use to us!'

'You're right, of course,' said Fox, still not moving.

'We can stay here until this storm is over, at any rate,' Badger reassured him. 'Nobody will be about in this rain – not even farm workers.'

'When it stops we shall have to look for food,' Fox said. 'However . . . yes, we'll stay here for the present, and rest.'

Tawny Owl alighted in the doorway. 'Kestrel's in one of the plum trees, keeping a lookout,' he announced. 'Pheasant's agreed to relieve him in a while. I'm joining you until dark.'

The owl fluttered up to a vacant piece of shelf and there he perched. For a time he watched the animals preparing their nests from the straw; then he closed his eyes.

Badger, having finished his own arrangements, directed the voles and fieldmice in forming their own little ball of straw.

The larger animals laid out a generous, thick expanse all over the floor, and lay down side by side. Even Adder was content to entwine himself round some of the strands.

## THE STORM

The squirrels, however, objected to sleeping on the floor. 'It's just for now – just this time,' Badger told them. 'There's not time enough to build a proper nest on the shelf.'

So Weasel and Mole joined Badger in the corner, Fox lay down with the rabbits and hedgehogs, Hare and his family joined the squirrels, and Toad snuggled up with the mice. Only Adder found that no one wished to sleep near him.

As they listened to the rain lashing down outside, the animals from Farthing Wood were all the more grateful for the snug dryness of the storehouse. One by one they dropped into sleep, forgetful of their empty stomachs.

There was not one of the party left awake when Kestrel arrived on the threshold having completed his watch, his dry feathers showing that the furious storm had at last abated.

As Kestrel joined his sleeping friends, the safety of the party was now entrusted to Pheasant.

# XII

# TRAPPED!

Tom Griggs had been in a black humour all that morning. He had lost another chicken the previous night, from right under the nose of his guard dog, a big bull mastiff. The animal was worse than useless; it always seemed to fall fast asleep just when it was needed most. This latest theft had brought the total of stolen chickens to four. And now the hens were in such a frightened state that they would not lay. Oh, if he could just get his hands on the guilty fox!

To cap it all came the storm. After weeks of drought which had dried up his crops, those that had survived were now being beaten flat by this merciless rain. 'I shall be ruined, Betsy, I'm sure of it,' he muttered angrily to his wife, as he stood watching the storm dash itself against his windows.

Mrs Griggs could offer him no comfort. Weather was its own master; mere humans had no control over it. She went on preparing the midday meal, keeping silent except for an occasional word to the farm cat, which sat shivering in the kitchen, soaked to the skin.

The rain finally stopped as Griggs was moodily munching the meat pie his wife had made. He pushed his plate away. 'No more for me, my dear,' he said. 'I must go out and have a look round.'

He got up, ignoring the protestations of his wife concerning the unfinished meal, put on his gumboots and mackintosh, and, taking up his ancient shotgun from the corner, went outside.

The sky had lightened considerably, but the ground was awash with puddles.

The bull mastiff strained at its leash as it saw its master. 'Down, Jack!' called the farmer. 'You're no use to me!'

It lay down again, sadly, and watched him out of sight.

It took Griggs about an hour to examine his fields for damage, and he found what he had expected to find. This put him into an even blacker humour.

As he trudged unhappily back through his small orchard, a gaudy cock pheasant rose up from the long grass, and, putting his gun to his shoulder, he shot clean through it. The glossy, multi-coloured bird crumpled, and plummeted to the earth.

At the sound of the shot, the pheasant's dull-marked mate also took to the air, uttering a loud, startled clatter. Griggs promptly fired his other barrel at the hen pheasant, and she, too, dropped to the ground.

He collected the two limp bodies and then, noticing his wife standing by the storehouse, with the now unleashed Jack by her side, he called out, 'We're in luck, Betsy! A brace of pheasant!'

'You come and see what I've found!' she called back.

Griggs was somewhat struck by the way in which his dog remained by the shed, bolt upright, and did not bound towards him at his approach.

'Look through the window if you want a surprise,' said Mrs Griggs, indicating the storehouse.

Her husband put his face to the glass, and a gasp escaped him. For a moment he remained immobile, then he moved away and looked at his wife, round-eyed.

'It's . . . it's full of animals!' he said in a tone of disbelief, handing the pheasants to her absent-mindedly.

'Including your fox,' she added meaningfully.

Griggs looked at his gun. 'Caught him red-handed,' he whispered.

'I came out to give Jack his dinner,' his wife informed him. 'I just chanced to wander round here, and there was our store-shed full of animals – and birds – all fast asleep. When I saw the fox, I quickly shut the door on 'em all.' She paused to examine the two unfortunate members of Fox's party who were not inside, and which her husband had just killed in the orchard. Then she motioned to the shed. 'There's an owl on the shelf, and a sort of hawk thing,' she reported. 'I reckon they must have all run in there out of the storm. Did you ever see such a thing?'

'No, I *never* saw such a thing,' said Griggs emphatically. 'And I won't ever again. The culprits won't get away from me this time.' He seemed to think the other animals had also played a part in the theft of his chickens.

'Now, Jack,' he admonished his dog, 'you sit there, and don't stir till I say so. We've got work to do.'

The bull mastiff did not show the slightest inclination to do anything but sit exactly where it was, its teeth partially bared in anticipation of its forthcoming moment of success.

'What are you going to do, Tom?' asked Mrs Griggs, following her husband indoors.

Griggs brandished his shotgun at her. 'I'm going to clean and oil this,' he said. 'Then I'm going to re-load her, and *then* I'm going to settle a little score with our friend the fox.'

'What about the other animals though?' asked his wife.

'Those we'll see about later,' he replied. 'There's plenty of time.'

Fox had woken with a start as he heard the door close on them. It was not a loud noise, and most of his companions continued to sleep unawares.

'Are you awake, Kestrel?' Fox whispered, as he saw the bird stir.

'Yes,' Kestrel whispered back. 'Was that the wind?'

'No, I can hear someone outside,' Fox replied. He walked to the door and tried to peer through the crack underneath. At once there was a loud growling noise. Fox quickly retreated.

'There's a human and what sounds like a very large dog,' he informed Kestrel.

'We'd better wake the others,' suggested Kestrel.

'No,' Fox said sharply. 'Not yet. We don't want any panic.' He sniffed all round the sides of the shed, pushing at various boards with his paw.

'Have a look at the windows,' he said finally.

'No latches,' Kestrel reported. 'In any case, none of you animals could climb up here.'

Fox nodded and went over to Badger's corner. A gentle prod roused him.

Badger noticed at once the door was shut. 'Oh dear,' he said. 'Now we're in a mess.'

'I'm afraid we are,' Fox said. 'But there *must* be a way out.'

Badger stood up, unintentionally disturbing Mole. 'What is it, Badger?' asked the sleepy animal, with a yawn. 'Are we going?'

'Sssh!' Badger cautioned. 'We're thinking. Go back to sleep, Mole, there's a good fellow.'

But Mole sensed there was something wrong. 'Oh! We're shut in!' he shrieked. 'We're caught!'

'Be quiet!' snapped Fox fiercely. 'Do you want everyone to wake up?'

There were sounds of stirring amongst the straw. They heard the lazy hiss of Adder's voice. 'Mmm. It seems our exit is sealed,' he drawled. 'I knew it was a mistake to put that stupid, vain bird on guard. Pheasants are only good for eating.'

'No use saying that now,' remarked Badger. 'What's done is done. What we've got to do now . . .' he broke off as they heard the unmistakable report of a gun.

The animals looked fearfully at each other. There was a brief silence; then they detected the alarm call of a pheasant followed immediately by a second gunshot.

'Sounds as if Pheasant's done for,' Fox muttered.

All the animals were awake now, milling about in the centre of the floor, and bombarding Fox and Badger with frightened questions.

Finally Fox shouted for silence. 'Please! Everyone, quiet!'

He began pacing up and down the shed, a few feet one way, then a few feet back. 'Now, I admit we're in danger,' he said in a low voice. 'There's no point in denying it.' His head was down, and he seemed to be merely thinking aloud, not addressing the others. 'But if you all keep calm,' he murmured, 'we'll think of a way out.' He continued to pace.

'There's only one way out, of course,' Tawny Owl observed.

All faces turned to him.

'Dig,' he said.

'Dig?' asked the squirrels.

'Dig?' asked the fieldmice.

'Of course!' exclaimed Fox. 'Dig! We'll dig our way out.'

At that moment they heard human voices calling to each other outside. It was Tom Griggs telling his wife about the pheasants, and she replying to him about her find in the store-shed.

The animals fell silent again. The next minute they saw the farmer's face pressed to the window. In his eyes they read amazement, then anger, and finally resolution. They saw him turn away, and heard his and Mrs Griggs's footsteps receding towards the farmhouse.

'Right,' said Fox. 'No time to lose. Who's our best tunneller?'

'Mole,' replied Badger.

The little creature visibly swelled with pride. At last he was to be of some use to the party. It was all he could have wished for.

'Come on then, Mole,' said Fox. 'Show us what you can do.'

'Just watch me,' said Mole ecstatically. Then he looked up at Fox in consternation. 'But where do I begin?' he asked miserably. 'I can't dig through that.' He pointed with his snout at the wooden floor. He was so disappointed that he could feel the tears beginning to collect.

'Leave that to us,' said Squirrel, and gathered the gnawing power of his party together.

'We can gnaw too,' said the hedgehogs.

They were joined by the rabbits and the voles and mice. Opening their mouths, they presented over a score of sets of powerful teeth to the floor and began to gnaw.

The din was terrific as they set to work. The bull mastiff heard the rasping and scraping of their teeth and began to growl again.

'They've left the dog behind,' Kestrel said to Fox.

'How are we to avoid him?'

'I think that's where I come in,' hissed Adder, and slithered towards the crack underneath the door. Here he stationed himself, keeping the farmer's dog at bay by alternately hissing and lunging at its inquisitive muzzle.

The thin planks of wood that formed the floor of the shed soon succumbed to the concerted efforts of the rodents. When the hole was big enough, Mole squeezed through, and began to dig vertically downwards through the soil underneath as fast as his expert claws could manage.

As the hole in the floorboards was enlarged, Badger was able to climb into Mole's pit, and, following in the tracks of his friend, he widened the tunnel as he descended. Presently he reached a junction in the tunnel where the industrious Mole had turned off horizontally, carving out a straight path that would eventually take him right underneath the shed, to emerge again in the orchard.

'Where are you, Mole?' Badger called softly as he stopped. 'Are you outside yet?'

'Not yet, Badger,' he heard a muffled voice reply from the darkness ahead of him.

'How do you know?' Badger asked. 'You'd better dig up to the surface to see.' He was afraid that Mole, in his enthusiasm for being useful, might get carried away and dig too far.

'All right,' he heard Mole answer him.

Badger waited patiently. A little later he heard Mole's excited squeak. 'Yes! I'm out! Badger, I've done it!'

'Good fellow,' said Badger warmly. 'Now, come back to me. If we work quickly, we'll all be safe in a few minutes.'

Mole, an elated expression on his face, returned along the tunnel to Badger.

'Now, I want you to go back to Fox,' Badger told him. 'Tell him to organize a chain of animals to pass the earth along that I'm going to dig out. He'd better stay at the entrance of the tunnel to pile the earth in the shed. Off you go!'

A moment later Weasel appeared. 'Fox said to go ahead,' he informed Badger. 'You push the soil back to me, and I'll pass it on to Hare. Behind him is Rabbit, then Mole, and finally Fox at the top.'

'Good.' Badger nodded. 'I'm going to dig fast, so be careful you don't get buried.'

Without another word he began to move forward along the tunnel, kicking large sprays of earth behind him with his powerful back feet. Weasel worked overtime to keep his part of the passage clear, furiously pushing the earth behind him to Hare.

As they progressed down Mole's tunnel, more animals were needed in the line to keep the soil moving all the way back to the entrance, where Fox was busily spreading it over the floor of the shed. By the time Badger reached the point where Mole had started to dig towards the surface, nearly the whole of the party was helping with the work. Only the tiny animals, the voles and fieldmice, the very young, and Toad and the birds remained in the store-shed, assisting Fox where they could.

Adder had remained at his post all the while, and had succeeded in holding the attention of the bull mastiff so well that the dog remained completely unaware that the animals had almost tunnelled their way to safety.

Badger soon saw daylight ahead and cautiously inched his way to the surface. Pushing out only his head, he saw that he was back in the orchard, about six feet from the shed. Only a matter of inches round the corner sat the bull mastiff. Badger sniffed elaborately in every direction, and then stepped out of the hole.

Looking down into the tunnel, he could see Weasel, his fur

and face covered in lumps of earth, climbing up towards him.

'Pass the word back to Fox that we've finished,' Badger whispered, 'and that he must get everybody through the tunnel as quickly as he possibly can. I'll stay here at the exit to help everyone out.'

Weasel turned to whisper the message to Hare, then joined Badger on the surface. The procedure was repeated by all of the animals in the tunnel, so that when Hedgehog, who was the last in the line, finally repeated Badger's words to Fox, most of the party was already hiding in the long grass of the orchard, ready to race for safety.

Fox had just finished distributing the last quantity of earth over the floor. 'Down you go, my little friends!' he called to the youngsters, who descended into the tunnel under the care of the voles and fieldmice.

Toad, Tawny Owl and Kestrel went close on their heels, the birds half fluttering and half walking along the tunnel.

Fox glanced towards Adder. 'Can you hold on just long enough for us to get clear?' he asked.

'Of course,' replied Adder. 'We must all play our part.'

'We won't forget this,' Fox assured him. 'We'll wait for you as soon as we reach a safe spot. I'll send Kestrel back to show you the way.'

'You'd better get going,' Adder hissed. 'I can see the farmer on his way back.'

Fox called a final farewell and leapt into the tunnel.

# XIII

# Pursued

Now left entirely alone, Adder prepared himself for escape. He stretched his full length tight against the wall, so as to be as inconspicuous as possible. As soon as the farmer and his dog entered the building, he would slip through the crack while their backs were turned.

He could still watch the approach of the farmer towards the shed, but now all he could see were his boots trudging ominously forward. He heard Griggs call to the bull mastiff; then the footsteps stopped, and the door was swung back.

The dog bounded inside, barking furiously. Then, seeing that the shed was empty, it began to run round, nose to the floor, whining in frustration.

'What the devil . . .!' was the unfinished exclamation from

the farmer as he stepped into the shed, his gun half raised to his shoulder. He stood staring in disbelief at the earth spread evenly over the floor, and the neat hole in the floorboards.

Behind him, Adder slithered under the open door and out on to the path, making as fast a pace as he could manage towards the nearest long grass. He could hear the commotion in the store-shed, as the cheated farmer cursed and shouted angrily at his dog. The shouting was followed by a loud yelp, which, Adder decided, was the result of a well-aimed kick from the farmer.

He reached a patch of cover adjacent to the orchard, and hid himself in some wet twigs and leaves amongst a clump of couch-grass. Here he intended to stay until he judged it was safe to proceed further.

The farmer came out of the shed like a bolt from a gun, his miserable dog slinking at his heels, its tail held low. He went straight to the orchard, where he fell to scanning the grassy ground. His eyes soon picked out what he was searching for – the exit hole of the animals' tunnel. With an angry snarl, the farmer directed the muzzle of his shotgun down into the hole, and fired both barrels. Some clods of earth flew upwards, followed by a thin wisp of smoke.

'That'll teach 'em!' growled Tom Griggs, and he stumped off, frowning hideously, back to the cottage where his wife was waiting at the door.

The bull mastiff continued to skulk around the hole as if it did not intend to be fooled twice.

Adder, in his temporary hideout, wondered how far away his friends were. He knew that they would have put as much distance behind them as they were able before they rested.

Through the network of twigs and grass stems in front of his red eyes, Adder saw the bull mastiff suddenly turn its head from the tunnel and put its muzzle to the ground. It sniffed vigorously over the grass, and having picked up a scent, followed it closely under the trees of the orchard. Adder was sure the dog was now on the trail of Fox and his party.

The bull mastiff increased its pace, and barked excitedly. It was a deep, throaty bark; a fearsome noise.

Adder decided the coast was clear, and slithered into the open. He wound his way to the next piece of cover, an isolated patch of stinging nettles, where he paused to consider what he should do next.

After some serious contemplation he decided there was really very little he could do, except wait for Kestrel. He had no idea in which direction his companions had gone, and there was no way in which he could warn them that they were being pursued. In any case, the dog was making enough noise to wake the dead. They would have plenty of time to get out of its way. Having reassured himself on that point, Adder settled down patiently for a long wait.

\*

It had taken a matter of only a couple of minutes for Fox to race through the tunnel, clamber up the exit shaft, and prepare the waiting animals for immediate flight. It needed only a short consultation with Toad before they decided on their direction.

On Toad's advice Fox led them out of the bounds of the farmer's land, on to a footpath that wound its way past several neighbouring farmsteads and orchards, on to a stretch of open common land, where it then led sharply uphill.

'Are you quite sure this is the right way?' Fox asked, as they rested for a minute amongst some shrubbery at the foot of the rise.

'Oh yes,' declared Toad. 'I recognize all this. Of course, it took me an age on my own to cover the same ground.'

'I don't much like the look of what's ahead,' Fox admitted. 'We can be seen far too clearly, for my liking, as we climb that hill.'

'Don't worry about that,' Toad answered. 'It's a very stony, uneven path. Humans don't use it much, I would guess. In any case, the sensible ones are still indoors after that storm.'

'I hope you're right,' said Fox. 'What's on the other side of the hill?'

'The path drops steeply down to a sort of copse. Beyond that there are more farm dwellings and fields. When we've got those behind us, there are green meadows ahead, as thick and lush as you've ever seen. They will lead us to the river.'

'Can we reach the copse today?' Fox asked briskly.

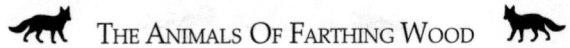 

'Oh, it's not too far,' Toad assured him. 'We'll be quite safe in there. Nothing but a few rooks to bother about.'

Fox looked round at his friends, most of whom were too tired and hungry to talk. 'One last effort now and we'll soon be able to rest and eat at our leisure,' Fox promised them. 'Can you do it?'

All the animals nodded, some more wearily than others.

Fox took the lead as they moved up the hill at walking pace. As they climbed, rain began to fall again. But this time it was gentler; there was no fury in it, and it refreshed them.

Wearily they plodded on. Tawny Owl and Kestrel flew to the brow of the hill and called back encouragement to their struggling companions.

'You can see the river from up here,' Tawny Owl cried. 'It looks just like a tiny stream in the distance.'

'You're nearly up,' Kestrel called. 'Keep going.'

When they were about halfway up, Fox suddenly stopped. 'Did you hear anything?' he asked Badger, who was behind him.

'No,' said Badger.

'Keep going! Keep going!' Kestrel shrieked. His hawk's eyes had picked out an ominous shape way back on the footpath. 'Don't stop now!' he cried. 'Make haste!'

Fox knew now that he had not been mistaken. A faint bark came to him from the distance. 'It's the farmer's dog,' he said to Badger. 'We must hurry.'

Standing to one side Fox egged on the other animals to fresh exertions. Eventually they all passed him, and he was left watching their ascent anxiously.

'Badger, I must entrust you with the party again,' he called after him. 'You get them to the copse. I'll try and delay this customer.'

He added in a lower voice, 'Well, Toad, I'm afraid you'll have to make your own way for a bit. I'll join you as soon as I can.'

'Of course, I understand,' Toad replied, and instantly leapt to the ground from Fox's back, and hopped after the main party as quickly as he could. 'Look out for yourself!' he called back over his shoulder.

The bull mastiff was just beginning to climb the slope, so Fox descended part of the way to meet it. Needing all its breath for running uphill, the dog had at last ceased to bark.

'Here I am!' Fox shouted down, standing his ground. 'I'm the character you're after! You can ignore the others!' He glanced quickly behind him to see how his friends were progressing. They were about three-quarters of the distance up the rise.

'Yes, it *is* you,' gasped the dog, looking up towards the small chestnut figure. 'You're . . . the . . . culprit. My master . . . wants you . . . dead.'

'Your master wants every fox dead,' came the reply. 'I could see the hatred in his eyes when he saw me in the shed.'

The bull mastiff paused, a few yards from Fox. 'He wants

*you,*' the dog replied. 'You killed his chickens. He wants his revenge.'

'He's got the wrong animal,' Fox said calmly. 'I never killed a chicken in my life. They don't suit my tastes at all – too many feathers.'

'A likely story,' growled the guard dog. 'Strange isn't it, that you should be found lurking just round the corner from the chicken coop?'

'You may call it strange,' said Fox. 'I was not lurking, as you suggested. I and my friends merely entered the shed to shelter from the storm – and were shut in.'

'I don't believe a word of it,' the bull mastiff said savagely. 'Oh, I know you foxes are all supposed to be very cunning and clever. But you don't fool me. I'm taking you back. Then perhaps I'll get some thanks, for once, from my master.'

It advanced a step towards Fox, warily.

'I'm afraid you'll find you're mistaken, if that's what you're expecting,' Fox said evenly.

'What do you mean?' growled the dog, hesitating a fraction.

'Your master doesn't want *you* to obtain his revenge for him. He, and only he, wants that satisfaction. Nothing else will do. Believe me, I know all about human feelings.' Fox shrugged. 'You domesticated creatures are blinded by humans' generosity. They feed you, groom you, give you a home. You don't notice their faults. Now we wild animals are different. We observe human ways from a distance, and we understand them better. Animals, and their needs, are of little consideration when they conflict with their own. That's always been the way of it, and it won't alter. So I say again, you'll get no thanks from your master for killing me.'

The bull mastiff seemed to waver. With less confidence in its gruff voice it said, 'Then I'll take you back alive.'

'That's quite impossible,' Fox replied at once. 'I'm no match for your size and strength, but if you want to take me back, you'll have to kill me first.'

'Confound your clever talk!' the bull mastiff swore. 'My master blamed me for not catching the fox that killed his chickens. Now I *have* caught a fox, it seems he won't want it.'

'You should have caught the right fox,' said Fox smoothly. 'I've got nothing against you,' he went on. 'Every creature to its training. But whatever killed those chickens was clever enough to elude you. It won't help you now to kill the wrong animal.'

With wonderfully contrived coolness, Fox turned on his heel and walked off up the slope after his friends, who had now disappeared over the brow of the hill.

He steeled himself to continue at a sauntering pace, knowing full well that this show of confidence would convince the bull mastiff once and for all that it had made an error.

At the top, Fox found Toad waiting for him. Only then did he permit himself to look back. The bull mastiff was standing, with a baffled expression on its once fierce face, looking up the slope towards Fox. It had not moved one inch forward. As it saw Fox turn, it slunk away, back the way it had come.

Toad was unable to contain his excitement. 'Fox, you were superb!' he exclaimed. 'I heard everything. It was magnificent. Wait till I tell the others about it. Such coolness and poise. Well, you certainly browbeat him!'

'When you live by your wits and senses, as we wild creatures do,' said Fox, 'it's not so difficult to win an argument with one of his sort.' He smiled. 'Now, come on. Up you get, my friend. We must catch the others up. It's a long time since we ate, and I bet there are all sorts of good things to be found in that copse.'

# XIV

# THE COPSE

Badger and the rest of the party made much of Fox when he and Toad caught them up. The respect and admiration which they already felt for their leader was now heightened by his latest success.

Dusk was falling as they entered the copse. Rooks were circling the tree-tops, cawing noisily in their evening ritual, before settling one by one, on their nests for the night.

The immediate objective of the animals was to satisfy their gnawing hunger, and, after establishing their camp amongst some elm shrubbery, they set off on their separate forays.

The squirrels were so overjoyed to find tall trees which they could run up and down, that their quest for food was temporarily suspended as they chased one another up the trunks and along the branches. The sleepy rooks cackled irritably.

When the animals had all found and eaten as much as they needed, they made their way directly back to the camp. Fox called a council of the leaders of each group, and they decided unanimously to remain in the copse for some days, to rest and build up their strength. After the danger and hardship which they had encountered in the last few days, when they had run from one crisis to the next, all the animals agreed that they had found the ideal haven of safety for the time being. Here they could comfortably prepare themselves for the many hazards that lay in their oncoming travels.

'What are you going to do about Adder?' asked Weasel.

'Adder!' Fox exclaimed. 'Good heavens, we've forgotten him! Whatever will he be thinking of us!'

'Leave it to me,' volunteered Tawny Owl. 'It's pitch black now. I'll fly back to the farm and find him. Don't worry.'

He flew off through the trees and into the open country.

'You mustn't blame yourself,' Badger said to the downcast Fox. 'You've had a lot on your mind.'

'But I promised him,' Fox said miserably. 'He depended on me.'

'It's much safer for Adder to travel at night. The two of them will be far less noticeable,' Weasel said comfortingly. 'Tawny Owl will get him here by the morning. You'll see.'

All afternoon Adder lay hidden amongst the thick stinging nettles, wondering, while he felt comparatively safe himself, about the safety of his friends.

He watched the farmer's bull mastiff race away on their trail, bellowing horribly. The dog's barks had gradually dwindled into the distance, and Adder was left wondering what the fate of Fox, Badger and the others would be.

He would not admit to himself that he was worried, but he found it difficult to maintain his chosen character of an uncommitted, unfeeling individual. He felt decidedly uneasy. This feeling grew as the time wore on; in fact until the time he saw the bull mastiff return.

There was something so altered in the manner of the dog, as it slunk through the long grass of the orchard on its way to its kennel, that Adder guessed at once that it had been bested in some way by his friends.

His feeling changed to one of mild excitement, and he felt sure he could soon expect the arrival of Kestrel.

The rain stopped again, but the sky remained cloudy, and soon it was dusk. Adder began to hope Kestrel would not be long in arriving; otherwise, if it grew too dark, they would certainly miss one another.

But Adder was still alone when night fell. He decided it was pointless to remain any longer under cover in the darkness, and he sallied forth to search for food.

He kept well away from the bull mastiff's kennel, and slithered round the other side of Farmer Griggs's cottage, keeping close to the wall. There was an old water-butt at one corner, and next to that an ancient vegetable box, full of potato peelings and other scraps. Here Adder was fortunate enough to catch himself some supper in the shape of a rat, which had been looking for its own supper amongst the kitchen leavings.

He decided to eat his meal in comfort, away from the human dwelling where there would be no fear of being disturbed. So, with the rat clutched firmly between his jaws, Adder made his way back to the patch of stinging nettles.

In the middle of his meal, he was interrupted by a familiar hooting sound. So Tawny Owl had come for him! He made

haste to reach the orchard where Tawny Owl was flitting to and fro like a huge bat, calling him softly in his flute-toned voice.

The bird's powerful eyes soon discovered Adder signalling him from the grass.

'Glad to see you, Adder,' said Tawny Owl.

'Likewise,' drawled Adder. 'What kept you?'

Tawny Owl related all that had happened.

'I'm just finishing my supper,' said Adder afterwards. 'Have you eaten yet?'

'Only lightly,' Tawny Owl replied.

'Will you join me?'

'With great pleasure.'

They both repaired eagerly to the stinging-nettles, and made short work of what was left of Adder's meal.

'I'll catch you another,' said Tawny Owl, 'and we'll share it out. One good turn, you know . . .'

Adder described where he had made his catch, and Tawny Owl flew away.

He was not long in returning with a second rat, and Adder complimented him on his prowess as a night hunter. They set to together, and devoured their additional snack in companionable silence.

'Now I think we should get under way,' said Tawny Owl. 'It's going to be a fairly long haul for you, Adder. I'll swap some hunting yarns with you as we go.'

In the early hours of the following morning, just before daybreak, Adder and Tawny Owl paused on the crest of the hill, before their descent towards the copse. Tawny Owl took the opportunity of relating to Adder how Fox had triumphed, by persuasion, over the fierce farm dog.

Adder enjoyed the tale. 'Yes,' he said afterwards, 'he's a clever chap, that Fox. I shouldn't be at all surprised if he sees us safely through after all.'

Tawny Owl, whose wisdom even Fox admired, was a little envious of the praises heaped on his friend, considering that he himself had played a leading part in the animals' escape from the farm by his suggestion of digging.

'He *is* clever,' admitted Owl, 'but I'm sure we've all been of some assistance, at one stage or another, on the journey.'

Adder could see where Tawny Owl's thoughts lay, but, a trifle spitefully, pretended ignorance to afford himself some amusement.

'Of course,' he hissed, 'there's no question of anyone else assuming the leadership of the party.'

'Er . . . no, of course not,' said Tawny Owl.

'And yet, if Fox should fall sick or something . . . there would have to be some changes,' Adder went on. 'I suppose Badger would step into his tracks in that case.'

'I really couldn't say,' Tawny Owl said shortly. 'Badger has a good heart, and he's kind. But I don't know if he's got *all* the necessary qualities . . .'

Adder could not resist replying: 'But then who else is there?'

'Well,' Tawny Owl said, ruffling his feathers importantly, 'I . . . um . . . would always . . .'

'You were perhaps thinking of yourself?' Adder suggested.

'Well, Adder, you know I myself would never have mentioned it,' said Tawny Owl, 'but as you began on the subject . . .'

'Did I?' said the teasing snake. 'Yes. I must have done. Ah well, I suppose we all have our aspirations, but whether we ever succeed in them is another matter.'

Tawny Owl felt that Adder was making him look foolish. He tried to retrieve some dignity. 'For my part,' he said, 'I shall be content to act as counsellor when called upon to do so. Fox, I know, relies on me in that respect.'

'Oh, quite,' returned Adder. 'Er . . . shall we move on?'

As they continued towards the copse, Tawny Owl was uncomfortably aware that, without any distinct confession on his part, Adder had exposed a very private feeling of his, the existence of which he had scarcely acknowledged to himself.

It was dawn as they entered the copse. They found their friends astir, their slumbers having been interrupted by the first noises from the rookery. They were greeted with enthusiasm by the whole party, but as soon as possible they pleaded tiredness and went away to find resting-places. For Tawny Owl, in any case, it was customary to sleep during the daylight hours, so

this arrangement suited him admirably. The other animals busied themselves exploring the copse.

Thus the best part of the day was spent, and when most of them, apart from the squirrels, had returned to the elm scrub after their wanderings, they were joined by several visitors.

These were a number of the male rooks who, flying down from the elm-tops, came waddling towards the animals, their iridescent purplish plumage reflecting the shafts of late sunlight that broke through the thick greenery. Naturally they were curious to know what had brought such a miscellaneous group of animals to their particular copse, but there was no trace of resentment in their tone.

Fox explained why they were there, describing their travels as he did so.

'I must tell you,' said one of the rooks, interrupting him after a while, 'that we did wonder if you could be that party of animals we had heard about.'

The animals exchanged surprised glances.

'Word spreads quickly in the bird world,' said the rook, 'and, of course, such an event as a fire is soon common knowledge in the neighbourhood. We've all heard of your escape from that, and how you ran through the storm. But I've never heard tell of a White Deer Park, so there must be a good long way ahead of you yet.'

This observation brought Toad into the conversation, explaining that he was acting as guide because he had already travelled the distance once on his own.

The rook shook his head in admiration. 'I wish I had your pioneer spirit,' he said. 'But I'm too old for that sort of thing now. This rookery's been my home all my life, and I expect to end my days here.'

'Oh! we're not all youngsters in this party,' chuckled Toad. 'Badger and I have both reached double figures, you know.'

'Then I admire you all the more,' said the rook, who seemed to be the patriarch of the copse rookery. 'But now that you're here,' he added, 'I hope you won't leave us too soon, despite your long journey. We don't see many ground folk here, and we rooks always enjoy a good chat.'

'We've already decided to spend a few days here,' Fox told him. 'We need some uninterrupted rest before we move on.'

'You've made a wise decision,' replied the rook, who failed to recognize the veiled hint in Fox's remark. 'It's secluded and peaceful here,' he went on. 'Nobody ever comes near the place. We're really delighted to have your company.'

He looked round at his companions. 'Are we singing tonight?' he asked.

'It was fixed for tomorrow,' replied one of the younger rooks.

'We fellows have a bit of a sing-song some evenings,' the old rook explained to the animals, 'when the ladies are in the nest with the young ones. We gather under the trees. If you'd care to join us tomorrow evening under the tall elms, we could have a longer chat too.'

'I'm sure we'd all like to come,' said Fox. 'How kind of you.'

'Till tomorrow then,' said the old rook, opening his wings for flight.

'Till tomorrow,' said Fox.

## XV

# THE RIVER

The animals were made so welcome by their new friends the rooks, that they were all very reluctant to leave the copse. The days drifted by, free of any danger, and all the members of the party were able to enjoy their first freedom from intrusion since before they had left Farthing Wood.

Badger found an old disused set, part of which he soon cleaned and lined for his own quarters, while the rabbits occupied some of the other chambers.

Mole, Weasel, and Fox, too, slept in the old tunnels leading to this group of chambers. The voles and fieldmice made their home under the exposed roots of an ancient sycamore, and Toad contented himself with retiring into a discarded jam-jar that he had found amongst some ground-ivy.

The squirrels, of course, built makeshift dreys of old leaves and twigs in the tree-tops, but far enough from the rookery for them to enjoy some privacy.

Only the hedgehogs and hares remained on ground level, and Hare found it necessary to accommodate his family on some dry grass well away from where the hedgehogs collected to sleep, owing to the fact that they *would* snore so.

Nobody knew where Adder hid himself: one or other of the animals would sometimes stumble across him sunbathing in a warm spot in a glade, but he seemed never deliberately to seek anyone's company.

Kestrel hunted by day, in the open country and farmland that surrounded the copse, and in the evening he returned. When it grew quite dark, Tawny Owl flew away on his nocturnal wanderings, and between them the two birds kept the party informed of anything outside the copse that could pose a threat to the continuance of their journey.

It was so easy for them all, now they had the opportunity, to slip back into their usual habits of foraging, eating and sleeping, and with the occasional diversion of a party and a conversation with the rooks, many of the animals began to wonder why they had to move on at all.

Fox, however, saw the danger of their being lulled into a false sense of security, for he felt quite sure there was something significant about the absence of any resident animals in the copse. So, one morning about ten days after they had first

arrived, he made a tour of the copse and rounded everyone up, including Adder, telling them to be ready to leave at dusk on the following day.

That night they had their last sing-song with the rooks, and, despite their friends' efforts to persuade them to stay a little longer, they made their farewells.

At the appointed time, the animals gathered in the elmscrub, and when they were all present, Fox led them out of the copse, to a chorus of good-luck caws from the rooks, who had stayed up late to see them off.

Their way took them first through a wide area of farmland. After their recent experience with the bull mastiff, the animals were far more cautious of straying too near human dwellings or livestock enclosures, where other fierce dogs might be on guard.

Following Toad's directions Fox led them on a route that skirted most of the farm buildings, and which always had sufficient cover for them to lie up in during the day.

Emerging from their communal hiding-place at dusk each day the animals would spend some time searching for food. They would eat together, as far as this was possible, and then set off for their night's travel, stopping to drink on the way as soon as they found the opportunity. Water was no longer a problem as, ever since the May drought had ended, showers of rain had fallen regularly.

For as long as Toad informed them that they were still in the vicinity of human habitations, their pattern of movement and rest never changed, and as the days wore on they drew close to the river.

Finally, one night, they passed the last farm on their side of the river, and when they rested at daybreak the animals could see the green meadows, many dotted with vivid yellow buttercups, sloping gently away from them down to the water's edge.

They looked their fill at the peaceful scene, before finding a corner in one meadow, overgrown with thick shrubs, nettles and dock, where they could sleep during the day.

As they settled down to rest, Hare asked Toad what they would find on the other side of the river.

'More meadows,' replied Toad. 'When we've passed those, as far as I can remember there's a long stretch of common land. Don't worry, it'll all come back to me when I see it again.'

'Is the river very wide?' asked Vole.

'Not very,' said Toad. 'None of us will have any trouble crossing it. There's a stretch of water, just a few yards along the bank from where we will arrive, which is almost still, the current there is so slow. Leave it to me, I'll see we all get across at the right point.'

This assurance satisfied all the immediate queries regarding what lay ahead of them, and, without further ado, the animals prepared for sleep.

Kestrel declared he was tired of hunting at dusk, when his piercing eyesight was of little use, and that now the sun was coming up, he was going to make the most of it.

'Poor old Kestrel,' Tawny Owl sympathized. 'I'm getting the best of the arrangement at the moment, travelling at night, sleeping by day. It doesn't suit him at all, of course. It's a complete reversal of his usual habits.'

'We have to plan every move with an eye on safety,' said Fox. 'I myself am not averse to a spot of daytime hunting for a change; but for a party, it's far safer to go off foraging when it's dark, and, of course, to journey by night.'

'Dusk,' hissed Adder, 'is the best time for hunting activities. I've found that it's then that all the tastiest little creatures are stirring.' Here he was unable to avoid casting a meaningful glance at the fieldmice, making them quail. 'And it suits me . . . er . . . right down to the ground, as you might say.'

The larger animals and Tawny Owl chuckled at this quip, but the fieldmice and the voles shifted uneasily. They were still unsure of the snake's intentions towards them, even as travelling companions, and were more than glad of the reassuring presence of Badger and Fox.

As the sun rose higher, bees and butterflies began to appear, skipping from one buttercup to another, or settling on the white clover flowers. Weevils and beetles, grass-hoppers, ants and earwigs were all busy amongst the grass stalks, and the morning was filled with their rustlings and murmurings.

Drowsiness soon fell on all the animal band, and they gratefully shut their eyes.

Another day passed, and Fox led them through the cool meadows to the bank of the river. They paused, looking down into the clear water that reflected the starry night sky in its blackness. Then they drank greedily before they undertook the important crossing.

Toad led them upstream a short way, looking carefully for the spot where he himself had crossed before. Eventually he came to a halt.

'I'm sure this is it,' he told them confidently. 'There's a hole in the bank here just like the one I hid in last time. It must be the same one.'

The animals drew themselves up into a bunch, and all of them started to jostle at the water's edge in their efforts to examine the state of the river.

'You're right, Toad,' Fox declared. 'The water here seems scarcely to be moving.'

'It looks a long way to the other bank,' squeaked Fieldmouse.

'Don't worry,' said Toad kindly. 'I'll go across first. You can watch me. I'm about your size, and if I can do it . . .'

'You go ahead,' Fox told him. 'The rest of us will take to the water together, and help each other. Good luck!'

Toad gave them a smile and sprang from the bank, landing

in the water with a modest little plop. The animals watched as the regular backward-kicking of his strong hind legs propelled his small body across the river in a series of jerks.

As he reached the middle, he was lost to their view, but a few minutes later they heard his croaks of triumph from the opposite bank.

'I've done it! I've done it!' he called. 'Come and join me! The water's lovely.'

Fox sent Kestrel and Tawny Owl across to join him. The animals paused on the brink, waiting for directions.

'We'll all go together,' Fox repeated. 'Line up along the bank, everyone.'

The voles and fieldmice took the middle position, flanked by the squirrels and hedgehogs. The rabbits, Hare and his family, and Badger took up their positions on the far right. Weasel, Fox, Mole and Adder were on the far left.

To Toad's encouraging cries, the long line of assorted animals entered the inky water together.

Mole and Badger were soon ahead of the rest, both being excellent swimmers, and the hares and hedgehogs found no difficulty in paddling their way across. Fox and Weasel swam well within their capabilities in order to keep an eye on the rest, who were not faring so well.

Strangely enough, of the slower swimmers the voles and fieldmice were the most adept. It was merely their size and comparative weakness that made the crossing of the river a daunting task. Yet they kept bravely on, their tiny heads poking above the surface, and their even tinier pink feet paddling furiously.

Adder, who was not really a keen swimmer, seemed to be making reasonable progress. The rabbits and squirrels were the slowest.

These animals were the jumpiest and the most nervous of the party. Although they all possessed the ability to swim, once they were in the water they seemed to lose their heads. Instead of striking out for the opposite bank, they went round and round in circles, thrashing the water in a kind of panic, and paying no heed to Fox and Weasel who attempted to calm them.

Toad watched the proceedings with considerable anxiety. Although he had been able to see all of his companions when they lined up on the bank in the moonlight, once they had entered the blackness of the water he could see only the reflected stars and the heads of the largest animals, Badger and Fox. The only evidence of the presence of any other animals in the river was the noise of their splashing, and the widening rings on the surface of the water that had been caused by their entrance. It was only when some of them reached what was about the halfway point, that Toad, peering over the water, could distinguish their features.

He spotted Mole, swimming dexterously, alongside his friend Badger. 'I can see you, Badger! I can see you too,

Mole!' Toad shouted excitedly, and in another minute he was welcoming their dripping bodies as they pulled themselves on to the bank.

Badger shook himself like a dog, and sent a shower of water over Tawny Owl. Ignoring the bird's protests, he turned back to see how his companions were managing.

The hedgehogs, who actually seemed to be enjoying the swim, had almost reached the shore. Behind them, in the gloom, Badger noticed Hare's mate, swimming comfortably, while Hare himself was paddling between his two young ones, holding them on course.

Soon the members of the party safely on the bank numbered nineteen, including the two birds, and with the arrival of the undulating Adder, the number became a round twenty.

Next into sight were the voles and fieldmice, who had formed one closely packed mass, so that they appeared to Badger like one creature, with an infinite number of heads.

These brave little animals could hardly find the strength to climb out of the water after their exhausting efforts but, needless to say, their friends on the bank all rallied round to help them up to safety.

'I knew you could do it,' said Toad, 'if courage played any part in the matter. You'll be surprised to see that a lot of the larger animals are still in the river; so you've really set them an example.'

'Wherever can Fox be?' asked Badger, with a note of concern in his voice. 'I can't see him at all.'

Straining his weak eyes for a glimpse of his friend, he walked along the bank a few steps, and then returned to go in the other direction, a puzzled expression on his face.

'Fox!' he called. 'Are you all right? We can't see you.'

The only sounds that reached his ears were the continuing splashes that had been audible ever since they had all first entered the river.

'Fox!' he called again, more loudly. 'Are you there? Rabbit! Weasel! Can you hear me?'

A muffled reply from he knew not whom followed his cries. He could not distinguish a single word.

'What was that?' he shouted. 'I can't hear you.'

Just then Weasel's head appeared out of the darkness, and the squirrels were with him.

'Bit . . . of . . . difficulty,' he panted, as he paddled nearer. 'The rabbits . . . took fright. Swam in . . . all directions, except . . . the right one. Fox is . . . trying to calm . . . them down. Squirrels . . . all right now.'

Badger called the rabbits all sorts of names under his breath.

'Can he manage?' he asked, as the squirrels, somewhat shamefaced, and Weasel joined the throng.

'I don't know for sure,' replied Weasel. 'He's tiring. I told him to leave them, but he wouldn't.'

'Just like Fox,' said Badger. 'Perhaps I should go and help him,' he added. He scrambled down to the water's edge.

'Let me come too! I'm a good swimmer!' cried Mole.

Then, suddenly, Hare shouted: 'There they are!'

The heads of the rabbits and of Fox were at last visible. Fox was swimming behind them, trying his best to keep them on course; for even at this stage the rabbits were still in a state of alarm at finding themselves in deep water, and none of them was swimming in a straight line.

The weary Fox was paddling furiously to one rabbit, who was threatening to swim away from the group, only to see that, having put *this* animal straight, another, at the other end of the line, had started to swim back to the far bank.

Badger and the rest of the party who had successfully made the crossing, were absolutely amazed at the rabbits' stupidity, and in their sympathy for the gallant Fox, began to shout angrily at them.

'Where are you going? This is the way!' shouted Weasel.

'What are you turning round for?' Vole called in his shrill voice.

A chorus of protests were directed at the jittery rabbits. Fox looked pleadingly at the animals on the bank, but the damage was done. At the sound of the shouting voices, the already nervous rabbits really panicked. Pandemonium broke loose as they all set off in different directions, colliding with each other, and pushing the young ones under the surface with their struggling bodies.

The despairing Fox swam into the midst of the mêlée, and tried to shepherd the frightened animals towards the bank.

Badger was still poised on the edge, in two minds whether to enter the water to assist Fox, wondering if one more animal in the river would only add to the rabbits' confusion. He happened to look upstream, and what he saw made him shudder.

A huge mass of debris, containing twigs, leaves, grass and even whole branches, was drifting in the middle of the river, and bearing down directly on Fox and the rabbits. It was so large that Badger saw it when it was more than thirty yards off.

If Fox had been alone in the water he would have been in no danger, for the debris would be slowed down considerably

by the slack water of the crossing-place, and he would have had ample time to reach safety. But Badger knew that Fox would never abandon the rabbits, and so, unless he acted quickly to save his friend, all the animals in the water would be carried away downstream, and perhaps drowned in the swifter currents.

'Quick, friends! They're in danger!' he cried. 'Every able body into the water. Each one of you must rescue one rabbit; I don't care how. I'll look after Fox. Be quick, lives are at stake!'

Badger dived into the river, just ahead of Weasel, Hare, Mole and the hedgehogs. Even Toad followed, determined to help if he could.

Each of them singled out one rabbit, and, with one eye on the approaching debris, either coaxed or forced the animal to the bank. Toad took one of the youngsters in charge, and eventually, by some means or another, all the animals were within striking distance of the river bank.

Only Fox and Badger were now left in danger. Fox had used all his strength and stamina in his heroic efforts to save the rabbits, and when Badger reached him in mid-stream, he was on the point of sinking with exhaustion. With Badger's assistance, he was able to manage a painfully slow paddle.

The debris was about ten yards away. Badger noticed with relief that all the other animals were now safe on dry land. They seemed a long way away. He looked again at the approaching mass. With a feeling of horror he realized he and Fox could never reach the bank in time. Fox knew this too.

'Badger, please,' he begged, 'leave me. You've still got time to save yourself. Go back to the others. They'll need you . . .' He could not manage any more words.

Badger did not reply, but steeled himself for the coming impact. He heard the alarmed voices of Tawny Owl and Weasel, and the various squeaks of the mice and voles, and of Mole. Then a cold, sodden mass struck him on his left side, and enveloped him completely.

He was pulled underwater, his legs and head entangled in the choking mass. He fought to free himself, but was dragged further and further down into the dark depths of the river.

## XVI

# A New Leader

The animals on the bank watched with horror the drama taking place in the river. The sight of Fox, the leader of their expedition, and Badger, whom all, except perhaps Tawny Owl, acknowledged to be his deputy, in such grave danger of drowning, sent a shudder through every one. They could all see that the mound of floating debris was about to engulf both the swimmers; and there was nothing they could do about it.

They saw Badger's head disappear under the surface, while Fox caught a blow from one of the floating branches, and was carried away downstream, his feeble struggles being powerless to prevent it.

In one mass movement the animals raced along the bank to keep Fox in sight, while Tawny Owl and Kestrel flew directly over the river, following its course.

After some twenty yards or so the debris reached the swift-flowing water, and in no time Fox was hurled away out of sight of the animals, though the birds continued to follow overhead.

There was a large rock in the river at this point, and the debris broke into two pieces, half of it rushing past one side, and the other piece on the opposite side. A lot of the grass and leaves caught against the rock, and were trapped there.

The animals were about to retrace their steps along the bank, all of them in the depths of despair at the tragedy.

'Stop!' cried Toad. 'There's something amongst that mass of vegetation out there.' His voice rose in a feverish excitement. 'It . . . I think it's . . . Badger! Yes, I can see him! Badger's there!'

The animals held their breath. Sure enough, there in the thick of the swirling grass and weed, was the unmistakable striped head of Badger – motionless.

'Is he . . . is he . . .?' faltered Mole, in a shaking voice.

'I'm afraid there's little hope of his still being alive,' said Weasel, and did his best to comfort Mole, who began to sob inconsolably.

'Look! Look!' shrieked one of the young rabbits. 'He's moving!'

'Come on, Hare,' said Hedgehog. 'We must get him out.'

Without hesitation he jumped into the water and, using all his strength to combat the faster current, struck out for the rock. Hare and Weasel were not slow to follow his action.

# A New Leader

To the smaller and weaker animals on the bank it seemed an age before Badger's rescuers managed finally to reach the dead water behind the rock. Weasel tore savagely at the vegetation round Badger's body to free him, and when he had cleared a space, he and Hedgehog got on either side of Badger's head, and using their small bodies as props, kept it just clear of the water. Hare, the strongest of them, took up his position directly behind Badger, and as they began to swim for the shore, he pushed the helpless body along with a series of nudges from his shoulders.

At last, to the intense relief of Mole, all four reached the bank again. They had to push Badger to safety, as he was unable to stand.

He was a pitiful sight. His eyes were barely open, his coat matted with mud and rotting grass, while his sides heaved violently as his lungs gulped in air. Presently he coughed up about a pint of water.

The animals surrounded him, touching his aching body affectionately, while Mole leant his little black velvet head against one of Badger's legs, and wept as though his heart would break.

'Now, Mole,' Adder reprimanded him. 'Badger's safe now. That's enough of that.'

'It won't help him, you know,' said Rabbit.

Weasel turned on him fiercely. 'How dare you utter a word,' he snarled. 'You, and your cowardly kind, are to blame for this.'

Rabbit quailed before Weasel's furious glare, and coughed uneasily.

'Well, we all panic at times,' he muttered uncomfortably, looking away. 'We rabbits don't like flowing water – we're not good swimmers, you know. You're more fortunate . . . Ahem! I'm sure we're all very sorry for the . . . um . . .'

'Please,' Badger managed to gasp. 'Don't let's quarrel. We're all . . . all safe now.'

Weasel looked at Hare, and Hedgehog exchanged glances with Toad. Badger was obviously unaware of the fate of Fox. Weasel made a little sign to them all that they should keep quiet about it for the present.

'What you need more than anything is a good rest,' he said to Badger kindly. 'You'll feel better after some sleep, and we'll have something ready to eat when you wake up. Do you think you can manage a few steps to the clump of undergrowth just over there?'

With help from all his friends, Badger reached the shelter and fell into a deep sleep as soon as his head touched the ground.

The animals went off to look for food, and when they returned they found Tawny Owl waiting for them.

'We lost him,' he told them. 'Kestrel's snatching some sleep – I left him back there. He's going to continue to search when it's light . . . far better eyesight than mine.'

'Surely Fox will be far away by then?' said Hare.

'Kestrel flies like a bullet,' said Tawny Owl. 'It's not long to daylight; he'll soon make up lost ground. I suppose . . . no news of Badger?'

The animals had forgotten that Tawny Owl was still ignorant of Badger's rescue. They all started talking at once.

Tawny Owl was both pleased and relieved to hear that Badger was restored to them, but there was, nevertheless, a certain reserve in his reply that was probably only recognized by Adder.

'When Badger wakes,' said Weasel gloomily, 'someone will have to tell him about Fox.'

The animals looked at each other. There were no volunteers for the task.

'Don't despair,' said Tawny Owl. 'Let's keep our spirits up, at least until Kestrel returns. He may have some good news for us.'

'What will we do if it's bad news?' asked Mole.

'Carry on,' said Toad. 'We must.'

'Without Fox?'

'If we have to – and we ought to face the possibility of it.'

'Of course. What else can we do?' said Tawny Owl. 'We'll manage – Badger and I – somehow.'

A crafty grin spread over Adder's face. Without intention, Tawny Owl found his eyes turning towards the snake's, and when their glances met he turned away again uncomfortably.

'I'm sure we'll *all* play our part,' Weasel remarked, a little huffily. 'I don't believe Fox ever named a deputy.'

Adder's grin became wider. 'It seems,' he drawled, 'that we have several pretenders to the throne.'

'Badger will lead us,' declared the loyal Mole stoutly. 'Fox has already relied on him once or twice to lead us in his absence.'

'Well,' said Tawny Owl, looking at his feet, 'I really don't know if Badger will be quite fit enough. Not at once, I mean,' he added hastily.

'How can you all stand there arguing about who is to be the new leader?' demanded Toad. 'Surely you're forgetting something? Our first concern is for news of Fox. He may even now be on his way back to us.'

'Well said, Toad.' Hare remarked. 'He's only been out of our sight a matter of hours. What *would* he think if he could hear us?'

'I suggest we all retire straight away,' said Hedgehog, to change the subject. 'Kestrel will soon wake us on his return.'

'How will he know where we are?' asked the short-sighted Mole.

'You obviously don't know the expression "eyes like a hawk",' said Tawny Owl. 'He'll spot us a mile off.'

The animals began to make a move to join Badger.

'Aren't you sleepy?' they asked Owl.

'I'll join you later,' he replied. 'I've a spot of hunting to do.'

The animals woke of their own accord during the following day. From the position of the sun, Adder, an expert in such matters, judged it to be about noon. Only Badger remained sleeping, and as Tawny Owl was nowhere in evidence, they decided he, too, must still be dozing in one of the nearby willow trees.

They immediately began to discuss the plight of Fox but none of them could feel very hopeful about his return.

Toad decided to go for a swim while they were waiting for Kestrel. Out of bravado, Mole said he would accompany him.

'You'd better come with me to the slacker water,' said Toad, and they set off along the bank.

When they reached the spot where they had made the crossing, Mole asked, 'Will it be safe here in the daylight?'

'Yes, if we stay near the bank,' answered Toad, 'We're both small enough not to be noticed.'

They went in together, and splashed around happily. Toad began to enjoy himself, frequently diving out of sight, and then surprising Mole by surfacing right in front of him.

'I wish I could do that,' said Mole enviously.

'I'll show you if you like,' said Toad. 'Now, watch me.'

He performed two small dives, and Mole tried to copy him but without success.

Toad dived again, and was gone for some minutes. Mole was just beginning to feel worried, when Toad reappeared with an alarmed look on his face.

'Quick, get to the bank,' he said urgently, and Mole obeyed without hesitation.

When they had pulled themselves clear, Toad blew out a long breath. 'Phew! That was close,' he said. 'Look!'

Mole peered into the clear water, and saw a huge pike, about three feet long, skimming about with its cruel mouth jutting forward as it sought for food.

'It didn't see me; I hid behind some weed,' explained Toad. 'Thank goodness it was not around last night.'

Mole shuddered. 'Perhaps we'd better get back?' he said.

'This very minute,' agreed Toad.

When they arrived back at the camp, the two animals found Badger awake, and surrounded by his friends. They were told that he had woken refreshed, and had made a reasonable meal of roots and grubs. He had told everyone that he felt a great deal better, and of course had enquired about Fox. Tawny Owl had volunteered the information of Fox's disappearance, trying to sound as hopeful about his return as he was able to.

Badger was now describing his own experience in the river. 'As I was drawn under the water, deeper and deeper,' he said, 'all I could think of was that if I drowned Mole would have to find someone else to carry him.'

'How kind you are,' said Mole, nestling close to the fatherly Badger, 'to think of others when you yourself were in such danger.'

'Well, you know,' Badger went on, 'I really thought I *was* going to drown. I was literally bowled along by the pace of the water, and my limbs were fettered by that ghastly mass of vegetation. My lungs were bursting. Then there was a sort of jolt, and everything became still. The hateful weed seemed to be pulled away from me, and I felt myself floating upwards. The next instant my head broke the surface, and I was gulping in air as fast as I could.'

'That was when we saw you,' said Hedgehog.

'Not quite then,' replied Badger. 'I remember striking the surface, but nothing after that. I must have passed out. I do recall feeling rather light-headed. Then . . . nothing.'

'We found you by that large rock,' Weasel pointed out.

'Exactly,' said Badger, with some excitement. 'That rock was my saviour. The weed caught against it, thus freeing me. I don't mind telling you, it was a near thing.'

While Badger had been talking, Rabbit had been shifting his gaze from the face of one animal to another, and then back again. Never once did he look at Badger. Finally, when Badger stopped speaking, he shuffled forward sheepishly.

'I . . . er . . . that is, on behalf of all,' he began, 'that is, all the rabbits. I mean . . .' He stopped, looking very confused. Nobody spoke. He struggled on. 'What I was trying to say,' he mumbled, 'was . . . um . . . we all hope you'll forgive us, Badger, for being such nuisances yesterday. We . . . er . . .'

Badger relieved him. 'It's all forgotten,' he promised graciously. 'We all have our weaknesses. We'll say no more about it.'

Rabbit's expression changed to one of gratitude. He smiled at Badger, and Badger smiled back.

'I wonder how long Kestrel will be,' said Mole.

'Patience,' admonished Tawny Owl. 'He won't come before he has something to tell us.'

As the minutes passed, and then the hours, all the animals stopped talking. Instead they sat together, scanning the sky. Some of them fell asleep as they waited.

At long last their patience was rewarded. Hare spotted Kestrel, just a speck in the blue, speeding towards them.

'It *must* be Kestrel,' he declared. 'Only he flies so fast.'

They craned their necks. Kestrel hovered and, as swift as an arrow, swooped in to land. When he saw their expectant faces turned eagerly towards him, his heart sank.

'It's bad news,' he forced himself to say.

'I managed to find him,' he told them, 'soon after dawn. I kept him in sight for a long way. He was still floating on the surface, half clinging to the driftwood. There was a weir. But Fox came through it, still on top of his wood, although the debris had broken up. After that the river broadened. There were boats – small ones and pleasure steamers. Somehow Fox's little pile avoided them all. Then it floated under a bridge. I waited on the other side, but he never came out. All I saw was a small boat, a motor one, but no pieces of driftwood, and no Fox. I waited and waited, but he didn't reappear.'

'Lost!' whispered the animals in horror.

'I even flew under the bridge, and I looked everywhere,' said Kestrel. 'He was not there.'

There was an awful hush. None of the animals dared speak. Mole wept silently against Badger's side. Rabbit looked ghastly. He stumbled away, with his relatives following, and sank to the ground in misery.

'I can't believe he's gone,' Badger whispered. 'Surely, Kestrel, you're mistaken? He couldn't just have disappeared?'

Kestrel was unable to speak.

After some minutes, Badger shook himself.

'We'll move on tonight,' he said. 'There's no point in staying here. Do you hear me, everyone? The journey continues. Be ready to leave tonight.'

There was a new authority in his voice which was unmistakable. Tawny Owl said nothing. There *was* nothing to say. Badger had recovered, and he was the new leader of the party. It was as simple as that. No one wanted to dispute the fact, and, strangely enough, Tawny Owl felt himself quite content with the situation.

# XVII

# WHICH WAY?

As dusk fell, the animals set out on the next stage of their journey.

Badger informed everyone that he was fully rested, and assured Mole he would not feel his weight on his back. Toad climbed up on Hare, and the party moved off silently, all of them with their minds full of thoughts of their missing leader.

It was a cool, breezy night with clouds chasing overhead, behind which the moon struggled to shed some light.

The rabbits looked a particularly forlorn bunch, for, despite Badger's forgiveness, they still felt the rest of the animals held them to blame for the loss of the courageous Fox. They shuffled along in the rear of the party, faces down, not caring to meet the eyes of their companions.

The grassy meadows they were passing through smelt sweet and lush, and some of the rabbits, mostly the younger ones, paused to nibble at the scented stalks.

'Come along! Come along, you youngsters!' called Rabbit harshly. 'No dawdling! We don't want any more trouble.'

After some time had elapsed the animals began to feel the need to talk. It was Weasel who broke the silence.

'Somehow,' he said, 'I still have the feeling that Fox is not lost. Perhaps even now he's making his way back to us.'

'Swimming *up* river?' suggested Adder sarcastically. He had no time for those who would not accept facts.

'No, no, of course not,' said Weasel. 'It's just that . . . well, nobody knows for *sure* what happened to him.'

'But we *are* sure he's no longer with us,' Adder persisted, 'and we should therefore get used to the idea that we have to reach our destination without him.'

'Now, Adder,' Badger felt obliged to cut in, 'there's no harm in hoping, you know.'

'Oh, as to that,' the snake replied in a whisper, 'I hope for a lot of things.'

After this exchange silence prevailed again for a spell. The animals entered the last meadow.

'What do you see ahead, Owl?' Toad called to the bird, who was fluttering a little in advance of the band.

'Looks like open country,' Tawny Owl called behind him after a moment.

'Good,' said Toad. 'It's as I expected.' He raised his voice so that all could hear. 'A stretch of easy going now,' he announced. 'Cheer up, everyone. Things aren't so bad. We've come a long way.'

'Yes. *We* have,' Mole said pointedly, in a small voice.

'Try not to distress yourself too much,' said Badger to him. 'Fox wouldn't want that, you can be sure.'

'I'm sorry, Badger,' said Mole. 'I know he would wish us to go on. But . . . Oh dear!' he sighed miserably, and stayed silent.

'I'll get you there,' said Badger encouragingly. 'You'll see.'

The animals left the meadow and found themselves on wide, open downland. Underfoot the rich grass rippled beneath the breeze with a gentle waving motion. The air was bracing, the grass springy and soft to walk on. The little party found their spirits lifting despite themselves.

Toad and Mole were determined to share the exhilaration of their friends, and took to their feet, walking side by side.

Hare, freed for a while of responsibility, could not resist the urge to run and jump about, and he called to his mate to join him. Together they gambolled about, chasing each other and racing away at breakneck speed, their long hind legs and lean bodies as supple and elastic as if they were on springs.

All the animals relaxed and travelled at an easy pace. They forgot the anxious moments of the past, and, confident that for the present no danger or hardship was at hand, were determined to enjoy their new sense of freedom.

## WHICH WAY?

Badger looked up at Tawny Owl. 'Won't you join me for a moment, Owl?' he asked. 'Come and have a natter.'

Tawny Owl obliged willingly, and fluttered to the ground by Badger's side. 'I'll walk a few steps with you,' he said.

'You know,' said Badger, 'this is the first time since we left Farthing Wood that I haven't wished I was back in my old set. I really feel a sense of adventure at last.'

'I know what you mean,' agreed Tawny Owl as he strutted along, his wings folded comfortably on his back. 'I think we've really put our old life behind us now, haven't we?'

'Yes,' said Badger. 'And I'm glad we weren't there to witness the wood's final destruction. At least we have our memories untainted.'

They strolled on, talking of the old days. The party had scattered and spread out into little groups of two or three, but a few walked alone like Adder and Weasel. For once the animals did not feel confined; they were enjoying the extra space.

Suddenly Toad halted, and looked all about him. He looked puzzled. The others stopped too. Some yards away Hare and his mate sat down and looked back.

'Anything wrong?' asked Weasel.

'It's strange,' Toad muttered. 'I'm sure we go straight ahead here, and yet something is nagging at me, drawing me away to the left.' He shrugged and hopped on in the same direction. His companions continued slowly, keeping their eyes on him.

He halted again after a few more yards. 'It's no good,' he said. 'This feels wrong to me. I'm not comfortable. My legs want to turn left. And yet . . .' He looked all round again. 'Can't understand it,' he murmured.

'Perhaps we've taken a wrong turn somewhere?' suggested Squirrel.

'No. No, that's just it. I remembered everything quite clearly as we came along.' Toad was emphatic.

'Shall we try the other direction,' Badger asked, 'if it seems right to you?'

'All right,' said Toad, and swung left. The animals re-formed into a bunch and followed him.

But Toad did not look happy. He shook his head in a puzzled way, although he did not stop.

'This should prove interesting,' Adder drawled. 'Looks as if our guide has lost himself.'

'Good gracious!' exclaimed Badger. 'I hope not.'

Toad ignored this remark, but continued on with a somewhat grim expression, continually turning his head in all directions, as if searching for a clue.

In the face of Toad's doubt the travelling began to lose its enjoyment.

Tawny Owl rejoined Kestrel in the air. Kestrel honoured his return with an aerial loop. Tawny Owl was unimpressed. The hawk's dexterity in the air was a simple matter of fact to him. Now it was night, he, Owl, held sway in his natural element.

The next moment Kestrel's words seemed, unbidden, to acknowledge the situation. 'I'm afraid I can't be of any use in the dark,' he began, 'but you can see. Why not fly on ahead and spy out the land? Then Toad will know if we're on the right track.'

'Surely you don't imagine I hadn't already decided that for myself,' the owl replied haughtily.

'You said nothing,' retorted Kestrel. 'I'm merely trying to help.'

He watched in annoyance as Tawny Owl flapped his powerful wings harder, and flew away without a word. 'Can't bear to be told anything,' Kestrel muttered in disgust.

'Where's Owl off to?' Mole inquired of Badger.

'We shall soon see,' replied Badger. 'Tawny Owl never does anything without a reason.'

Toad had no need to ponder over the owl's action. He realized at once what the bird was doing. He felt relief, and at the same time alarm. If it should prove he was leading the party in the wrong direction, he knew they would all feel he had let them down. Would they not then lose faith in their guide? Toad shuddered. Every one of them depended on him so much – on his memory. They had trusted him completely so far, and he had not made one error. And now? He longed for, yet dreaded, Tawny Owl's return. Nevertheless, the strange unseen influence that had made him turn left still beckoned. He plodded on.

Badger could sense Toad's anxiety; he could feel a definite tenseness in the air.

'Don't worry,' he said kindly, and so quietly that only Toad could hear. 'If you've made a mistake, no one is going to blame you.'

Toad looked up at the familiar striped head and smiled as their eyes met. He could not bring himself to say anything.

'I suggest we stop for a bit,' Badger said more loudly. 'We'll wait for Tawny Owl.'

Toad nodded unhappily and the animals came to a halt behind him. Most of them stretched out at their ease on the soft grass. Kestrel joined them.

They did not have long to wait. Tawny Owl's grey shape appeared in the gloom. Every eye was turned on him as he came to rest amongst them. Only Toad failed to look up. His flat, broad head was bowed, as he waited with bated breath.

'It's the wrong way,' Tawny Owl announced with an air of finality. A medley of gasps and sighs followed his words. 'We're almost back at the river. We've travelled a complete circle.'

Toad felt all eyes were on him, accusing him. His error had cost the animals precious time and effort. Time and effort that was completely wasted.

'I . . . I'm sorry,' he sobbed.

Badger was about to speak, while Mole nuzzled their miserable guide, but Tawny Owl had not finished.

'No need to be sorry,' he said. 'It's quite obvious what's

happened. Your homing instinct has begun to work, just as it did when you were captured before and then escaped on your own. It's leading you back to your pond at Farthing Wood – your birthplace.'

Toad looked up. 'Of course,' he murmured. 'The irresistible urge – pulling me the wrong way.'

The other animals felt they had become victims of a mystery; an age-old mystery over which they had no control.

'What . . . what do we do now?' asked Fieldmouse.

'Simple,' said Tawny Owl. 'Turn round and retrace your steps.'

'But what about Toad?' said Vole. 'How can he guide us now?'

'Fortunately, Toad still has his memory,' replied Tawny Owl. 'He can no doubt remember what lies ahead of us on our route.'

Toad nodded.

'But,' said Tawny Owl, 'in future you will have to rely on my guidance by night . . .'

'And mine by day,' said Kestrel.

'Will it work?' asked Squirrel.

Tawny Owl drew himself up. 'Of *course* it will work,' he said pompously.

# XVIII

# THE BUTCHER BIRD

The travellers, in fact, made little progress under the guidance of Kestrel and Tawny Owl, but through no fault of theirs. Several of the mother voles and fieldmice presented the party with additions to its number during the next rest period, and these events proved to be a turning point in the journey.

It was obvious to all, particularly to the despairing Badger, that the vole and fieldmouse parents concerned in these births would no longer be able to travel, and a conference of the group leaders was arranged in the resting-place they had chosen in some heath scrub.

'It looks as if our ranks are to be depleted further, then?' said Weasel.

'There's no other solution,' Badger said miserably. 'We can't put a halt to our journey until these young ones grow up.'

'It was bound to happen,' remarked Fieldmouse, 'but nobody ever mentioned the subject.'

'If we had reached White Deer Park I would have been delighted with the whole thing,' said Badger.

'But we haven't,' said Tawny Owl.

'Oh dear,' sighed Badger. 'I wonder what Fox would have done.'

'That question shouldn't arise,' said Tawny Owl impatiently. '*We* have to decide.'

'There's really no decision to make,' Adder chipped in. 'If we're to continue on our way these new broods of our friends the mice must be left behind. If we can't bring ourselves to do this, then we must all stay here and sing silly songs while they grow big enough to walk. Believe me, there's no doubt in *my* mind what we should do.'

'If it had been left to you, none of *us* would have been here in the first place,' said Vole angrily, steeling himself to ignore the horrific leer which served as Adder's reply.

'Please, please,' Badger interrupted hastily, 'this isn't getting us anywhere.'

'Adder's right, of course,' said Tawny Owl emphatically. 'The parent mice concerned will have to do the best they can for their babies, and that is to stay behind. We can help them to look for a home in the area. Then we *must* go on. All of us are committed to it.'

'Well, Owl, you know,' Badger nodded his head as he spoke, 'I must admit I'm in agreement with you.'

'Well, I am *not*!' retorted Vole. 'The issue is not so cut and dried as far as we voles and mice are concerned. These creatures are our kith and kin, and we can't just abandon them here.' He looked at Fieldmouse for support. 'I say, if some of the mice stay, we *all* stay.'

Badger looked distinctly alarmed. 'Please don't take that view, Vole,' he begged.

'Well, you *must* realize, Badger,' said Fieldmouse, 'there will be no second opportunity for these animals to press on to White Deer Park – even when their babies have grown. I can see Vole's point of view. How *can* we take the responsibility of leaving our relatives behind to await – who knows what fate?'

'*I* will take the responsibility,' said Bardger stoutly. '*I* am your leader now.'

'But you're not a vole or a fieldmouse!' snapped Vole. '*You* don't see the situation in the same light.'

'I really don't see,' drawled Adder, 'why everyone is getting so concerned about something they had no part in.'

Vole and Fieldmouse glared at him.

'I think you're forgetting something, Adder,' said Badger. 'Before we began our journey we all swore an Oath, including *you*. That Oath meant that the safety and well-being of any member of the party was the concern of all the others. You should reflect on that,' he finished in a schoolmasterly tone.

It was not in Adder's nature to apologize. He merely grinned disarmingly.

Vole and Fieldmouse turned to Badger again.

'Then *surely*, Badger,' Vole said, 'if that Oath meant anything at all, how can you talk about leaving even one of us behind?'

'Because, Vole, you know as well as I do that the parents with their babies can't attempt to travel. But, for the safety of the *whole* party, we must complete our journey as quickly as possible; and, having come this great way, the rest of you mice should be moving on with us. We'll do everything possible to find them a safe home here,' he added. 'I'm sure they'll be quite comfortable, you know. It's a secluded spot.'

'Thank you, Badger,' said Fieldmouse, who was inclined to be more reasonable than his cousin. In a persuasive tone he said to Vole, 'Badger's in a difficult position, don't you see? He didn't ask for this to happen, and he has to think of everyone.'

'At this moment, *I* am thinking primarily of my own kind,' said Vole. 'You should be, too, Fieldmouse. We have to stand by them. I can't go on if any of them stay behind.'

'I'm sorry, Badger,' Fieldmouse muttered. 'I'm afraid Vole is right.'

'If that is your decision I shall have to accept it,' said Badger sadly. 'But our priority is to reach our destination. In Fox's absence, I have to see that the rest of us succeed. I'm sorry.'

Vole shrugged and left the meeting without another word. Fieldmouse lingered, as if in two minds, but finally followed his cousin.

'It's natural they feel so concerned,' said Weasel.

The conference broke up with the intention of searching for the best settling-place for the voles and fieldmice as soon as it was daylight.

Badger wandered off alone to think. The break-up of the party that had already travelled so far preyed on his mind, and he found himself thinking how happy he would have been if he had had Fox to consult. But the animals depended on *him* now, and he must see them through.

As soon as it was light, a number of the animals, led by Badger, set off to look for a new home for the mouse contingent. It was not a difficult task, as these small creatures' requirements were modest.

On the advice of Fieldmouse they chose a spot in a thicket of birch scrub, where the leaf litter was thick and soft, and there was plenty of cover in the way of twigs and bracken. Vole agreed that the sunny hillside nearby would make the area ideal for his group, and the animals hastened back with the news.

The mice and voles were soon comfortably installed in their new home and, after all the farewells had been made, the main party continued on its way with Kestrel as guide.

As the sun rose higher, the day grew hotter and hotter, and the animals' pace became correspondingly slower. They were relieved to find a little stream at which to quench their thirst, and the shallow gurgling water was so inviting that several of the animals followed Toad's example and stepped into it to cool themselves.

The countryside seemed so empty and peaceful that Badger decided to pause awhile, until they were all completely refreshed.

Kestrel and Tawny Owl flew on ahead to spy out the land, and the sunny, quiet day lulled the animals into a state of drowsiness. Toad was floating blissfully on the stream's surface, buffeted gently by the ripples, his limbs spread out, and his beautiful jewelled eyes glinting as they reflected the sun. He was half asleep.

Suddenly he returned to full consciousness with a jolt. He heard a violent squeaking noise and saw a small, fierce bird flying overhead with a tiny, wriggling fieldmouse clamped firmly in its beak.

Toad paddled briskly to the bank, and watched the grey-headed bird making off with its prize. Badger, Weasel, Hedgehog and Hare came running.

'It might be one of our mice!' cried Toad.

'Quickly!' said Badger. 'Hare, Weasel, come with me. Hedgehog, will you stay here, and get everyone under cover? Oh, *where* are Kestrel and Owl?'

The three animals raced off in the wake of the robber, Hare at once taking the lead.

Burdened by its victim, the bird fluttered along slowly, and the fleet-footed Hare was soon directly beneath it. He slackened his pace, and was about to cry out. But, as he looked up, he saw that the poor mouse was dangling limply from the bird's cruel hooked beak. It was quite clearly dead.

Hare knew it was useless to follow further. The bird looked down with an air of invincibility, and uttered a muffled 'chack'. Then, turning its handsome chestnut back on the powerless Hare, it flew triumphantly away, disappearing into the very birch scrub where Hare knew the voles and fieldmice to be.

He looked round. Badger and Weasel were still a long way off. He followed the bird into the scrub. An excited 'shrike, shrike' betrayed the creature's whereabouts, as it was greeted by its mate from a prominent perch on a birch sapling. What followed made Hare's blood run cold.

The chestnut-backed bird made for a neighbouring blackthorn bush, and, with a vigorous stab of its beak, skewered the tiny mouse on one of the projecting thorns. It then promptly rejoined its mate on the branch where they clacked excitedly, wagging their long tails from side to side.

Hare found himself drawn towards the thorn-bush, almost against his will. A few feet away he stopped, scarcely able to credit the horror of what he saw. The bush was covered in bodies: bumblebees, large beetles and grasshoppers, and tiny, almost furless mice, all neatly impaled on the sharp thorns.

Hare whispered to himself: 'The butcher bird!' All wild creatures had heard tales of the horrible 'larder' of mutilated victims which was kept by the red-backed shrike, the 'butcher bird'.

Hare shivered. He was struck by a thought he hardly dared acknowledge. Where *were* the voles and fieldmice? He began to search amongst the leaves and twigs underfoot, more and more desperately. He looked everywhere. None of the mice was to be found.

He heard Badger calling. 'Hare! Where are you?'

He quickly left the scrub. The shrikes were both sitting bolt upright on their perch, turning their heads jerkily in every direction, searching for fresh morsels to catch.

Hare was determined that Badger should not see what he had just seen. It would be in that kindly animal's nature to blame himself for what had occurred, and if he saw that awful larder he would feel he had sent the voles and fieldmice, or at least their helpless babies, to their death.

'There you are!' cried Badger, as Hare emerged into the open. 'Where did the bird go? Did you see?'

Hare sadly shook his head. 'The little mouse – whoever he was – was dead,' he said. 'I saw *that*.'

'What kind of bird was it?' demanded Badger.

Hare had to think quickly. 'Well, I'm not sure,' he said evasively. 'It had a red back, grey head, and a hook-tipped beak.'

'The butcher bird,' said Weasel immediately.

Badger looked at him in horror. 'Ghastly creatures,' he said. 'There used to be a pair on the borders of Farthing Wood . . . more dangerous than Adder when it came to hunting small creatures.' He stopped talking and looked round.

'But the mice . . . the voles . . . where are they?' he muttered, moving towards the scrub.

Hare held his tongue, but lamely followed him. Inside, Badger looked around again.

Suddenly they heard the rustling of leaves underfoot, and, from beneath a pile of leaf litter, one by one, came the voles and fieldmice.

'Is it safe?' whispered Vole.

'Yes, come quickly,' said Hare; and he, Badger and Weasel, shepherding the mice between them, ran from the birch scrub towards a hollow tree. Once inside, they rested, panting heavily. No one spoke for a while.

Then Badger said, 'You see, Vole, what happens when you leave the safety of the party? You small creatures are too vulnerable to be left on your own. How many have died?'

'All the babies,' Vole said brokenly. 'I'm sorry, Badger. I should have known you were really thinking of our good.'

'We'll stay with you now,' said Fieldmouse. 'The poor parents are agreed – otherwise there'll *be* no voles and fieldmice.'

'Come on,' said Badger resolutely. 'We can't leave Hedgehog any longer. Who knows what other dangers threaten us?'

The animals made their way back to the stream, where Hedgehog trotted out to meet them, 'All safe here,' he announced.

Badger explained what had happened. 'It's been a tragedy,' he admitted. 'But this won't happen again. You have my word on it. From now on we shall travel in close formation – and we shall stop only to drink and eat and sleep. One of the birds will always be on guard in the air, where they will be able to detect the approach of any foreign creature.'

He looked all round. His voice took on a warm, benign tone. 'There will be no more lives lost while I'm in charge; I promise it. I hope now you will all trust in me?'

The animals responded unanimously to his plea.

'I thank you all,' said Badger. 'Adder, you look as if you want to say something?'

Adder's face took on a sardonic grin. 'A very moving vote of confidence,' he drawled. 'I'm sure if it were possible for me to applaud, I should do so now.' He chuckled noiselessly.

But nobody took any notice of him. For there *was* a new confidence in the party, despite the recent setback. They had survived the catastrophe of the river crossing and the loss of Fox who, a natural leader, had seemed irreplaceable.

They felt that Badger had now stamped his authority on the leadership and would rise to the occasion. Whatever hardships were still in store for the animals, they sensed that, having come so far, it was unlikely they could now be diverted from their joint purpose.

Ignorant of the fate of Fox as they were, most of them could not believe him dead, and still felt in their bones that, eventually, he would rejoin them. Yet, with or without Fox, however long it might take, the determination of each creature was now reinforced. Their journey could end in only one place – within the boundaries of White Deer Park.

# PART TWO

## JOURNEY TO WHITE DEER PARK

# XIX

# Fox Alone

From the middle of the river Fox watched a huge mass of driftwood and debris floating downstream towards him. He was tired – terribly tired – and he knew he was too far from the shore to avoid the impact. In a few seconds the mass was upon him, engulfing him. One of the larger pieces of wood dealt him a sharp rap on the head, and he was carried away on the current.

Despite his struggles, he was unable to resist the pressure exerted by the heavy brushwood, and he was carried helplessly along. In a last, frantic, backward glance, he saw his friends on the bank running, trying to keep pace with him, but he knew it was impossible for them.

In a few minutes, Fox was entirely alone. All his effort was concentrated on keeping his head above water.

Eventually he was carried into a stretch of calm water, and here he managed to ease himself a little. He was able to pull himself far enough out of the river to rest his front legs on the collection of large sticks and branches surrounding him. In this position he travelled a considerable distance, while day gradually dawned.

The water was cool and refreshing, and as he was not able to swim – enmeshed as he was in the driftwood – he had very soon recovered a good deal from his previous exhaustion. But as he floated downstream on his tiny island, farther and farther away from his friends, Fox wondered if he would ever feel solid ground underfoot again.

The wood-pile carried him over a weir, from which he emerged none the worse except for a fright and a good ducking. He floated into less peaceful water, becoming more and more of a speck in the broadening river. He drifted past anglers and picnickers, past houseboats and rowing-boats; he drifted underneath overhanging willows and alongside big pleasure-steamers thronged with passengers in thin summer clothes. But nobody saw him. Nobody remarked on the waterborne fox.

He had begun to feel quite convinced that before long he would be washed out to sea – that vast, terrible expanse of water he had heard tales about – when his situation suddenly changed.

As he floated under a bridge, there, directly in his path, was a small motor-boat. The man inside had obviously been fishing, for he was getting the last of his tackle aboard. The wood surrounding Fox caught against the outboard motor, and finally came to rest.

Fox did not dare to attempt to climb into the boat, although it was low in the water, but he thought there might be a chance for him to reach the bank at last, if the angler was going to moor his boat.

When he was quite ready, the man began to paddle his boat in a leisurely fashion out from the bridge without once looking behind.

A little further on the river split, flowing either side of a large island. The man paddled into the left-hand channel, and Fox saw ahead two large wooden gates, right across the water. As they approached these gradually swung open, and the man continued to paddle right inside.

Suddenly the boat was motionless. Fox found he was in a narrow channel of water, locked in by two tremendously high, slime-covered walls on either side, and two sets of great double doors, before and behind. Looking directly upwards he could see human faces peering over the tops of the walls.

He heard a gushing sound, and the next thing he knew, he was slowly being raised upwards on the water. The green slippery walls slid past on either side of him, and the faces above came nearer and nearer. Surely they would notice him!

All at once he heard a child's excited cry. The faces peered further over the walls. Fox began to feel nervous and vulnerable. He heard the sound of human voices growing louder, and he saw the man stand up in the boat, and look towards him.

Fox tried to shrink back against the branches and sticks, hoping to camouflage himself. But he was too late. More and more faces were staring down at him. Hands and fingers pointed excitedly. The chattering voices increased in number. Fox was almost on their level.

The water was rising more slowly now. The man in the boat had been obliged to sit down again, and prepare to move his craft. The lock gates in front of him were swinging open, and he was taking hold of his paddle.

Fox saw that unless he did something quickly, he would be towed on down the river. His head was now level with the top of the wall. Arms reached out to him, but he did not wait to see if they might be helping arms. He snapped his jaws twice, viciously, and the arms were withdrawn. With a half-leap he scrambled clear of the brushwood and, for a fleeting moment, balanced himself before jumping on to the pathway.

Legs, human legs, everywhere. Straight through them he dashed, before anyone could prevent it. He saw the river bank and raced for it. Then he ran as he had never run before in all his life, away from the humans and their noise, and straight for the first cover he could find.

But humans seemed to be everywhere. Shouts followed him. Humans were in front of him as well as behind him. They were strolling, sitting or lying on the grassy bank. Some did not even notice Fox dash past. Others stepped back in amazement, uttering little shrieks.

Fox sped along the tow-path, with the river on his left and fences, hedges, walls, houses on his right. He was hemmed in, but still he kept running.

Soon, looming in front, was the bridge he had floated under only a short time ago. The path ran directly underneath. Fox did not stop.

The sun and the air were drying his fur, wet for so long. He felt strong and refreshed and courageous, and was spurred on by the thought of the friends he was running back to join. Suddenly the fences ended, and there on his right were trees and wide fields with cows or horses in them.

He turned into the first field. The grass felt cool and supremely soft under Fox's feet, and as he put the human path further behind him, he felt secure. A little, winding stream ran through the field, and he drank from it in great gulps.

A Friesian cow that was drinking a little further upstream raised her head and looked docilely towards him. 'You're a bold one,' she said. 'Farmer's in the next field.'

'I . . . I was lost,' Fox replied. 'I'm trying to find my way back.'

'Are you far from home?' the cow asked.

'I'm a long way from what I used to call home,' answered Fox. 'I have no home now. I'm on my way to a new one, only I've been separated from my friends.'

The cow wanted to know if she or her companions could be of any assistance.

'You have been already,' said Fox gratefully. 'I shall avoid the next field. I must get on – I've a long way to go.' He thanked the cow, and ran off, skirting the neighbouring field, and entering the adjacent one, keeping the river in sight in the distance on his left.

There was a solitary black horse in this field, and from its grizzled haunches and neck, Fox could tell he was old. He was leaning peacefully against a chestnut tree, blinking his eyes and lazily swishing his threadbare tail against the flies.

'Good day!' Fox called pleasantly, as he trotted past.

The old horse started and looked down. 'Oh, hullo!' he wheezed. 'Must've been dozing again. Very warm today.'

'Isn't it?' said Fox, stopping for a moment to snap up a stag-beetle that was lying on its back, all six legs waving feebly.

The horse turned his head away in disgust. 'Ugh! Don't know how you can,' he protested.

'That's the first morsel I've had for a good many hours,' Fox replied.

'If you're hungry, my manger's half-full over there,' the horse said hospitably. 'My teeth are going – I can't crop grass so well now. And my appetite's not what it was.'

'Very kind of you,' said Fox, 'but I don't really go in for that sort of food.'

'Oh well, come and have a chat anyway,' wheedled the ancient horse. 'I get so bored here by myself all the time.'

Despite his haste to rejoin his friends, Fox felt it would be impolite to refuse the invitation, especially as the horse was behaving very civilly towards him.

He wandered over to the chestnut tree and lay down, panting, in its shade. The sun was very hot.

'That's right,' nodded the horse. 'Make yourself at home. It's cooler under here.' He continued to lean against the trunk of the tree. 'I don't get much company these days,' he went on, turning his rheumy eyes on Fox. 'Not since my old pal, the bay, died last summer. After the wife went, we became very close, although, of course, he was only working class.'

'The bay?' asked Fox.

'Yes. A draught horse, you see.'

'And you are . . .?'

'I *was* a hunter,' replied the black horse. 'Best in the stable, with a long pedigree. Seems funny, my talking to you like this, after a long career chasing foxes.'

Fox started and pricked up his ears. 'Fox hunting?' he whispered.

'That's right. Oh, I don't uphold it. It's a wicked sport really. But the racing, the leaping, the scarlet coats – that part of it's grand.'

Fox shuddered. The old horse's words took him back to his childhood, and the terrifying tales he had heard from his father of the mad, baying hounds, the thundering hooves, and the torment of the exhausted, solitary fox forced to run to its death.

The old horse noticed Fox's discomfort. 'You must excuse me,' he said humbly. 'Just an old creature's thoughtless reminiscences. Believe me, I used to be as relieved as you would be, when the animals I chased got away.'

'That's good of you,' said Fox. 'I never suspected anything else. Only humans could practise such cruelty as exists in hunting any smaller or weaker animal to its death.'

'I agree with you,' the old horse nodded. 'And yet, those same humans have always treated me well – like a lifelong friend.'

'Well,' Fox shook his head. 'A different relationship, I suppose.'

'Of course.'

'Thank heaven, I've never been involved in a hunt,' said

Fox. 'But my father told me of his experiences. He was lucky, but *his* father and mother were both caught. The hounds tore them to shreds.'

The black horse nodded his grizzled head. 'I can give you a word of advice,' he said seriously. 'I shouldn't stay in this part of the country any longer than you can help. It's all hunting country for some miles round here. I wouldn't want anything to happen to you.'

'Thank you, but don't worry,' said Fox. 'I'm just passing through. I'm on my way back to rejoin my friends up river. I was separated from them last night.'

'Really? What happened?' the old horse wanted to know.

So Fox explained that he had been swept away while trying to help some frightened rabbits to cross the river. Then, seeing the look of disbelief on the horse's face, and feeling that it would do him good to rest for a little while longer, Fox settled down to tell the whole story.

He explained how all the animals of Farthing Wood had been driven from their homes by the humans, and how, having heard from Toad of a wonderful place, White Deer Park, a Nature Reserve where they could live in peace again, they had banded together to make the long and difficult journey. Fox trembled as he recounted the various dangers they had met on the way, remembering particularly the terrible fire they had survived, and the storm, and the angry farmer with his gun – and, finally, the horror of the river crossing. Stirred by renewed anxiety for his friends, Fox brought his story to an end as quickly as he politely could, impatient to be on his way again.

The horse had listened in silence, except for the occasional snort of disgust. When Fox stopped talking, he commented sadly, 'It's happening all over the country. You wild creatures are being driven back on all sides. Humans have always been greedy, particularly where land is concerned. But it's to the credit of those among them who appreciate your existence that they're setting aside at least a few chunks of land where you can live in peace. I've heard about this White Deer Park you mentioned. For a horse it wouldn't be a long journey from here. But if it's necessary for you to travel at the pace of mice, then obviously it's another matter.'

'I sometimes wonder if any of them will reach our destination,' admitted Fox. 'The journey is really too harrowing for such small animals.'

'I wish you luck,' said the horse feelingly. 'I mustn't detain you. Your friends will be worried.'

'You've been good company,' said Fox politely. 'Perhaps one day you'll hear news of our success.' He got up and shook his coat.

'I hope so,' said the horse. 'I'll be thinking of you every day.'

Fox opened his lips in a smile. 'Goodbye,' he said.

'Goodbye, my friend,' said the horse. '*Bon voyage!*'

Fox left the field without a backward glance. He had a long run ahead of him still.

As he trotted along, keeping as much as he could behind a screen of undergrowth or shrubs, he recognized various landmarks he had passed as he floated down the river. Some of the boats were certainly familiar, and, looking across the broad stretch of water to the other side, occasional aspects of the landscape brought again to his mind the thoughts that had occupied him as he passed the spot earlier.

Most of the time he had been endeavouring to think up some means by which he could get out of his predicament, but the plight of his friends, without their leader, had also been uppermost in his mind. He had constantly hoped, too, that Badger would send Kestrel to search for him, and as he retraced his journey, he kept scanning the sky for a sight of the bird. His friends seemed so far away.

After some hours, Fox knew he would have to stop for a rest. Although he could not really afford time to sleep, he realized that it was essential to refresh himself with a nap, in order to have any chance of rejoining Badger and the others. Apart from a few minutes when he had fallen into an uneasy doze as he drifted helplessly along, trapped amongst the brushwood, Fox had been far too alarmed to sleep properly. He started to look round for a likely spot of cover.

There were still many anglers and picnickers too close for comfort, so he kept going at a slackened pace. Traffic on the river was confined at this point to one or two small motor or rowing-boats, and Fox thought he could see that the opposite bank had drawn just a fraction closer. Presently he came to a spot where a thick grove of willow trees grew right down by the water's edge. Here it was impossible for any human to approach the river from the bank, and so Fox decided it was an excellent place to hide himself.

He crept under the trees and laid himself down under the thick leaves of a tree whose boughs bent so low that some of them brushed the ground. Here Fox was sure he was invisible from the river too, and he gratefully laid his head on his paws and let out a long sigh. A few hours' rest and he would be fresh on the trail again. He was so sleepy that he was able to ignore the pangs of hunger that had begun to make themselves felt in the pit of his stomach. A gentle breeze rustled the willow leaves, causing them to stroke his fur. In another moment Fox had fallen into a deep sleep.

## XX

# THE VIXEN

It was completely dark when Fox was woken by a strong breeze blowing through the sheltering willow trees. He got up, feeling refreshed but appallingly hungry. After stretching all his limbs in turn, he emerged from his bower and set about finding something to eat.

In his ravenous state, Fox had no scruples about snapping up any small creatures that happened to be abroad. Beetles, slugs, worms, snails were all tasty titbits to his keen appetite. When he had taken the edge off his hunger, Fox continued on his way at a smart trot, remembering the warning of the old horse.

At night the river was quiet; there were no longer any noisy motor-boats about, and no humans sitting or strolling on the river's banks.

A complete day and night had now passed since he had been swept away by the river debris, and he had seen no sign of any of his companions coming to look for him. He realized that the distance he had been carried in the water was far too great to allow anyone but one of the birds to set out in search. He wondered if he might have missed Kestrel while he had been sleeping, but as many hours of daylight had passed without any sign of the bird before he had stopped to rest, Fox gradually became certain that his friends had given him up for lost. He felt terribly alone.

As he went on, he reflected that the sort of community life he had been living during the last month or so on the journey had changed him. He had lived in a rather solitary style in Farthing Wood – a typical fox's life, sleeping during the day for the most part, roaming and hunting alone at night. Of course, Badger had always been his friend, and there had been other acquaintances, notably Tawny Owl. But, in those days, he had not been in the habit of inviting the company of others. Now Fox found himself so in need of companionship that he could feel a definite physical ache inside. What worried him most at that moment was that, if the other animals had indeed decided he was lost to them, they would move on, continue their journey, leaving him further behind. The one consolation was that, alone, he could travel a great deal faster than the party, obliged to travel at the pace of the slowest. He increased his pace to a canter, which he knew he could maintain quite easily.

He still cherished a faint hope that, now it was night, Tawny Owl might be on his way to him. But as time wore on, this hope waned.

Constantly wondering about the fate of Badger and the rabbits, who had still been struggling in the river when he was swept away, Fox suffered real anguish in his ignorance. There was very little to take his mind off these thoughts as he travelled through the cloud covered, breezy night.

He felt he was making some recognizable progress when he spotted the weir a little way ahead of him. The sound of the furious, swirling water made him shiver again, and he forced his tiring legs to a still faster pace.

Soon pale streaks of grey appeared in the sky, the clouds seemed to lighten in hue and with the approach of dawn, the breeze dropped.

As the light gathered, Fox's weariness became more acute.

These two things progressed together, so that the thought came to Fox's mind that as soon as it was broad day, he would drop from exhaustion.

At length he stopped running, and, his head hanging between his legs, his breath came in long panting gasps. He descended the river bank, and lapped up the cool, treacherous water, while his weakened legs quivered like a hovering kestrel's wing-beats.

When his great thirst had been slaked Fox knew he could go no further. If he was ever to catch up with the friends who needed him, he must keep his strength up by eating and sleeping sufficiently. He felt satisfied with the progress he had made during the night, and started to look round for a resting-place.

There was nowhere with sufficient cover by the riverside, so Fox moved further away from the water, towards the fields and meadows where there were thick, concealing hedges. In a corner of one field, under the hedgerow, he found a large burrow. He first sniffed very carefully all round the hole, and then put his head inside and sniffed again.

He thought he could smell fox, but as there was no sound, he very cautiously ventured inside. The hole was dark, warm and empty. It could indeed have been a fox's earth, he decided, but how recently it had been occupied he could not tell. He went back to the entrance once more and looked out. There was no sign of any animal nearby. Fox turned his back on the daylight and made himself comfortable on the bare earth floor. It was quite soft enough to send him off to sleep almost at once.

He awoke with a jump as he felt something touch his body. In the darkness it was some time before he could see what it was, but his strong sense of smell conveyed to him at once the unmistakable scent of a female fox. He scrambled to his feet.

'Don't be alarmed,' said the vixen soothingly. 'Stay and rest as long as you like. It's dusk, and I must go in search of food.'

'I . . . I didn't know the place was occupied, you see,' Fox stammered, 'It was empty, and I . . .'

'It's only one of my retreats,' explained the vixen.

Fox looked puzzled.

'I haven't been in this area for some time,' she explained. 'I was passing, and I could hear your breathing.'

'I was very tired,' Fox explained.

'Have you been travelling? I don't think I've ever seen you before.'

'Travelling?' Fox smiled. 'Yes, I have. It's a long story.'

'I'd be interested to hear it – if you feel like telling me.'

'I should enjoy it,' said Fox. 'But you said you were about to go hunting. I haven't eaten either – and . . . well, perhaps we could hunt together and bring our food back here. Then, after we've finished, I'll tell you how I came here.'

'That's a marvellous idea,' said Vixen. 'Shall we go straight away?'

'Rather,' replied Fox emphatically. 'I'm ravenous.'

Vixen led the way from the earth, and Fox trotted beside her, experiencing a new feeling of companionship, quite different from anything he had felt before.

As they crossed the darkening fields, Fox now and again glanced at his new acquaintance. He thought Vixen was the most wonderful creature he had ever seen, and he intended to make her aware of it when the time was right.

Together they hunted, and together, through the moonlight, they slipped back to the earth with their catch. All this time neither of them uttered a word.

Safe underground again, they devoured their supper and Vixen invited Fox to tell his story. So he told her of Farthing Wood and his friends, of their journey to White Deer Park, of the calamity in the river, and how he was on his way to rejoin the band as their leader.

Vixen listened with the greatest interest and admiration for their exploits. 'How brave you all are,' she murmured when Fox had finished.

'And you?' asked Fox. 'Tell me your story.'

'Oh no!' Vixen laughed, and shook her head. 'There isn't any story really. I've always lived in this part of the country. Fortunately *my* home has not been taken from me by the humans, although I've had my brushes with them.'

'The Hunt?' Fox asked in a low voice.

'Yes, but I've been lucky. I've heard it in full cry more than once, but always in pursuit of another animal.'

'Poor creatures.' Fox shuddered.

'It's part of our existence.' Vixen smiled. 'We learn to live with it. One day it might be my turn, but until then . . . I'm free.'

'I can't bear to think that you . . .' Fox began – but broke off.

'What were you going to say?' Vixen asked gently.

Fox did not reply at once. Then he said, 'I couldn't help but look at you while we were hunting. You're the most marvellous creature I've ever seen – so swift and lithe. How your eyes shone! And your coat is beautiful – glossy and soft.'

Vixen was silent. She looked away shyly . . .

'I wish you were my mate,' said Fox. 'Then you'd have nothing to fear. I would protect you – from everything.'

Vixen looked up and smiled. 'I believe you would,' she said softly. 'Gallant Fox.'

'Then will you come with me as my mate, and help me to find my friends?'

Vixen fell silent again, and stared down at the earthen floor as if thinking. Fox held his breath. Eventually she looked up and met his eyes in the darkness.

'I will travel with you until you find your friends,' she said finally.

Fox's spirits sank. Her reply was less than he had hoped for.

Vixen sensed his disappointment. 'I cannot promise more at present,' she said. 'But as we travel, by and by I shall make up my mind.'

Fox understood her at once. He had to prove himself to her. For her caution he admired her even more.

He made a resolve. 'I shall be worthy of you,' he said solemnly under his breath. Aloud he said, 'Then I can hope?'

Vixen laughed. 'Of course,' she said. 'I shouldn't want it otherwise.' She lay down on the floor.

'You must be tired,' said Fox. 'I've rested, and I'm ready to start. But you must have your rest, too. While you sleep, I'll speak to the night creatures. Perhaps they will have news of Badger and the others. I'll return before dawn. Sleep well.'

'I shall,' said Vixen, resting her head on her paws.

Fox left the earth and made for the nearest wood. If the local owls were about they would be sure to have some knowledge of the Farthing Wood party. He *must* find out which way his friends were heading.

The wood was quiet and very dark, save for silvery patches of moonlight filtering through the gaps in the trees. The mellow, liquid notes of a nightingale assailed his ears, and he quickly followed its direction. He found the songster perched on a hawthorn branch.

'I compliment you on your voice,' said Fox diplomatically, 'and I wonder if you could help me?'

'Thank you,' replied the nightingale, 'I *am* reckoned to be the finest ballad singer in these parts. I certainly haven't heard a finer.'

Fox, who did not have a lot of faith in the good sense of songbirds, was not particularly surprised at the empty answer he had received. He decided to have another try.

'I can well believe it,' he continued. 'I think some friends of mine might have passed this way recently, and they would certainly have appreciated such music. I wondered if you might have seen them?'

'What do they look like?' inquired the bird without much interest.

Fox described the leading members of the party.

'Humph!' returned the nightingale indignantly. 'Snakes and toads and such-like have no ear for music. Only birds such as myself can be relied on to judge such things. No, I haven't seen your reptilian friends.'

The absurdity of the bird irritated Fox, but he wasted no more time on him, for he had espied the ghostly form of a barn owl flitting from tree to tree. He hurried over as it alighted in the fork of an old ash.

The owl looked down at him with its huge eyes.

'I'd like a word with you, if you've the time,' Fox called up.

'Certainly,' came the prompt reply. 'On what subject?'

'I'm trying to trace my friends,' said Fox. 'Have you seen anything of a group of animals travelling through these parts?'

'I'm afraid I haven't,' said the owl. 'I don't seem to see many foxes in the wood these days.'

'Not foxes,' Fox corrected him. 'A mixed party of animals

– a badger, a mole, a weasel, rabbits, hares, squirrels and so on, all travelling together and accompanied by a tawny owl and a kestrel.'

'Ah! Now I'm with you. No, I haven't actually seen all of them. But your friend the tawny owl was around . . . oh, a couple of nights ago. I had a conversation with him.'

'Are they all safe?' Fox asked quickly, suddenly recalling with a jolt that he had no idea what had happened to Badger. 'Was there a badger with them?'

'Oh yes. Your friend the badger is their leader, is he not?' replied the owl, who had no reason to assume he was only a deputy. 'The tawny owl mentioned some mishap, but I think they're all safe now.'

'That's good news,' said Fox. 'So I am on the right track.'

'You've all come a long way,' the owl commented, 'according to your friend. But how did you come to be separated from them?'

Fox explained.

'I understand.' The owl nodded, blinking his great eyes. 'Well, I hope you find each other again. It would be a shame if your adventure failed to end happily.'

Fox asked the owl if he could give him any idea of the direction the party had taken. The bird shook his head. 'On that point *your* owl was not forthcoming,' he replied, 'and I imagine that his hesitancy was deliberate. After all, the less their plans are known the safer will be their journey.'

'It's true our route was known only to one member of the

group all along,' Fox admitted. 'And, of course, it is better kept that way. But at least I know I'm in their vicinity.'

'I'm sure your sensitive nose will prove more than equal to the task of discovering them,' said the owl. 'Good luck to you.'

Fox thanked him and, without pausing for words with any of the other denizens of the wood, returned to the earth. Vixen was peacefully asleep.

## XXI

# VIXEN DECIDES

The morning was warm and sunny when Fox and his new companion left the earth and set off towards the river.

Their swift pace and alertness helped them to avoid the few humans dotting the riverside that day. In a few hours they had reached the piece of slack water where the Farthing Wood party had swum the river, and where Fox's troubles had begun.

Fox, however, now had reason to think differently about his misfortune in the water. Although it had separated him from his old friends, he had found a new one, and he felt grateful to the river for enabling him to meet Vixen.

His loneliness had disappeared, but he was more anxious than ever to catch up with the other animals. He felt so proud of his beautiful new companion that, for a reason he would not have been able to name, he wanted his friends to meet her and like her.

As they trotted, nose to tail, along the river bank, Fox felt he wanted only one thing more to make his happiness complete – for Vixen to see him leading the animals into White Deer Park.

Every now and then he would steal a glance at her, or turn quickly to meet her eye. In the bright sunlight he thought she looked even more beautiful. Her silky fur seemed to glow, and her eyes sparkled with liveliness and intelligence.

When they reached the crossing-place, Fox bade Vixen keep out of sight while he searched for some clue as to the direction his friends had taken.

The first thing he found was the animals' sleeping-quarters, where the long grass had been flattened by their bodies. Shortly afterwards, he detected a narrow track through the first meadow, beaten down by many assorted pairs of feet. He barked a signal to Vixen, and they continued on their way.

Using his sharp eyes and sense of scent, Fox was able to keep on his friends' track. During the afternoon the two foxes left the last meadow behind them and found themselves on the open downland.

Rather than press on until they caught sight of the other animals, Fox decided it would be better to look at once for a resting-place, and to make an early start again the next morning. Had he been able to foresee the consequences of this decision, he would have continued his journey that day, and all the following night too, even to the point of exhaustion.

However, in the late afternoon, Fox and Vixen his themselves in a thick growth of bracken, and dozed during the remaining hours to dusk.

When at last it was dark, Fox was on his feet first. He stretched – first his front legs, and then his hind legs. He looked down at Vixen who was still napping. When he shyly nuzzled her, she awoke.

'Are you hungry?' Fox asked.

'Very.'

'I'll see what I can rustle up for you,' said Fox. 'You stay here; I won't be long.'

'You're very kind,' said Vixen, and smiled at him.

Fox felt a warm glow spread under his skin, and he smiled back. Jumping over the fern-fronds, he ran off into the darkness.

While Vixen awaited his return, a gentle shower of rain fell, sharpening the rich smell of bracken and the scent of grass, and producing an intoxicating fragrance of damp leaves and soil.

Fox returned, carrying a generous supper in his jaws, and his fur sprinkled with glistening raindrops.

'I'm sure we shall catch up with them tomorrow,' he said as they ate. 'I can sense we're close.'

'What a surprise they will have,' said Vixen, 'if they think that you were . . .'

'. . . lost,' finished Fox. 'Oh, it'll be so good to see them all again! Dear old Badger, and Owl, Kestrel, Toad – even Adder! They're *all* my friends.'

'You're lucky to have so many,' remarked Vixen. '*I* never did . . . not many . . . well, until you . . . turned up.'

'And now you'll have a lot more,' promised the beaming Fox. His voice dropped. 'That is, if you agree to come with me, as my mate.'

'I'll give you your answer tomorrow,' said Vixen.

The two foxes rose with the dawn and slaked their thirst at a cool puddle in a hollow of the ground. They were soon on the animals' trail again. They had not been travelling for long when Fox suddenly stopped and looked all round with a puzzled expression. Then he sniffed the ground closely, to the left and right of him, for some distance.

'That's very odd,' he remarked. 'The trail seems to divide here. They can't have split up!' He sniffed more closely. Then he shook his head. 'No, the same scents run in each direction. For some reason they must have made a turn, and then doubled back. Perhaps something was after them . . .'

'Could it have been a wrong turn?' suggested Vixen.

Fox looked up. 'Yes, you're probably right,' he agreed. 'The question is, which is the right way? If we take the wrong direction we're going to waste a lot of time.'

'There's only one thing to be done then,' said Vixen. 'We must separate; I'll go left, you go right. If you are on the wrong track, turn back as soon as you realize it, and catch me up. If I go wrong, I'll do the same.'

'Vixen, you're wonderful,' said Fox with admiration. 'What an asset you could be to our party. Oh, if you would only join me!'

'We'll see about that,' said Vixen mischievously. 'But I must wish you farewell for now.'

'But not for long?' begged Fox. 'Now that I know you, I couldn't bear to lose you.'

'You may not have to,' said Vixen with an impish grin as she turned away.

Her reply put new heart into Fox, and he took his direction in a joyful mood.

As he paced over the downland, following the familiar

scent of his friends' trail, he occasionally stopped and turned, expecting to see Vixen in the distance, running towards him. Then, as the gap widened and he still did not see her, he began to expect to find very soon that it was he who was on the wrong track.

Nevertheless, he plodded on faithfully, and eventually came across a sign that pointed without any doubt to the fact that his friends had indeed travelled *his* route. On reaching a patch of birch scrub he found that the scent he had been following all along continued past it. But a second scent, which smelt to him fresher than the other, led right into the scrub itself. It was not long before the smell of carrion made him stop and look around in alarm. A few yards away he saw a thorn-bush littered with bodies, amongst them tiny, new-born voles and fieldmice.

As Fox moved nearer he noticed, to his horror, that two of the baby voles bore a striking resemblance to those with whom he had been travelling only a few days ago. Shocked, he noticed two adult voles, who a few days ago had actually been travelling with him, impaled on the cruel thorns. There was no doubt in his mind now – his friends had suffered some misfortune. Perhaps they *had* lost their way, or been split up?

Fox felt he could not rest until he knew what had happened. He was convinced that at least *some* of his friends were very close, and he had to find them.

He thought of Vixen. *Surely* she must have discovered by

now that she was on the wrong track. He dashed out of the scrub, confident he would see her running towards him, but she was still not in sight.

He was torn between retracing his steps to collect her, and leaving her to make her own way back to him while he pressed on in pursuit of the other animals.

With each passing minute he was becoming more worried about the fate of his friends, and he felt that to double-back now would be to waste vital time.

With a heavy heart, Fox decided in favour of his old friends from Farthing Wood. He picked up the trail again and followed it as swiftly as he could.

When the scent Vixen had been following ended abruptly, she realized Fox had taken the correct trail, and that she must rejoin him as they had agreed.

She sat down and pondered. Now was the time to make her decision. Did she wish to rejoin Fox or not? If she did, there was no time to lose. If she did not, then here was her chance to leave him without causing him the pain of rejection.

It took Vixen but a few seconds to read her own heart. Of course she wished to rejoin him! He was kind, handsome and courageous. She wanted to go wherever he led. Yet still she did not move.

While every muscle in her body prepared to spring her forward in the direction Fox had taken, her mind would not

give the command. Something at the back of it told her she was losing her freedom. She had always been completely free. She had lived the life of the wild with only herself to consider, only her needs to satisfy. If she followed Fox now, that freedom – to go where *she* chose to go – would be lost.

But in the end, Vixen's heart decided the matter. At the moment that Fox, with anguish, decided not to go back for her, Vixen was already running after him.

Sadly, her moment of hesitancy was to put her life, and that of Fox, in the gravest danger.

# XXII

# THE HUNT

Fox had been quite correct in assuming that his friends from Farthing Wood were not far ahead of him.

On that very morning Badger had led his somewhat dejected party out of their night shelter in a nearby ditch, on to the downland again.

Their journey now took them up a rising piece of ground, the slope of which was very steep, and because of the voles and mice progress proved quite slow.

Rabbit had begun to mingle with the other leading animals again, as the recent distressing event convinced him that his and the other rabbits' part in the loss of Fox, was now forgotten.

'You might be interested to know,' he remarked to Hedgehog, 'that if it weren't for us rabbits, this grassland would

all grow out of control. No sheep round here, you notice. What do you think keeps the grass nice and short like this?'

'Cattle?' suggested Hedgehog.

'Nonsense! No cattle about. It's rabbits!'

'I always felt sure you creatures must have some usefulness,' replied Hedgehog, 'though I could never think what it might be.'

'Hmph!' snorted Rabbit. 'More use than any hedgehog,' he said witheringly.

'On the contrary. The place would be overrun with insects and slugs if we didn't find them so tasty,' said Hedgehog.

Rabbit's argumentative nature was not equal to finding another retort, and he contented himself with muttering peevishly beneath his breath. Hedgehog left him and joined Weasel.

Badger and Mole were in conversation. Mole had been dismayed to hear Badger's gasping and panting as he plodded up the steep slope.

'Oh dear,' he thought to himself. 'Here I am, on Badger's back, and he's finding it such an effort.'

Then, aloud, he said, 'If you stop for a moment, Badger, I'll get off.'

'Don't be silly . . . not much . . . further,' panted Badger.

'Please, I'd like to walk for a change,' said Mole.

'Not worth stopping now,' replied Badger. 'Wait till we get to the top.'

This was just what Mole was trying to avoid, so without speaking further he leant to one side, and slid down Badger's coat, finally dropping the last few inches to the ground.

'Ow! Don't tug so, Mole!' complained Badger. 'You just stay put.'

'Oh dear, he thinks I'm still on his back,' Mole said to himself, and hurried in his attempt to keep up with the larger animal's strides.

He heard Badger continuing to talk, but he had already dropped behind so much he could not hear what his friend was talking about. He dared not make it obvious that he had played a trick on him, for it would only make Badger look foolish. So Mole, as he struggled upwards, bellowed, 'Yes, Badger,' and 'No, Badger,' or 'Just as you say, Badger,' at intervals, hoping Badger would not discover him.

Mole's pace was so slow that gradually all the other animals, including the mice and voles, passed him. In the end he was left cursing his own misplaced good intention of lightening Badger's load, while he watched the rest of the party leaving him further and further behind as they mounted the steep slope.

He knew that Badger would be very cross indeed when he reached the top and found he had been talking to himself for most of the way. As Mole's eyesight was so very poor he eventually lost sight of the other animals altogether, and this made him feel as if he were climbing the hill completely alone.

Supposing they left him behind? He reassured himself quickly. That could not happen. Badger, or somebody, would notice he was not with them. Badger would come back for him. But by the time he was missed, they might be miles ahead! No, no, surely they would pause for a rest at the crest of the rise?

'Oh dear, oh dear,' Mole wailed, as he inched his way upwards. 'I'm always causing trouble! If I had only done as Badger said, this wouldn't have happened.'

Suddenly his small velvet-clad body froze to the ground. His sensitive feet and acute hearing had caught a series of vibrations. The vibrations strengthened. Mole knew it was not the light tread of his friends that he could sense. The vibrations were too many, and too loud. They increased at a tremendous rate.

Then Mole heard voices – human voices – and the excited

bark of dogs. At the moment they were still distant, but with every second the noise, and the thudding of the ground, increased.

Mole looked round in horror. Of course he could see nothing. But that tremendous din, that thud! thud! thud! approaching so swiftly, the scattered barks and human cries, could mean only one thing. The sound that every creature of the wild, however great or small, dreaded beyond all else. The sound of the Hunt!

For a moment Mole's senses reeled in panic. He was terrified, not for himself, but for his friends – particularly Badger and the hares. He knew he could dig himself to safety in a matter of seconds, and in any case the Hunt was not interested in such small quarry as he represented. But what about the others?

With all his strength, and the added speed of fear, Mole hauled himself up the hill after his friends.

He was almost at the top when the first of the dogs appeared, cutting across the side of the hill. Others followed, tongues lolling. Mole sighed thankfully as he watched them make their way down the slope. His friends on the summit were safe.

The scarlet coats of the huntsmen, and the black coats of the women riders came into view on bay, black and grey horses. But the animals were at a mild canter, and Mole realized that the hounds had not yet found a scent; their pace was far too leisurely, and their cries, though excited, were without any trace of that awful frenzy that typified, more than anything, the terror of the Hunt for wild creatures.

At the top of the hill Mole found a small spinney, and from the confines of the trees in hesitant pairs, or singly, appeared the forms of his friends.

'Oh, Mole! You're safe!' cried Badger. 'Whatever made you do it? We all thought you were lost again.'

'I'm sorry, Badger,' Mole said contritely, 'but I did it for a very good reason. Please believe me. It was for your sake.'

Badger could say nothing more. He merely gave Mole an affectionate, understanding nuzzle.

'Did you see . . . the . . . Hunt?' Mole faltered.

'We heard rather than saw,' said Weasel. 'We buried ourselves among the trees.'

'I fervently hope no foxes are abroad today,' said Toad.

The other animals all turned to him, the eyes of every one of them showing that they were occupied with the same thought.

Suddenly a startling new cry was borne to them on the breeze. The hounds were giving tongue in a wild, unearthly baying. The animals rushed in a body to the edge of the slope and peered down.

They saw the hounds now racing over the downland, the riders galloping after them with coat-tails flying, in the direction of a small wood.

'They've picked up a scent,' said Tawny Owl grimly. 'Some

235

poor creature's got the race of his life ahead of him.'

It was in fact the unfortunate Vixen, on her way back to join Fox, who had attracted the interest of the pack. In an attempt to make up for lost time, she had taken a short cut through a wood, expecting to be ahead of Fox when she emerged on the other side of the trees.

Halfway through the wood, she heard the hounds. Her first thought was that they were on the track of Fox, and she was engulfed by a feeling of mingled horror and helplessness, so much so that she stopped stock still.

Then, in mounting waves of terror, she heard the baying and the galloping coming nearer, and she knew that it was she they were after!

Her first reaction was to turn about and run back the way she had come. Then, in a moment of startling clarity, she realized that, once in the open again, she would have little chance. By far her best manoeuvre would be to remain in the wood and, amongst the close-knit trees and saplings and shrubs, to zig-zag, feint and double-back, in and out and around the undergrowth and groups of trees, so that she would tie the hounds up in knots and break up the pack, while the horsemen would be constantly impeded by the low branches. Then, when she had got them into such a state of confusion that they would waste many priceless minutes extricating themselves, she would streak for the nearest edge of the wood, and with the lead she would have earned, race so fast across country that she stood a fair chance of losing them for good.

With wildly beating heart, Vixen forced herself to stay still until the first hounds should reach the wood and locate her. While all her senses and every nerve screamed at her to run, to fly, she retained an outward composure.

The horrible, deafening baying grew nearer . . . nearer . . . nearer . . . Soon she could even hear the jingling of the harness of the first horses. Then, with a crash, a shock, the hounds were into the wood, sending clouds of leaves, twigs and mould into the air, and trampling down undergrowth and seedlings beneath their furious feet.

Away spurted Vixen, away from their baying and their gaping mouths, away from their gleaming fangs. She ran under the taller trees of beech and oak, and dived into a thick shrubbery of elm and holly bushes. The hounds followed her.

Emerging swiftly from this, Vixen made a complete circuit of the shrubs, so that she was in effect then behind the leading hounds. With a swift glance she saw the main body of the pack threading its way through the trees on her right. She rushed off towards a thick stand of birch saplings, slowed enough as she entered them to make sure the hounds followed her direction, and then looped her slim body first round one trunk, then another, in and out, with the suppleness of a snake.

She heard the hounds yelping frustratedly as they attempted to push their bigger, stouter bodies between the close-packed saplings, and she heard the curses of the riders

who had ventured into the wood as shoulders were buffeted, or heads assailed by the protruding branches of large trees.

She broke from the group of saplings, and ran exultantly into the more open part of the wood. Her plan was proving successful. Now she saw ahead a thick screen of brambles and ferns. If she could once enmesh the maddened hounds in its clinging prickles and stems, she would still have breath and strength enough to run out of the wood and race far and fast across the open downland.

She had achieved her main object of separating the hounds. They were coming after her singly now, or in pairs, with long gaps between them. Others were barking in bewilderment, trapped amongst the saplings; some that had broken free had lost considerable energy in doing so, and their continued baying was at half-strength. Some again had lost all sense of direction and were sniffing the air, or unthinkingly following the lead of other hounds and becoming in turn entangled in the shrubbery.

But now the greatest test of courage faced Vixen. For to ensure that a good number of the hounds followed her into the undergrowth, she herself would have to delay entering it until they were but a few feet from her. Otherwise their training would tell them merely to bypass this obstacle, surround it on the outside, and wait for their quarry to be forced into the open by their master.

Her heart thudding madly, Vixen allowed her pace to slacken, gradually, until, as she neared the undergrowth, she had almost stopped moving. Now the hounds gave tongue to a new note, as if they sensed their triumph. Their baying became shriller in its excitement, and they increased their pace. Some of the bewildered hounds began to make straight for this corner of the wood as they saw and interpreted the leaders' commotion.

Vixen glanced behind and, despite herself, felt fresh waves of fear explode through her body. The hounds were almost on her! With a tremendous bound she leapt forward, and landed in the midst of a thick mass of fern. At once she began to inch and crawl her way through the intricate mass of stems.

She heard the hounds scrambling after her, and knew that if she could just manage to pull her body through the tugging

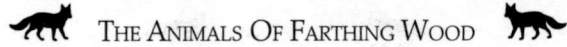 

heap of undergrowth without trapping herself, she could almost certainly escape.

As the minutes passed the confused and furious noise behind her told her that more and more of the foxhounds had penetrated the brambles and bracken. Angry human voices – calling voices – ordered the remainder of the pack away. Vixen continued to edge forward, at times with her stomach almost flat to the ground.

A little more, a little further, and she would be free. She saw, through the tunnel of undergrowth, bright sunlight ahead, and an absence of trees. She was about to emerge on the other side of the wood! There were only a few feet of undergrowth remaining for her to pull her body through! Brambles had torn at her fur and skin, springy ferns had struck her face again and again, making her eyes stream water, but ahead was clear, open space. She struggled on.

The next time Vixen looked up, her heart almost stopped: In that wide empty space of downland she had almost reached, she now saw a forest of horses' legs, stamping the ground impatiently as their riders waited for her inevitable appearance. Between those legs were blazing eyes and open mouths – cruel, red tongues and bared, snapping teeth. Foxhounds!

Despite her superb cunning, the humans had bested her. Realizing the futility of remaining in the confining wood, they had ridden back into the open, and moved round the outside of the trees to the very spot she had been working towards, unaware. They had taken with them those slower hounds which had been prevented from entering the undergrowth.

Now Vixen saw her stupidity in underestimating the skill and experience of the huntsmen. Behind her the hounds who were struggling in fury through the brambles and ferns were inching closer. The game was up.

# XXIII

# Fox to the Rescue

The noise of the Hunt had, of course, soon been picked up by Fox as he ran across the downland, hoping every minute to see some sign of his old friends.

When the first yelps of the pack reached him he stopped dead, just as Vixen had done. His ears pricked up, and he sniffed the air cautiously. He judged the Hunt to be some distance away, but directly in the line of his present path.

Like Vixen, Fox wanted to run as far as he could in the opposite direction – to keep running until those ghastly sounds became memories only. But he had already decided once that day, that to be reunited with his friends was his most important objective. Those friends, who needed him, were somewhere ahead, and not far from him.

Now Fox realized that to reach them, he would have to run the risk of encountering the Hunt. He had one advantage. He was upwind from the pack, and if he made a wide skirting movement from his present course, he might well avoid detection.

He looked behind him again, and stood for some moments, motionless, but there was still no sign of Vixen. Fox suddenly experienced a feeling that he might never see her again, but he immediately cast it from his mind, and set off on his decided route.

As he ran on, the noise of the dogs and the hoofbeats of the horses became louder. Soon he heard the frenzied baying of hounds following a scent. For a moment Fox felt that selfish feeling of relief produced by the knowledge that it is another, and not oneself, in danger. Then he wondered whose scent they might be following.

Fox had no doubt that there were a good number of foxes in the vicinity, any one of which might be the unfortunate animal now being pursued. He was thankful that Vixen was behind him, out of danger's reach. But suddenly his protective instinct told him he ought to find her and make quite sure she was safe. After all, he did not know for sure where she was at that instant.

The realization of this struck Fox with the impact of a heavy blow. He felt dreadfully afraid, not for himself, but for his lovely companion who, it now appeared, he might have abandoned at the very time she needed his presence and protection the most.

He wanted to run back then and find her at all costs. But what if she were not behind him? If she had been, surely she would have caught him up sufficiently to be visible in the distance at least? The awful thought that his beloved Vixen might at that very moment be the quarry of the hounds made Fox shudder with horror. The more he tried to shut the thought out, the more he became convinced that that was the dreadful truth.

He raced back on to his old path, and made a bee-line for the direction of the Hunt. Fear lent wings to his feet. 'I'm coming!' he called, while knowing full well nobody could hear him. Then to Vixen he vowed in a low voice, 'They won't catch you while I'm still alive!'

Soon he could see the wood, and the dogs plunging into it, the riders following more cautiously. For a few minutes they were out of sight, under the thick screen of the trees. Bound by bound Fox lessened the distance between them.

When he had only a few hundred yards to run, he saw the scarlet coats emerging again from the darkness, and spurring on their horses as they raced round the side of the wood, taking with them a bunch of eager, dancing hounds.

Fox saw them pause at a point on the east side of the wood, all of them looking down expectantly, and he set himself to run right into the teeth of danger.

He seemed to feel no fear at all as he spurted across the springing turf towards them. His mind, his whole existence, was occupied with one idea – to save Vixen, whose scent at that moment he himself detected for the first time.

They saw his coming with surprise, pointing and shouting their astonishment to each other. They had not expected a fox to appear from that quarter; and so headlong and fierce was his rush that the hounds themselves were taken aback, and gave way.

Fox dashed straight between the impatient legs and hooves of the horses. The amazing sight of a wild animal actually running to meet them had quite thrown the hounds off balance. But with Fox's russet back now turned to them, the hounds regained their composure.

The horn blew, the dogs howled, and the horsemen prepared once more to give chase. None stayed to await the emergence of Vixen from the undergrowth. They were no

longer interested in ambush, but only in the glory of speed, in skilful horsemanship, the feel of the wind dashing against their faces, the vibrations of thundering hooves: all the excitement and exhilaration of pursuit.

Fox kept close to the trees, and continued to run round the perimeter of the wood. He felt strong, fresh and keen. He felt confident no hound could ever catch him. He would show them what *real* running was!

Nevertheless, he was not going to make it easy for them by staying in open country. Like Vixen, he realized the value of trees in impeding the progress of the hounds and, particularly, the horses and their riders. He entered the wood through a wide gap between the trees.

Of course, the Master called off the dogs from following into the wood a second time. He was not going to have this tactic repeated, with its accompanying frustrations to pack and riders. However, by electing to stay on the outside of the wood, he was at a loss as to which direction to take, as there was absolutely no knowing from which side the fox would appear again, and there was no way of surrounding the whole wood.

In the end, he realized he was temporarily beaten. He would have to allow the hounds into the wood again; otherwise, what possible chance was there of getting his quarry to leave it?

So under the trees they went again, baying continually. But the Master had lost this round of the battle. His indecision had given Fox a valuable lead, and he had already run through the length of the wood, and was now in the open again on the other side, going full-tilt across the grass towards a steep rise he saw ahead of him.

In the meantime Vixen, who had of course been a witness to Fox's heroic action of leading off her ambushers, found the coast clear again. Scrambling free of the thick undergrowth, she burst into the open only seconds before the hounds who had followed her into the brambles also broke free.

And so the pack was now neatly divided into two sections, each giving chase to different foxes and each group unaware of the existence of the other. Here was a problem for any Master of Foxhounds, and the one concerned was at that moment following the hounds in the wood, ducking gingerly to avoid low branches and beginning, like the rest of the riders, to think it a very bad day's hunting.

However, Fox was not to have it all his own way. Strong as he was, he had made a grave mistake in heading for the grassy slope he saw ahead. For it was steeper than he had imagined, and a short way up he began to tire. His heart pounded horribly, his legs quivered, and his breath became more and more laboured.

And now the hounds began to gain on him. They were out of the wood and, after their brief rest, they were running better. Had it not been for the start Fox had on them he would have been in a hopeless situation, for the hounds' greater stamina made light of climbing the slope.

For the first time Fox began to feel the likelihood of being caught, and at the thought of what that meant his blood turned to ice. He was only a little more than halfway up the slope, and now he could hear the hounds' harsh breathing as well as their usual din.

Then, as if in a dream, he heard well-loved, almost forgotten voices shouting to him in familiar tones from the top of the slope. Badger, Mole, Weasel, Hare, Tawny Owl, Kestrel, Adder, Toad, and all his other friends had been watching from the very beginning the fluctuations of the Hunt in unbearable excitement, little realizing until now that the poor pursued animal was their own beloved Fox. They had believed him dead, and now, when he was on the point of being restored to them, he was in greater danger of losing his life than ever before.

It took the dazed Fox a little time before he could accept that what his senses were telling him was in fact real. He had found his friends again. Now everything would be all right.

With renewed effort, he managed a final spurt and reached the top of the slope, staggering into the protective circle of his old friends. At once they led him into the copse where earlier they had themselves hidden from the Hunt.

This time, however, the hounds were not passing by. The animals looked from Fox to the approaching yelling pack, and then back again. They saw Fox's exhausted form sink to the ground. How were they to save him?

'It's . . . no good,' the brave animal gasped. 'I'm done for. I . . . can't run . . . any more. Don't . . . stay with me. Hide yourselves. It's . . . me they want. Leave me!' He rose on to his tottering legs and took a few steps away from them.

They would not leave him.

'We haven't just found you to lose you again at once,' said Badger. 'Don't worry, Fox! We shall win yet!'

'They're coming! They're coming!' shrieked the squirrels who had, of course, taken to the trees.

Badger and the other animals, realizing their only chance was to fight to the death, instinctively surrounded Fox, and awaited the onslaught.

In agonized silence, their mostly defenceless little bodies frozen in fear, they waited. The painful throbbing of their hearts seemed to each animal like a continual thunderclap. They continued to wait; every second that passed seeming as if it would be their last.

Human shouts and galloping horses told them the riders had reached the top of the hill. Then the horn sounded, horribly close. Yet still no hounds appeared through the trees. They had even stopped barking.

The animals could not understand what was happening. They could not move. There was nowhere safer to go. The unbearable tension began to feel worse than the fate they had all expected.

'For goodness' sake, Kestrel,' Badger whispered hoarsely, 'put us out of this misery. Go and see what's happening.'

Even as Kestrel flew out of the copse, the animals heard more human cries, the hounds gave tongue again and, miraculously, these sounds and the horses' hoofbeats became fainter.

'They . . . they've gone,' whispered Mole in amazement.

'Yes.' Fox's weary voice came from the midst of them. He alone of all the Farthing Wood animals could guess the reason for the Hunt's change of course. 'It's Vixen,' he said.

The animals looked at him for an explanation. Weary as he was, Fox was obliged to tell them of his meeting with Vixen, and how they had travelled together.

'I thought I had saved her,' he muttered, in a tone of utter despair.

He had no time to say more. Kestrel was flying towards them in great excitement.

'There's another fox,' he said quickly. 'Some of the hounds were already following it. They must have broken off from the main pack that came up here. Now the Master has set all of them after it, and the horses are right behind. He stopped the hounds from coming in here – I don't know why. I suppose the Hunt can't chase two animals at once. Anyway, it's our lucky day. We must get out of here at once, while there's time. The other fox is making straight for this slope.'

'Where else is there for us to go? We can't possibly escape,' said Badger. 'How can our party outrun those dreadful hounds? They would tear us to bits.'

'Listen, Badger, listen,' said Kestrel impatiently. 'Don't you see? They're chasing the other fox, not us. As long as we get away from this copse, out of the path of the huntsmen, we're safe. They're bound to catch the other fox – it looks all in, though I've never seen such a fast runner before. Once it's caught, their sport's over for today.'

'How can you be so callous?' snapped Mole, who could see the groaning Fox, his head on his paws, weeping in the most pitiful way.

'You wrong me,' said Kestrel. 'You wrong me, Mole. I loathe and despise this human trait of hounding smaller creatures to death, with large numbers opposed against one solitary animal. But, don't you see, it's the law of the wild. This poor fox is sacrificed today to the humans' cruelty. But we can't stop it. I wish we could. Surely you believe that? I'm thinking now of our own party's safety. You can't blame me for that!'

'You want us to profit by another creature's misfortune?' said Mole.

'No. I merely want us all to escape,' said Kestrel, with a puzzled look. 'Is that wrong?'

'You mustn't blame Kestrel,' said Badger. 'He's thinking of us, and rightly so. He doesn't understand the situation.'

'What situation?' Kestrel asked.

'The other fox is . . . a female,' explained Badger with some awkwardness. 'She's our Fox's friend.'

'Oh no! How awful!' Kestrel exclaimed. 'Fox, do forgive

me. I didn't know.'

Fox was not able to reply.

'It's all right,' Badger smiled kindly on his behalf. 'You weren't to know. I know Fox won't hold it against you. But I'm afraid he's quite overwrought.'

'Look, Badger,' Kestrel whispered, beckoning him aside. 'Friend or no friend,' he went on, when they were out of earshot, 'I must say again, she will be caught. She'll never keep ahead up this hill, not after all the running she's already done. You *must* go now. Don't you see? Time's running out.'

'I do see,' Badger said gravely. 'But we can't leave without Fox. And he would never come with us, and desert her. He's obviously lost his heart to this vixen, poor fellow. Just look at him now!'

'Then it was a sorry day for our party when he did so,' Kestrel remarked, as he looked at Fox's pathetic form. 'For it means we shall probably all suffer her fate.'

'You are absolutely right in everything you've said,' Badger agreed. 'But we must stand by Fox now, come what may.'

They returned to the other animals, and as they heard the noise of the Hunt approaching yet again, led on by Vixen, Fox, despite himself, could not remain hidden. He felt bound to share her fate. He got up, and moved to the edge of the copse to watch her last gallant efforts. Behind him were the rest of the party.

She was nearer than he had expected her to be. Her head

was drooping in the extremities of exhaustion, and her tongue lolled lifelessly from her open jaws. From where he stood Fox could hear her hoarse, racking gasps for breath. He shuddered to hear it. Somehow her legs kept moving. It was a mechanical action, with no conscious effort behind it. The leading hounds were only feet away, their blazing eyes already anticipating the kill.

Amazingly, Vixen kept running. Inch by inch the hounds gained. She looked up, and Fox saw her glazed expression. Yet he knew she had seen him.

For a few seconds, her pace quickened perceptibly. The hounds, snarling in anger, lost a little ground, but by now the first riders were level with them, led by the Master, who urged them on.

Nevertheless, with each stride Vixen was drawing further away. The hounds, tiring rapidly, seemed to acknowledge that they were beaten. Their efforts were unavailing. Vixen was approaching closer and closer to Fox. Soon she was a matter of yards away.

And then, in horror, the watching Fox saw the treachery of human nature laid bare. By any natural laws, Vixen had won this race. If there was any fairness to be had in the dealings of humans, who regarded the drawing of innocent blood as sport, then she deserved to go free. But the Master thought otherwise.

Seeing that his hounds were beaten, he took the matter into his own hands, and spurred on his horse. Mercy was not to be shown by any rule in his book. He came up behind Vixen and raised his whip-handle, his arm poised for one heavy blow that would knock her gallant little body back into the hungry jaws of his hounds. He leant over the side of his horse, at the same time reining it fiercely back, to make sure of his aim.

Suddenly, in the grass under his mount's front feet, a glistening, mosaicked head reared up. It was Adder. With red eyes glinting, he lunged forward with the force of an uncoiled spring, and buried his fangs deep in the horse's left fetlock.

The horse let out a scream of pain, and reared on to its hind legs, its front ones pounding the empty air, and threw the unbalanced Master to earth with a sickening thud. He lay unmoving.

In the next second Vixen reached Fox, and all of the animals retreated once more into the copse. The hounds were halted by the band of huntsmen arriving on the scene. These looked down with concern at their companion, a vivid splash of scarlet sprawled on the green turf.

'My leg,' he gasped, his features white and drawn. 'I can't move it!'

His horse, with a frightened look, was limping about by his side.

'Perhaps an act of Providence?' one of the other riders was heard to whisper.

The day's hunting was finished.

# XXIV

# REUNITED

Behind the screen of trees, the animals watched the scene with bated breath. The huntsmen had called forward one of their number who was obviously a doctor, and this man was kneeling, grave-faced, by the injured Master. It was now the turn of the humans to be in difficulties. But the animals' only concern was to be quite sure that the Hunt was leaving.

They watched its slow retreat down the slope with its casualty supported as comfortably as possible, a limping horse in need of attention, and a pack of subdued hounds. Only when the last sounds of the assemblage had died away did the animals feel safe.

Adder came slithering nonchalantly towards them over the leafy soil. The whole party greeted him like a hero.

'You can save your breath,' Adder said sourly. 'What else could I do, when that monster was just about to tread on me?'

The animals ceased their praises at once, but Adder's excuse had not fooled any of them. They realized he must have deliberately positioned himself on the slope in the chance of being some help to the exhausted Vixen.

'This is indeed a happy day,' said Badger joyfully. 'Our dear friend, whom we thought to be lost, is restored to us. And now, it seems, we have a new member of the party to welcome too.'

He looked across to where Fox and Vixen, the latter still panting heavily, were sitting side by side, each content to feel the other's nearness without the need for speech.

Fox knew he would never have to ask Vixen that important question again. The adoring look her eyes gave him told him all he wanted to know.

Presently Fox looked up and smiled at all his friends. 'We've all got an awful lot to tell each other,' he said, 'but now isn't the time. I suggest we have a brief rest here. Then we should move to a safer spot. In addition, Vixen and I are consumed with thirst. I wonder if someone . . .'

'Leave it to me, my dear Fox,' Kestrel interrupted. 'I'll scout round for the nearest stream; it won't take me more than a few minutes.' He flew up towards the tree-tops and vanished into the steely blue sky.

The other animals found themselves automatically looking

to Fox again for directions. The usual pattern had soon been re-established.

Kestrel returned with good news. 'We're in luck,' he said brightly. 'There's a disused quarry about a quarter of a mile away, completely fenced off from the outside, and there's a great pond inside it with ducks and water birds and I don't know what else. We'll be quite safe there.'

And so, eventually, at a leisurely pace, the reunited party of animals, with Badger walking proudly by the side of Fox and Vixen at its head, made its way down the south side of the slope, with Kestrel hovering a few feet in advance.

When they had almost reached the quarry, Toad let out a cry. 'I feel right again!' he shouted. 'This is marvellous! I feel I'm going the right way at last.'

The animals looked at him curiously.

'Don't you see?' he croaked happily. 'My homing instinct is working again, only in the opposite way. Farthing Pond has no influence any more. I'm too far away. Now I can feel a pull to the other direction – the direction of White Deer Park!'

'Hooray!' cried Mole. 'Good old Toad! Now he can really guide us straight to our new home.'

'Hare, will you stop please?' said Toad gaily. 'I feel as if I can leap all the way myself.'

With a grin, Hare complied, and Toad sprang forward energetically in front of Fox and Vixen, determined to lead the column into the quarry.

The animals soon arrived at their temporary destination, but found the fencing to be of the net type, so that only Toad, the voles and the fieldmice could climb through. Adder was able comfortably to slide underneath.

'Leave this to me,' offered Mole proudly, and he began to dig a broad furrow underneath the fence. So quickly did he work that the leading animals found themselves unprepared, and were liberally sprayed with earth from top to bottom, as Mole kicked it back vigorously.

'Steady on, Mole,' protested Badger, giving vent to a sneeze, and hastily moving back a few steps.

The channel was soon deep enough to allow the hedgehogs and squirrels to pass underneath the fence and Mole, having deepened it considerably on the outside, went under himself to perfect the other end.

'That's it. It's done!' he squeaked excitedly, and the rest of the animals entered the quarry.

They saw before them a huge, deep pit of bare chalk with a wide, man-made pathway, now encrusted with weeds and bushes of gorse and broom, leading steeply down one side. In the centre of this crater was a large pool, dotted with islands of vegetation, where several varieties of water-bird seemed to have made their homes.

Fox and Vixen hastened towards the water, leaving the rest of the party to follow as they wished. Side by side the two foxes drank their fill, and in the clear water they had time to admire each other's reflections.

'Oh, it's so peaceful here,' said Vixen afterwards. 'I can hardly believe it's the same world.'

'All this countryside could be peaceful if only the humans allowed it to be so,' remarked Fox grimly.

'Yes, but let's be quite fair,' returned Vixen. 'There are many humans who detest the idea of hunting as much as we do.'

'The ones they call Naturalists?' asked Fox.

'Those, certainly. But there are others,' said Vixen. 'Otherwise why do they keep what they call pets?'

'I must confess I shall never understand humans,' Fox said, shaking his head. 'In the wild, certain animals prey on others who, in turn, prey on smaller ones. Every creature knows what is his enemy, and also what he has no reason to fear. But those humans, who a short while ago were clamouring for our deaths, will probably go home and play with their dogs and talk to their horses with real affection.'

'Well, at any rate, let's forget the Hunt now and everything connected with it,' said Vixen. 'We're lucky to be here, safe with your friends. Let's enjoy ourselves.'

'By all means, my sweet,' said Fox warmly. 'And don't forget – they're *your* friends, too.'

Vixen pointed, with a chuckle, to where, on the edge of the pond, Kestrel and Tawny Owl were busily ruffling up their feathers, preparatory to enjoying a bathe. The two birds squatted down in the shallowest part, and scooped the water over themselves using their wings. They made little flurried movements, sending a procession of ducklings out to a quieter spot in the middle.

Soon all the other animals were in a line by the pond edge, lapping and sucking water greedily. Toad found a quiet place where he indulged in his favourite pastime of bathing.

As the sun began to sink, the pond took on a wonderful reddish glow, like a huge molten ruby. The animals had remained in its vicinity, and they stood transfixed by its beauty.

'How quiet and still everything is,' Hare's mate remarked. 'This place is a sanctuary. Why is there any need for us to go further? We could live here quite happily.'

'Impossible, I'm afraid,' said Squirrel. 'No trees.'

'Hares don't need trees,' she pointed out. 'Neither do most of the other animals.'

'Well, we've come this far. Seems a bit faint-hearted to stop now,' Squirrel persisted.

'He's right, my dear,' Hare said. 'Of course, I see your point. But Toad was saying earlier there isn't much further to go. I think we should carry on.'

The discussion was interrupted by the approach of a heron, a very tall fellow who had been standing motionless in one corner of the pond almost all day.

'I bid you good evening,' he said in a lugubrious voice to the animals, stepping jerkily forward on his stilt-like legs. 'Your friend the owl has been telling me of your exploits. I heard all about the Hunt.'

'We were very fortunate,' said Fox, not wishing to have the subject brought up again.

'You were indeed,' replied the heron. 'A lot of foxes have been killed round here recently. I heard the racket going on earlier.'

'Actually, we're trying to forget the whole incident,' said Badger diplomatically. 'It was a frightening experience for all of us.'

'Oh yes,' said the heron, 'I can imagine. I was shot by those humans once, you know. Look.' He opened out one vast wing which had a neat hole through the middle.

'Gracious! Can you fly?' Kestrel asked.

'In a rather wonky fashion, yes,' the heron chuckled. 'The wind makes a lovely whistling noise through that hole when I flap my wing.' He beat it up and down a few times to demonstrate.

The animals let out little cries of surprise.

'My friends all call me the Whistler,' the tall bird went on. 'They always know when I'm coming.'

'It's a good thing you don't hunt in the way I do, then,' remarked Tawny Owl. 'I'm quite noiseless, of course – have to be.'

'Everyone to his own trade,' said the heron. 'I'm a great fish-eater myself. There are plenty in this pond: carp, tench and perch. I've always preferred carp.'

'Fish would certainly be a welcome change to *our* diet,' said Fox.

'Really?' exclaimed the heron. 'Tell you what, I'll catch you a few tomorrow, if you like.'

'Would you? How very kind,' said Vixen.

'Oh, no trouble, I assure you,' said the heron. 'I enjoy the sport. Perhaps we can take breakfast together?'

'Do please join us,' said Fox. 'But don't wake us too early,' he laughed, 'it's been a very tiring day.'

'You can rely on me,' said the heron. 'I'll say goodnight, then.'

'Goodnight,' said the animals in chorus.

They watched the blue-grey back of the lofty bird as he stepped away towards his own resting-place. Then, as if by common consent, the whole party of Farthing Wood animals, with Vixen, huddled together into an intimate circle and listened as Badger and Fox exchanged stories of their adventures while they had been separated.

Some of the drowsy youngsters amongst the squirrels and mice fell asleep against their parents' sides. One of them forgetfully leant against a hedgehog and was given a rude awakening.

But the adult animals and birds, despite their tiredness, talked far into the night about the hardships they had survived, and of what might lie ahead. Exhausted as Fox and Vixen had been earlier, the talk and good company revived them, and nobody retired until Tawny Owl broke up the party by saying he wanted to stretch his wings, and glided off into the night.

The following morning the animals were awakened by a persistent whistling sound. They had slept in the open, without any need for cover, so far from danger did they feel now. They all stumbled to their feet to find their new friend the heron waving his damaged wing vigorously, and pointing his beak towards a glistening pile of freshly caught fish.

There were many cries of enthusiasm at this sight, but the vegetarian animals, after greeting the heron, went their own way to find some breakfast.

'As I caught them I brought each one up here,' Whistler explained. 'Early morning's the best time for fish, I find. I could see dozens of 'em dashing about. Anyway, there's plenty for everyone, I think. I don't know about you, but I'm starving.'

'You *have* done well,' Fox congratulated him.

'Well, have a look and take what you fancy,' said the heron generously.

Fox chose some plump carp for Vixen and himself, and Whistler, with his long beak open in a grin, his rigid stance making him look as if he were standing to attention, watched as Badger, Weasel and the hedgehogs took their share. Kestrel and Tawny Owl followed, and even Adder ventured to swallow whole some of the very small fish. Mole said politely that he thought such rich fare might upset him, and went to dig for worms with Toad at the pond side.

The heron began hungrily to stab his beak into the pile that remained, and the animals were intrigued to see the way he tilted his head right back and gulped the fish down his capacious throat.

When all the animals had satisfied themselves, they lay back on the ground to allow their digestions to operate comfortably, and congratulated themselves that there was no need to be moving on that day.

'Mole and Toad must be hungry,' Badger remarked with a chuckle. 'They're still eating.'

Mole, who was not far away, heard him. 'I didn't know Toad had such an appetite,' he squeaked in amazement. 'As soon as I dig the worms up, he pounces on them. I've hardly had a look in.'

At that very moment Toad snapped out his long tongue and dexterously flicked up another worm, then used both his front feet to cram the protruding ends into his mouth. He gulped it down, inch by inch, in a series of huge swallows that shook his whole body, and at each swallow both his eyes closed in ecstasy.

'You'd better catch *yourself* some,' laughed Weasel, 'otherwise old Toad will burst himself in a minute.'

Mole's breakfast was eventually assured by a fall of rain. The raindrops caused a change to come over Toad. He abandoned the worms, and took on a distinctly lively air as he felt the moisture on his skin.

'I always feel like singing when it rains,' he declared, and began to jump about every time he felt a fresh raindrop. He broke into song with a rather high-pitched series of croaks, which resembled the cries of the ducks on the pond.

Mole paid him no heed, but ate all the worms he could dig up. For some ridiculous reason, he had felt a little stab of jealousy when the other animals had laughed at Toad's good appetite. He felt that his own reputation for voracity was being obscured and, perhaps because this was his only noteworthy feature, he started at once to reinstate himself as the greatest worm-eater.

It was a vain move because, as the rain grew heavier, most of the animals looked for shelter, and his greediness was unobserved.

Toad's antics, meanwhile, had carried him into the water. As he paddled about, he did not notice the dark shape beneath

him, but suddenly he was seized by a fish, whose great size betrayed its age.

This old denizen of the pond, unable to get a good grip on Toad's slippery body, tried to gulp him down its throat as quickly as possible. This proved difficult, since the huge quantity of worms that Toad had put away had considerably distended his stomach, and he was too plump a morsel to swallow whole.

So Toad, half in and half out of the old fish's jaws, croaked loudly for help. He was not able to call out for long as his captor's next move was to dive promptly for the depths of the pond. As Toad felt the water close over his head, he decided his time was up unless he quickly wriggled free, and he kicked manfully. Not an inch did he gain. He was held fast. Although he could last without air for a few minutes, he knew the old fish would remain on the mud bottom now until he was drowned.

Luckily, though most of Toad's friends had not noticed his disappearance, one creature had seen everything, and this was Whistler. He quickly alerted Fox and Badger and then waded into the pond, peering down into the water, his view partially obscured by the raindrops.

'Can you see anything?' Fox asked anxiously.

The heron did not reply, but Badger gave Fox a meaningful nudge. He knew silence and stillness were of paramount importance now.

After what seemed an age, Whistler suddenly lunged downward with his long break, and when he drew it up again, there was the old fish, a great carp, threshing in its grip, with Toad (a very limp Toad) still held fast in its jaws.

'Bravo, Whistler!' cried Badger, as the heron deposited the fish far up on the bank, where it squirmed and wriggled like an eel. It was not long before it was obliged to open its mouth, and Whistler immediately snatched up Toad and laid him gently at the feet of Fox and Badger.

Eventually Toad recovered his breath and got unsteadily to his feet. 'My dear Whistler,' he panted, 'I . . . I'm indebted to you.'

'Entirely *my* pleasure,' replied the heron.

Toad looked at the dying fish, gasping out its life on the bank. 'I wonder,' he said, 'if you could perhaps do me another favour?'

'You only have to ask,' murmured Whistler.

'Then will you return that poor creature to the pond?' requested Toad. 'He is old, and I should like him to die peacefully when the time comes. For the old, a violent death is all the more terrible.'

'Do you mean it?' asked the heron in amazement.

Toad signified that he did, and without further ado the tall bird gently raised the fish in his beak, and stepped solemnly back into the water to release it.

'You're getting too soft, Toad,' said Adder, who had hitherto been a silent witness of the events. 'That creature would have been your death if it had had its way. To spare such a life is senseless. It merely gives the fish a second chance to try the same thing.'

'I know there's no streak of mercy running through your twists and coils,' said Toad coldly, 'but fortunately some of us have a gentler nature. Having just stared Death in the face myself, and been rescued, how could I ignore the plight of another creature in the same straits?'

'Even when it tried to kill you? Oh, that's *very* sensible,' Adder commented sarcastically.

'Now, Adder!' Badger remonstrated. 'An act of compassion is dictated by the heart, not the head.'

'Pooh!' said Adder. 'Don't talk such airy-fairy nonsense, Badger. When it's a question of survival you, like me, take the only course open to you. If another's death means my life continues, then so be it.'

'The difference being,' Toad remarked, 'that my life was already safe.'

'Don't be too hard on him, Toad,' Badger whispered. 'Remember the Hunt. He saved us all you know.'

'*I* haven't forgotten, believe me,' said Toad quickly. 'Only I think old Adder is trying to. There's nothing he likes less than being regarded as a hero, and he's doing his best to change our minds. His action was a blow struck for all of us, not just himself as he would have us think. It revealed a layer of sympathy in him, and he's trying hard to cover it up again.'

'I'm sure you're right,' acknowledged Badger. 'But at least we know now we can depend on him in a tight corner. I always wondered about it before.'

Adder slithered away in a huff, as Whistler rejoined the animals.

'To be fair to your friend Adder,' he said, 'I must say I agree with his view. Although I admire your request, Toad, it seemed an unusual one to me. In addition, that fat old fish looked a tasty morsel. I've been trying for years to catch him, the wily creature. Now I don't suppose I ever shall again.'

'For that I'm sorry,' said Toad contritely. 'It wasn't the right way to reward you for rescuing me.'

'You know,' said Fox, 'I think the dangers and hardships we've suffered on our journey have changed us. Back home in Farthing Wood, none of us, including Toad, would have allowed that fish to escape. But I suppose fighting for our continued safety every day was bound to bring about a change in our behaviour.'

'Live and let live?' suggested Whistler.

'Exactly.'

'I must say,' said the heron thoughtfully, 'the more I talk to you fellows, the more I begin to wish I were travelling with you. You've got a purpose in life. You struggle on, but there's a reward at the end of it. Of course, I'm quite safe here. But nothing ever happens. I'm inclined to wonder if there mightn't be a charming young female heron living in White Deer Park who would love to meet me.'

The animals laughed.

'You're perfectly welcome to join us,' said Fox. 'We've already acquired one new member of the party' – he looked tenderly towards Vixen – 'and one more would be no strain on our resources.'

'I could be of some use to you, perhaps, too,' Whistler said excitedly. 'Oh, I should love to come.'

'Then it's settled,' said Fox. 'Tonight we'll have a celebration and you can meet everyone personally.'

'What a wonderful idea,' said Whistler. 'By the way . . . um . . . will you be needing any fish?'

# XXV

# THE CELEBRATION

As dusk fell that day the animals began to gather. Close to the pond Fox found a comfortable area of soft grass, screened by reed tussocks. There the animals lay down where they wished and Badger, who was to be Master of Ceremonies, counted his friends as they took their places.

Whistler had been looking forward to the event all day, and had been striding up and down the pond side in an effort to disguise his impatience for things to begin.

Mole, whose unnoticed attempt to eat a record number of worms had caused him to feel quite sick, had found it necessary to drink vast quantities of water during the day, and he now felt as bloated as a balloon. With every hesitant step he could hear the pond-water slurping inside his stomach, and he decided to fast rigidly for the next twenty-four hours.

As for Toad, after his fright in the early morning he had not ventured to swim again, but had contented himself with sitting in the mud in a cool spot, enjoying the rain, and lazily flicking up mayflies and gnats that strayed too close to him.

But the rain had stopped in time for the celebration, and it was now a warm, still evening with a sky whose stars were obscured by scudding clouds.

'Has anybody seen Tawny Owl?' asked Badger. 'And where's Adder? I hope he's not going to be silly and stay away.'

'Tawny Owl's flying over the pond,' piped up one of the little hedgehogs. 'He looks like a great big bat.'

There was a chorus of giggles from the other youngsters, which was checked instantly by Owl's arrival, and a stern look from Badger.

'I would never have believed it!' Tawny Owl exclaimed, with an almost indignant look. 'It's just too ridiculous for words!'

'What is it, Owl?' asked Badger. 'Do find a perch, old fellow, and settle down.' The latter remark was addressed to Whistler, who had hurried up to hear the news.

'I don't perch very much,' he replied. 'I'm more a statuesque sort of bird. I like my feet on terra firma.'

'Just as you like, of course,' Badger said politely, 'but don't walk off again, will you? Now then, Owl . . .?'

'It's Adder,' Tawny Owl explained irritably. 'He's in the pond, swimming up and down and causing as much commotion as a miniature Loch Ness monster.'

'Whatever for?' demanded Badger.

'You may well ask. Adder doesn't take to water too readily. It's my guess he's after that fish.'

'Oh, surely not!' cried Fox. 'Adder's got more sense. He can't *see* anything.'

'But this is serious,' Whistler said slowly. 'If Tawny Owl's right, he's more likely to end up the hunted than the hunter. That old carp could soon bolt down a long, thin morsel like Adder.'

Badger and Fox glanced at each other.

'How can we get him out?' Fox wanted to know.

'Nothing could get him out while he's in that sort of mood,' said Tawny Owl.

'Yes, yes, there *is* a way,' Mole squeaked excitedly. 'Listen, please listen, everybody. I know, I know!'

Fox smiled at him in a patronizing way, and Tawny Owl did not look pleased with Mole's dissenting opinion.

'All right, Mole,' said the kindly Badger, 'let's hear you.'

'All the mice and all the voles must sing – as loud as they can,' Mole announced, 'and I . . . I'll join them, and perhaps Toad could join in, if he feels able.'

'And will that fetch him out?' Badger asked gently.

'Of course not!' Tawny Owl interrupted contemptuously. 'I know what idea Mole's got in his head, but it won't work. Adder wouldn't be able to hear.'

'Well, what *is* the idea?' enquired Fox.

Mole looked round at the mice and voles shyly, and then at Fox. 'It's a little difficult to say now, Fox,' he said awkwardly.

Tawny Owl was not so shy. 'No good beating around the bush,' he said. 'We all know Adder's very fond of mice in his diet. Can't resist them. Their squeaky little noises in the dark act like a magnet to him.'

The voles and mice in one mass began to jump around in alarm, making nervous twittering noises.

'No, no!' they cried. 'We won't! We won't sing!'

Mole looked at Tawny Owl with an expression that plainly said: 'Now look what you've done!'

'It's all right, calm down,' said the owl. 'You don't have to worry. If we all sang at the tops of our voices he wouldn't hear.'

'Then we have to leave him?' asked Fox.

Whistler began to flutter his damaged wing a little, producing a very slight whistle. 'Of course, there is one answer to it,' he said meditatively. 'I could always do a spot of fishing.'

Fox looked for a moment as if he might agree to the suggestion. Then his eyes looked away. 'No, I couldn't allow it,' he said. 'Adder would never forgive us for humiliating him – and in front of everyone, too.' He looked at the heron again. 'But it was a good idea,' he admitted.

'We shall just have to do without him,' said Badger resignedly. 'Will everyone take their places again, please?' He waited patiently while his friends, including the placated members of the mouse family, rearranged themselves comfortably.

'This is a double celebration tonight,' Badger began. 'We're celebrating the safe return of our dear friend here – Fox; and we're also celebrating the fact that we have made two new friends – our very charming Vixen and, more recently, the amusing Whistler.'

Here the droll heron bowed with a flourish, causing his damaged wing to make a long, solemn note, at which the small animals giggled loudly.

Badger went on: 'This will probably be our last opportunity for a proper break before we reach White Deer Park, so we must make sure we all enjoy ourselves tonight.'

He looked at Fox, who appeared eager to say something, and nodded.

'Thank you, Badger,' said his friend. 'I just wanted to say, everyone, before we show our neighbours the fish and the ducks how to sing, how lucky I consider myself to have such good friends. After wondering for quite a time if I should ever see you all again, now that we're so happily reunited, I value your company more than ever.'

There were cheers at this juncture, and many of the animals called, 'Good old Fox!'

Fox continued, 'We've been through such a lot together already that there's no doubt in my mind we shall eventually win through. After all, if we can survive the Hunt, I am sure we shall prove the match of whatever dangers lie in our path ahead.'

The animals shouted excitedly at Fox's fighting talk. Some of them felt they were as good as in White Deer Park already.

'Just one last thing,' said Fox, 'and then, I promise you, we'll sing all night if you want to. When I was on my own, I met an old horse, an ex-hunter, and he gave me some good advice. He told me that this open country hereabouts, and the neighbouring enclosed fields, is all part of a hunting area, and that I should get out of it as soon as I could.

'And so, my friends, that is what we shall do. Now we're all together again, and thoroughly rested, we should be ready to push on tomorrow night, at our swiftest pace, and to stop only when it's vital. We shall continue in this way every night, sheltering by day, until we've put this dangerous stretch of country behind us for good. It'll be hard going – there's no point in denying it – but I promise you this: if we all make the utmost effort, and help each other, we'll see it through, I'm sure of it. And then what stories we'll have to tell the creatures of White

Deer Park!'

Fox smiled as he saw the resolute expressions on the faces of his friends. From the smallest to the largest, they all looked as if they had decided that, having come so far, nothing could stop them now.

'Well, Badger,' he finished, 'I'll leave it to you now to put us in a more light-hearted frame of mind.'

'Thank you, my dear friend,' Badger returned. 'Well now, who's going to start the singing?'

'I am,' said a low, drawling voice from behind. And there was Adder, his tongue flickering busily as he slid through the grass, his scales gleaming with wetness. 'I feel in a musical sort of mood,' he hissed, making no mention of his recent aquatic activities. 'Tiddle-tum, tiddle-tum, let me see, how does the tune go? Ah yes . . .' And in a rather monotonous, unmelodic lisp he sang a song about the first snake who had ever lived in the world, and who had had six legs, each one of which had broken off when it had told a lie, until in the end it had been obliged to slither around on its stomach.

The animals all applauded politely, but Adder was no singer, and Tawny Owl was heard to remark, 'Same old thing; he doesn't know any others.'

'Well, I'm sure we all enjoyed that,' said Badger. 'Who would like to follow?'

'I'll sing you one,' said Kestrel, flying up to a prominent branch, where everyone could see him. 'This, of course, is a song about birds,' he announced, 'and in it I shall imitate a lot of birds' cries, so I want you all to listen very carefully and see how many you can recognize.'

He began to sing, but there were so many different bird calls in the song that there seemed to be more of those than the words, and they all came so quickly one after another that the animals found it confusing and forgot half of the ones they had already identified. However, they all laughed very much when Kestrel gave a beautiful impression of Tawny Owl's flute-like hoots, so that the rather pompous Owl thought they were laughing at him, and looked offended.

But he soon cheered up when Kestrel finished his recitation with a few whistles that sounded exactly like their new friend the heron.

'How many did you know?' Kestrel asked afterwards, and it was discovered that Vixen had the best ear for bird calls. She had remembered nearly all of them, and Fox was proud of her.

'That was marvellous, Kestrel,' Badger complimented the hawk. 'But now, let's have one with a chorus where we can all join in. Anyone got any suggestions?'

'I know one,' said Toad. 'It's the one we toads sing every spring when we gather in the ponds. The frogs have a slightly different version. It's called "The Song of the Tadpole".'

However, nobody seemed to be acquainted with the words apart from Toad, although Fox said he had heard the toads and frogs croaking away at it in Farthing Pond many times.

'There must be something we all know,' said Badger.

'What about that song the rooks taught us?' Mole suggested timidly. 'You know, the "Freedom Song".'

'Of course!' cried Badger. 'The very thing. Well done, Mole, old chap!' He beamed at the delighted Mole, and asked everyone to sing up.

'We all know this one,' he said. 'Ready! One . . . two . . . three . . .' And in a dozen different pitches that nevertheless blended beautifully, from the squeaks of the mice to Fox's bark and Tawny Owl's hoot, the animals happily chanted the verses the rooks had taught them underneath the elms of the copse.

From then onwards the feeling of comradeship glowed in every member of the party. Animal after animal volunteered to give a song. Some were solo songs, some had choruses, and the night air vibrated with their lively voices.

Even Whistler, who confessed he did not know any songs, agreed to give a recitation, which he accompanied with many varied musical sounds from his famous wing.

At length the water-fowl, unable to sleep, gathered from their damp nests and resting-places and swelled the number at the celebration, quacking or chirping good-humouredly with the others.

It was left to Badger to give the final performance of the evening. Before announcing his choice of song, he smiled in a paternal way at the company of happy birds and beasts before him, the younger ones amongst them already lulled to sleep; and the companionship and mutual trust that was visible on the faces of the motley collection of creatures moved him so much that he had to blink hard several times before he spoke.

'Well, friends,' he said finally, 'we've had a wonderful time, and now at last it's my turn to entertain you. I knocked a little song together this morning, while we were eating, and now is the moment to give it an airing.'

He cleared his throat very deliberately, and in a voice that was rather gruff and off-key, sang to them a song which was about their own travels. Not one incident was left out: the fire, the storm, the farmer's dog, the river, the chase – everything was included. And, very cleverly, Badger managed to give at least a couple of lines to everyone in the party, bringing in Vixen and Whistler at the end.

The song proved to be so popular that everyone wanted Badger to sing it all over again. But he declined, saying it was getting late.

'I'll tell you what, though,' he promised, 'as we continue our travels, I'll add a few more verses as we go along, and when we finally reach our destination I'll sing the whole thing to you.'

The other animals all declared that it was a bargain, and Mole remarked that it made him all the more eager to get to White Deer Park. So, in the best of spirits, the celebration broke up, and everyone retired, full of confidence for the next stage of their journey.

## XXVI

# THE MOTORWAY

The animals left the security of the quarry late the following evening. Fox once again took his place in the vanguard of their formation, carrying Toad. On one side of him he had Vixen, and on the other Hare with his mate and offspring.

Badger, carrying Mole, and Weasel guarded the rear, and Adder slithered along with them.

In the middle mass the rabbits and hedgehogs were at the front, voles, fieldmice and squirrels behind.

In the air there were now three members of the party, Tawny Owl, flying in advance of the daybirds, Kestrel and Whistler. The animals found that the regular, musical wing-beat of the heron above them was a reassuring sound of the party's compactness. But Tawny Owl secretly disliked this noise, past master as he was himself of stealth and silence.

When dawn first suggested itself it was the animals' task to find a safe resting-place as soon as they were able. Here they hid up and slept during the day. At dusk they would forage and drink, then, when it was quite dark, continue their journey.

They proceeded in this fashion throughout the month of June, and the beginning of July found them only one day's travelling short of the end of the downland where, Toad told them, they would have to cross a very wide, new road that was still under construction. Once across this obstacle, their troubles would be very nearly over, for the only remaining hazard they would have to encounter was a town, and this they must pass through in order to reach the Park.

During these weeks they had not seen or heard any further evidence of the fact that they were in hunting country. Their narrow escape from the Hunt, and the terror they had all experienced had, with time, become little more than a bad dream.

However, while in the resting-place Fox had chosen for their last daylight hours on the downland, the animals' memories were very suddenly and unpleasantly jolted.

It occurred during the afternoon while they were sleeping. Only Kestrel was awake. He never seemed to find it necessary to take more than a few hours' rest. He had left his friends snoozing peacefully in the midst of a thick stand of thorn bushes, and was enjoying his solitude, alternately soaring and floating in the cloudless July sky.

His superb eyesight picked out various objects moving across the green expanse far below him. There were little groups of people picnicking, couples strolling with dogs, other birds forever flying from tree to tree and point to point, and motor traffic, in a moving rainbow of colours, flashing like beacons as the glass and chrome reflected the sun.

Kestrel looked out for the new road that Toad had mentioned. He knew in what direction it lay, but it was screened from his view by a high bank and a long, straight swathe of trees. Had he seen it, he would have been obliged to report that it was not at all the sort of thing they were expecting. As it was, a blur of scarlet in the far distance in another direction was an abrupt reminder of a danger they had almost forgotten.

Kestrel hovered, trying to assess the distance of the threat. There was no doubt that it was moving slowly towards him; he could see the ripple of movement running through the tightly-packed mass of hounds, and the pattern was repeated by the horses carrying their scarlet-coated burdens. He decided they were at present far enough off for him to remain calm, but not far enough away to be ignored altogether. He flew back to the camp to wake Fox and put the matter to him.

Fox thought they should move at once to be sure they kept ahead of the hunters, but he woke Vixen for her advice.

'Yes, we *should* leave here at once,' she said emphatically. 'We can't afford to wait and hope they won't come this way. If we did, we might find we'd left it too late to get away.'

Fox nodded. 'My thoughts exactly,' he said. 'But there's no cause to alarm the others, is there?'

'I think they'd be less likely to worry if you tell them *why* we're moving on,' Vixen said.

'I expect you're right,' admitted Fox. 'You always are,' he added admiringly.

Vixen smiled and helped Fox and Kestrel to rouse the sleepers.

Some of the animals grumbled at first at their slumbers being interrupted, but Fox soon acquainted them with the seriousness of the situation.

'Now there's no need for any panic or alarm,' he pointed out coolly. 'As long as we keep to a good steady pace, there will be no danger. And when we've got safely across the new road, we'll have put the Hunt, and everything connected with it, behind us for good.'

'How long till we reach the road?' asked Hedgehog.

'I couldn't say exactly,' Fox answered, 'but it's just beyond that line of trees. Now, are we all ready? Come on, Toad, up you get.'

He looked all round to make sure everyone was with him. 'Mole, are you all set? Good, I think that's it, then. I can't see Adder. I suppose he's here?'

'I'm right behind you,' said the snake. 'If you remember, you woke me before anyone else, and I've been waiting ever since.'

'Yes, I'm sorry,' said Fox good-naturedly. 'All together then?'

With a tuneful whistle, Kestrel was accompanied into the air by Whistler, but Tawny Owl continued to hold himself aloof, keeping a few feet behind them now that it was daylight.

Keeping their target of the line of trees constantly in sight, the animals made good progress across the last stretch of downland. No sound of hounds or horns reached their ears, and, apart from a few cautious pauses and detours to avoid other humans who were out enjoying themselves, they had little to worry about.

However, as the outline of trees gradually assumed a more definite shape while they approached, another kind of sound became increasingly noticeable. It was the sound of motor traffic.

As the nearest road in that vicinity was the one Toad had seen being built, Fox became more and more apprehensive. Eventually he called Kestrel down, and asked him to go on ahead and investigate.

The animals watched the hawk diminish into a black speck in the sky, and finally disappear beyond the trees. In a few minutes he was back.

Whistler and Tawny Owl escorted him to the ground, and the animals stopped for his report.

'We might have guessed it,' was Kestrel's preliminary remark. 'Toad's new road has been finished, and it looks as if it's been so for some time. There are six lanes of traffic on it, with an island in the middle, and high banks on either side.'

Some of the animals looked accusingly at the dismayed Toad, as if he were responsible.

'Oh, heavens!' he croaked. 'I . . . I'm sorry, everyone.'

'Nothing to apologize for,' said Fox. 'It's a good while since you passed this way. Humans build quickly, as we all know to our cost.'

'What's to be done?' asked Squirrel nervously.

Adder chuckled without humour. 'We shall have to cross it, of course,' he drawled.

'But it's impossible! We'll all be killed!' wailed Rabbit.

'We wouldn't have much trouble getting across one half,' Kestrel told them. 'There's a big traffic jam on the side nearest us: a mass of cars and huge lorries stuck fast, nose to tail.'

Fox looked at him quickly. 'And they are not moving at all?' he asked sharply.

'Only at long intervals, it seemed,' answered Kestrel.

'But by the time we get there, who knows?'

'Surely it's safer to wait until night-time to cross?' suggested Weasel. 'The road might be almost clear by then.'

'There wouldn't be so *much* traffic,' Fox agreed. 'But this is obviously a motorway, and motorways are never entirely clear.'

'Even so, we'd have more chance then,' Weasel insisted.

'I'm not so sure about that,' Fox returned. 'If we reach the road while this hold-up continues, we have a very good chance of at least reaching the centre island safely.'

'Yes, and there we'd stay,' Weasel said a little irritably, 'while hundreds of human eyes looked on. No, I don't like that idea at all.'

Fox lifted up a back leg and scratched himself thoughtfully. 'We're in danger of forgetting one thing,' he said evenly, 'the thing that decided us in the first place to travel at this time of day instead of during the dark hours.'

'Well, we've heard nothing so far,' Weasel pointed out.

'Quite right,' agreed Fox. 'However, we must ascertain our position.'

Kestrel needed no bidding. 'If you'll just be patient for a

minute . . .' he said, and flew upward again to discover the whereabouts of the hunters.

What he saw was disconcerting. 'They're much closer,' he told Fox. 'I think the hounds might be on your trail again.'

'Right. That answers your question, Weasel,' said Fox decisively. 'Press on, everyone. There's no time to lose now. There's not much further to go, and they can't follow us beyond those trees. I think you'll agree a lot of stationary cars is rather less dangerous than a maddened pack of hounds?'

'Caught between two fires,' muttered Adder.

The animals kept moving as quickly as they could, and the traffic noise was soon really loud and very frightening to them. Fox tried to keep everyone calm, but the fact was that none of them was at all used to being so close to heavy traffic, and the nearer they approached to the line of trees, the more nervous they all became.

'This is ghastly,' said Rabbit. 'I don't see why we can't wait for the road to clear. Even if the Hunt should come this way, they're not likely to be concerned about us small fry. Fox and Vixen can go now if they want to.'

This last remark he made in a much lower voice, which showed that he did not have the courage of his convictions, and that it was intended to be unheard. But Hare swung round on him. 'You're an utter disgrace,' he said witheringly. 'Surely by now even your small mind has grasped the fact that Fox decides on the best course for all of us. There's to be no splitting up.

And I might add that *you* wouldn't get far on your own without others to think for you.'

As usual Badger was the peacemaker. 'Please, please, Hare, you know quarrelling is never any help,' he said beseechingly. 'And, Rabbit, you should try to be more unselfish. Fox is in a very difficult position.'

'I know,' admitted Rabbit. 'I'm sorry, Badger. I'm just feeling scared, I suppose.' Only to Badger would the animals admit their faults.

His old striped face lit up with a smile and he said, 'Of course you are, Rabbit. Nothing to be ashamed of. But we've been scared before, haven't we? Nothing new to us, h'm?' And he gave him a reassuring poke with his muzzle.

It was not long after this conversation ended that the animals heard for the first time proof that the Hunt was again on their tail, and closing the gap. The fear they had experienced on their previous encounter with the furious dogs and riders, when they had so narrowly escaped, returned to them in a moment, and Fox and Vixen unconsciously began to run faster.

Although the sounds of the baying and the shrill blasts of the horn were faint in the distance, all the animals knew only too well how swiftly this faintness became louder, and, taking no risks, every one of them began to streak across the remaining few hundred yards towards the trees.

Fox, Vixen and the hares were first to arrive, and they waited in the shade, in trepidation, as they watched their friends drawing nearer.

One by one they came up breathless, and Fox counted them all in. With all the little mice and voles safely arrived, only Adder was to come.

The animals strained their eyes to see him slithering through the grass, but no one could spot him.

Kestrel went off to discover his progress, and the rest of the party momentarily turned their attention to what lay before them. As they stood together under the shade of the trees they could see just a few yards more of grass in front of them, running up into a high bank that obscured the motorway at that point. Whistler volunteered to fly over the bank to report on the latest state of the traffic.

As he left, the animals looked back towards the downland they had just travelled through. There was no sign of Adder, but they could now see the first hounds breasting a slight rise, not half a mile away. They exchanged glances of alarm, but none of them spoke.

Mole broke the silence. 'Do you think they're coming for Adder?' he asked timidly. 'You know – in revenge?'

'Oh no, not at all,' said Fox. 'But we can't wait for him. He'll have to manage by himself,' and he involuntarily shivered as he continued to watch the hounds' approach. With a visible shake of his head, he tried to pull himself together.

'Come on, everyone!' he said peremptorily. 'Up to the top of the bank.' And he nudged Vixen forward.

Together, the animals ran across the last open space and up the grassy bank overlooking the motorway. The bank was topped by an open wooden fence, which was no obstacle to them. They merely passed underneath the lower rail, and once on the other side they felt considerably safer from the sound of the Hunt.

However, there were now no more barriers between them and the motorway itself, and the crossing had to be faced.

The bank sloped straight down in front of them to the margin of the road, and a few feet beyond that was the nearest lane of traffic: cars and lorries of all shapes and sizes stretching as far as the eye could see in either direction, and all unmoving. Two similar rows of such seemingly peaceful monsters were lined up parallel to this, their gleaming metalwork baking in the heat, and from the end of each monster there issued a constant feathery column of smoke, that hovered for a little in the air and then seemed to vanish.

Separating these ranks of motionless vehicles from those that were roaring by in the opposite direction, was a thin strip of paper-strewn grass and weeds bounded on both sides by low crash barriers.

In one spot of this narrowest of islands, comfortably standing between the crash barriers, was the imperturbable Whistler. His back was turned to his friends on the bank, and he appeared to be completely engrossed in watching the fast traffic on the far side, for his head was turning rapidly from left to right as each vehicle flashed past.

'He looks as if he's been mesmerized,' whispered Weasel.

The animals had taken in the scene before them at a glance, and at the sight of all the humans ranged in lines in their stationary cars so close to them, they instinctively dropped to their bellies, while the nose of every creature, big or small, wrinkled in disgust at the tainted air.

Fox knew they would have to make a move very soon. Save for Vixen, he more than anyone felt they could not risk remaining still, with the threat approaching them from the rear. Although he believed that the possibility of the hounds being allowed to go further than the line of trees was remote, that was enough for him.

Kestrel found them on the top of the bank, watching Whistler.

'I couldn't see him,' he said, referring to the missing Adder. 'I think he's done this deliberately, in case he might be needed again to halt the advance of the Hunt.'

'Hmph!' Tawny Owl grunted. 'That last exploit must have gone to his head then.'

'I don't think so,' Fox said soberly. 'Adder's not like *that*, whatever else you might say about him.'

Above the roar and whine of speeding cars and lorries, and the low hum of idling engines, the animals caught again the hubbub of barking on the air.

Fox got up and looked behind him, then quickly dived

down again.

'We'll have to move,' he said bluntly. 'It shouldn't be difficult. There's plenty of space under the backs of the cars. We can run in and out of those lines of cars and join Whistler before we've even been spotted.'

'But, Fox, supposing they start moving when we're half-way across?' demanded Fieldmouse. 'Even just a few inches' movement could squash most of us, particularly the tiny ones.'

Fox looked again along the lines of traffic in both directions before he answered.

'There doesn't seem to be any likelihood of that,' he said, 'but the sooner we go the better.'

'Perhaps there's a footbridge over the road somewhere?' suggested Rabbit.

'Yes, and perhaps it will have tiny little steps up to it made especially for the convenience of mice,' said Fieldmouse sarcastically.

'I hadn't thought about that,' said Rabbit with embarrassment.

Fox turned to Kestrel, who had perched on top of the fence running along the ridge of the bank.

'Kestrel, will you stay and keep an eye open for Adder?' he asked.

'Of course I will. Both eyes,' he said merrily. The present difficulty facing the animals, as indeed with most of those they had already surmounted, did not affect him or Tawny Owl in the least.

'Well, my friends,' Fox said, turning to the rest, 'will you come with me, then?'

He looked round with just a trace of shyness on his face. He knew that most of the animals felt they were safe where they were for the time being, but the thought of the Hunt was, naturally, never out of his own mind.

Without a word Badger got to his feet and, with a look, bade Mole take his place on his back. Hare rose too, and hustled his family together.

Vixen, who had caught the almost pleading expression on her hero's face, nuzzled his side sympathetically and lovingly licked his fur.

One by one the other animals stood up. The rabbits were the last to do so. Tawny Owl flew off first to tell Whistler the heron to stay put.

Then Vixen ran quickly down the slope, shepherding the mice and voles in front of her, and in a trice they were lost to sight as they threaded their way through the traffic, under bumpers and between wheels, until they emerged on the island.

Fox let out his breath in a sigh of relief. Gathering the squirrels together, he made haste to follow in the steps of Vixen. Hare and his family went close behind him.

Weasel joined the hedgehogs, and eventually the rabbits, who were at last persuaded that the crossing was not as hazardous as they had believed, condescended to move.

Badger and Mole brought up the rear, so that in the space of a few minutes the whole party had safely crossed half the motorway, and was gathered in the precarious haven of the island between the two crash barriers.

Only Kestrel remained on his look-out post on the fence, searching in vain for a sign of the missing Adder.

As Fox and the rest of the party sat amongst the litter and weeds pondering their next move, they could see human faces looking at them in astonishment from the imprisoning cars and the cabs of lorries. Excited children gesticulated to their parents, their mouths *oohing* and *aahing* in silence behind the glass. The line of traffic nearest to the island held humans who were a matter of inches only from the animals, and before long tentative arms groped towards them from open windows. Fortunately for the animals they remained just out of reach, and as the vehicle occupants were all aware of the law prohibiting walking on the motorway, they were safe from any interference.

However, they did not greatly enjoy the closeness of the humans, and they all looked despondently from the roaring traffic on the other side of the road to their audience in the stationary rows, feeling very exposed.

But unknown to the animals, a mile away, where the jam started, traffic was starting to move forward at last. Like an imperceptible wave rippling to the shore, the movement was passed back down the long queue until finally it reached the spot where the animals had crossed. So the vehicles inched forward, taking away the amazed passengers. The animals were soon forgotten as their various journeys and errands reassumed their prime importance in the humans' minds.

'They're going! They're going!' cried Mole.

'How right you were, Fox, to cross at once,' commented Weasel.

'I'm very thankful it has proved so,' Fox acknowledged.

'Not such good news for Adder, though,' remarked Toad seriously. 'He's more or less stranded now.'

'Hallo! Here comes Kestrel,' announced Badger. 'I wonder if he's seen him.'

Kestrel alighted suddenly on one of the crash barriers. 'The Hunt has turned back,' he said with an air of drama. 'The hounds were called off when they reached the line of trees. Now they're all going back the way they came.'

'Thank heavens that's the last we shall ever see of *them*,' said Hare grimly.

'I'm afraid Adder hasn't shown up,' said Kestrel, 'though once the Hunt has disappeared there's nothing to keep him in hiding.'

'Will you continue to watch for him?' asked Fox. 'Otherwise, if he can't see any of us, he won't know which way to come.'

'I'll go and have another search for him,' Kestrel replied promptly, 'but what about you? You can't get across there.' He motioned with his head to the speeding traffic that had not diminished in volume one jot.

'Not at the moment, no,' admitted Fox. 'But surely it can't go on like this indefinitely. There must come a lull sooner or later.'

'And then you'll risk crossing?' Kestrel asked in surprise.

'What else can we do?' demanded Fox. 'This strip of debris isn't exactly my idea of a sanctuary. We'll have to do it in bursts, when there's a long enough gap between bunches of traffic.'

Kestrel shook his head. 'I honestly wonder if any of you except Hare are fast enough runners. Don't forget you've got three times the width of a normal road to cross, and vehicles that initially appear far distant come up in a matter of seconds. Their speed is unimaginable to us wild creatures.'

Fox's brow creased with concern. 'We have no option,' he said gravely.

'I think I may be of some use here,' Whistler said. 'Should it prove necessary, I could do a sort of portering job with the smaller animals – you know, ferry them across in my long beak.'

'What a wonderful idea!' Fox exclaimed. 'But we can't start until this dreadful traffic clears a bit. There don't seem to be any gaps at all.'

The animals sat and watched in dismay the unceasing stream of fast traffic. Where they sat, the stuffy air was thick and heavy with petrol fumes. Some of the young rabbits and Hare's leverets began to feel sick.

Kestrel flew away to take up his perch on the top of the bank.

'Why is there any need for *me* to wait?' queried Whistler,

beginning to flap his damaged wing slightly, as if in preparation for flight. 'I can relieve these youngsters' discomfort straight away.'

'Where will you take them?' Fox asked.

'I'll unload them on the top of the opposite bank,' replied the heron. 'They'll be quite safe there, and the air will be a little fresher.'

'All right,' said Fox. 'Rabbit, Hare, get the little ones ready.'

'It'll have to be one at a time,' Whistler explained, and he advanced upon the first rabbit, beak at the ready. Then, with extreme gentleness, he picked up the furry little body, using the blunt middle part of his beak and, holding it with just sufficient firmness, flew off to the safety of the far bank.

One by one, in trip after trip, he carried the young animals to safety. Tawny Owl stood guard on the other side.

'I might as well do the job properly,' the heron observed to Fox, and began to ferry the voles and fieldmice across. Gradually the number of animals on the island dwindled in the face of Whistler's continuing return trips, until finally Fox and Vixen, Badger, Mole, Toad, Weasel, Hare and his mate, and the adult rabbits, squirrels and hedgehogs remained – about half the party in numbers.

Fox looked round approvingly. 'We're progressing,' he said.

'I haven't finished yet,' said Whistler. 'Come on, Toad – you're next.'

Mole followed Toad, and the slender, light Weasel

followed Mole. The squirrels, Whistler declared, were just about manageable, but once he had transferred all of *them*, he confessed himself beaten.

The party was now split into three groups across the breadth of the motorway. On the downland side were Kestrel and, somewhere, Adder; halfway across, the hedgehogs, adult rabbits and hares, and Fox, Vixen and Badger were waiting; and in complete safety on the far side all the youngest, smallest and lightest animals were gathered under the joint guardianship of Tawny Owl and Whistler.

This situation continued for a little longer, without any chance of alteration. Then, as was inevitable, the fast traffic began to thin out, and small gaps began to appear.

'Hare, you'd better be ready,' Fox warned him. 'There's a longish gap approaching.'

Hare and his mate accordingly slipped underneath the outer crash barrier, and prepared for a lightning dash. As soon as the last car was level with them they hurled themselves across the three lanes of road and, without slowing down at all, raced up the bankside to join the others. They reached the top of the bank before the next cluster of traffic went past.

'Fox, you and Vixen must be next,' said Badger. 'You're faster than me. I may have to wait a little while yet.'

Fox did not dispute this. He felt he should remain behind until he had seen all the party get safely across, but he was also concerned about Vixen's safety, and so held his tongue.

The two foxes positioned themselves on the outer edge of the island and, at the next gap in the traffic, streaked across. They were not as swift as the hares, and they had barely reached the other side before the next traffic came up.

'I don't think we've got much chance,' Hedgehog said gloomily to Badger.

These two, the other hedgehogs and the rabbits were now the only occupants of the island.

'We'll certainly have to be a little less adventurous than those four,' Badger said.

Another quarter of an hour went past. It seemed as if they might be stranded.

Whistler flew over with a message from Fox. 'He says, even

if we all have to wait for the rest of the day, you're not to budge until you're sure you can risk it.'

'Thank him,' said Badger. 'You can put his mind at rest on that point.'

Eventually Badger saw a really promising space open up behind a group of cars that were fast approaching, and he got all the hedgehogs and rabbits lined up outside the barrier, alongside himself.

'Go!' he shouted gruffly as the last car flashed past, and all of them began to run desperately for the bank, himself included.

Two of the older hedgehogs fell behind as the main bunch began to cross the second lane, and seeing the other animals increasing their lead, they began to lose heart. With such a small margin between danger and safety, a second's hesitation was fatal. Badger and the rabbits and the faster hedgehogs reached the bank and turned round to see if they were all across. The two slower animals were just crossing the third lane, but the whole party could see they were not going to make it.

As the first cars roared up, the two hedgehogs instinctively adopted their habitual posture of defence, and rolled themselves into balls; the very worst thing they could have done. It was all over in a trice. The rest of the party gasped in horror, and amongst them a deadly silence fell.

Another dangerous obstacle had been passed. The animals were one step nearer White Deer Park, but two more lives had been lost.

# XXVII

# SOME COMFORTING WORDS

Sadly, silently, Fox led the party down the other side of the bank and into the first field, a cornfield, that lay before them. Here the motorway was not only out of sight, but its awful roar and din had become just a murmur in their ears. Whistler alone remained on the bank top to watch out for the return of Kestrel.

The animals lay down together in the midst of the tall green corn, listlessly watching a group of tiny harvest mice climbing from stalk to stalk, using their little feet to balance on the stems as they ate. The thought of death lingered in their minds, and the hedgehogs were all wearing solemn, even severe, expressions. Only Toad, of all the animals, was feeling in good spirits, though he tried not to show it because of the others' demeanour. He was feeling excited because, now they had crossed the motorway, he knew they were really not far from their destination.

Whistler, standing like a sentinel on the ridge, kept his eyes fixed on the bank opposite, ignoring the traffic still streaming below. Kestrel suddenly swooped up from the direction of the downland and alighted on his piece of fence as before. He looked across the road and, seeing only Whistler, flew over to him.

'Yes, they're all over there in the cornfield,' Whistler replied to the hawk's first enquiry.

'No mishaps?' Kestrel asked.

Whistler told him of the hedgehogs.

'I suppose we should count ourselves lucky to have lost so few,' Kestrel said philosophically.

'And Adder?' prompted the heron.

'Oh yes. *He's* all right,' replied Kestrel. 'He should reach the top of the bank over there any minute. You might just manage to catch sight of him from here. He'd been hiding in a ditch – said he didn't want to be trampled. Of course he emerged once the Hunt had gone back.'

'Well, let's fly over and meet him,' said Whistler.

The two birds took to the air. When they reached the opposite bank, they could see Adder's sinewy body winding itself through the grass of the slope.

'I trust I shall not be expected to apologize for lateness,' he remarked drily as he arrived on the ridge. 'Four legs are faster than none.'

'Fox is waiting for us with the others in a cornfield on the other side of the road,' said Kestrel. 'If you're ready, we ought to join him at once.'

'My readiness doesn't have much bearing on the situation, I'm afraid,' Adder drawled. 'I fail to see how I am to venture on to a road such as that without immediately becoming transformed into an integral part of the tarmac.'

Whistler winked at Kestrel. 'You lead off,' he said. 'They're in the first field. You'll soon spot them from the air.'

Kestrel at once flew up high, the better to pick out his friends from the green mass of the corn, and Whistler, before Adder had comprehended what was to happen, opened his long beak and snatched up the startled snake from the bank.

The animals in the field had the double surprise of seeing Kestrel suddenly plummeting towards them from the empty sky, followed shortly afterwards by a whistling sound which announced the arrival of the heron, carrying an indignant Adder dangling from his beak like an enormous earthworm.

The amusement they derived from the scene served to divert their minds, at least temporarily, from the recent tragedy. They began to chatter again, while Toad chuckled in his croaky way quite openly.

With the return of Adder, the threat posed by the Hunt was at last over – for good.

The cornfield became the animals' resting-place for the following night.

The foxes were the last to settle down. Although Vixen was quite ready to fall asleep, Fox was very restless and seemed unable to get comfortable. Vixen watched his vain attempts, and knew there was something bothering him.

She moved closer. 'What's on your mind?' she asked quietly.

Fox turned his head to look at her as she lay down among the stalks of corn. 'Oh,' he said. 'I can't seem to relax. My head's going round and round, and I can't clear my mind of things.'

'You're worried about something, I can see,' said Vixen in a sympathetic tone. 'Can I help?'

Fox smiled. 'I don't want you worried as well,' he said.

'If I am to be your mate,' said Vixen with a touch of shyness, 'I must share everything with you.'

'That's very comforting to me,' Fox said. 'You are the dearest creature.' He licked her face affectionately.

'I can't stop thinking about those hedgehogs,' he explained.

'Oh, I suppose it was no one's fault. If anything, their age was to blame, poor animals. But whenever there's a mishap, you see, I feel responsible.'

'I know you do,' said Vixen, 'and it's understandable. But you can't control everything that happens. It's not in your power to prevent such occurrences. Fox, you must put all this out of your mind. Nobody is blaming *you*.'

'Of course, I realize that,' Fox conceded. 'They're all such good-natured beasts. Even Hedgehog himself has avoided the subject ever since . . . but . . . but well, it's just that I can't stop wondering now if it *would* have been safer if we had waited until dark to cross.'

'So that's it!' said Vixen. 'I thought as much. You're feeling guilty because your decision to cross was influenced by the Hunt.'

'Yes,' said Fox. 'You already know me pretty well, Vixen.'

'Oh, how can I convince you that you did the right thing?' Vixen cried. 'You think that the Hunt was only interested in you . . . and me?'

'They were,' said Fox in a low voice. 'The others might have been safer staying on the bank until dark. I can't rid myself of the nagging doubt that two lives might have been sacrificed . . . to me,' he finished in a barely audible voice.

'What nonsense!' Vixen exclaimed. 'Don't humans hunt hares . . . and badgers? And do you think those hounds, if they had caught us up, as they would have done on the bank, would have singled *us* out and spared all the others? The whole party was in danger, and you did the only possible thing. You removed the danger from all of us.'

Fox was silent for a long time. Finally he said, almost timidly, 'Do you really think so, *dear* Vixen?'

'I've never been more sure of anything,' she answered confidently. 'And the others would agree with me.'

'I'm so glad you feel like that,' Fox said. 'Perhaps I was right after all.'

'Dear old Fox,' said Vixen, nestling up very close, 'don't you know you're already a hero to most of the animals? Just remember what you've led them through. You could never lose their respect now. And in only a short while, all this heartache will be over.'

'Yes,' said Fox. 'I really do believe we're going to get there. How I long for that day!'

'So do I,' murmured Vixen. 'I long for the peace and rest it will bring us all, and the feeling of uninterrupted safety.' Her voice became a whisper. 'But most of all I long for the day when I can have you all to myself, to be just *my* hero, instead of everyone else's.'

'Am I not your hero already then?' asked Fox playfully.

'Why else do I follow you everywhere?' Vixen smiled and, laying her head against his, closed her eyes with a blissful sigh.

# XXVIII

# THE DEATHLY HUSH

The sound of humans close by woke the animals early the following morning, and they at once prepared to move on. Once again they found themselves surrounded by farmland – only this farmland was different from any they had seen before. There were no hedgerows dividing the fields, no thatched farm cottages and no ancient lopsided barns. Everything was conducted in this area in a far more calculated, professional manner. Vast expanses of cereals and root crops grew mathematically in unbordered squares, without a wild flower or grass showing its head, even in corners. All unnecessary plants had been totally cleared away, and the fields had a cold, clinical look about them which seemed unnatural. The few trees that still existed were giants which had proved, in this cost-obsessed world, too expensive to move, and so they remained.

The farmhouses were modern, brick-built and efficient buildings without so much as a leaf of ivy growing on their walls, and the lanes and paths were cemented or gravelled.

Animals – farm animals, that is – could be heard cackling or grunting to each other, but they were never seen. It seemed they had all been shut away in the long, low concrete and steel outbuildings that were prevalent. In the over-heated interiors they were probably quite unaware of the existence of lush green grass spread with buttercups, or blue sky, or the fresh feeling of a shower of rain.

Because of the lack of cover the local wild creatures appeared to have deserted the area completely, and only domesticated sparrows, blackbirds or pigeons were in evidence. The wild creatures from Farthing Wood found great difficulty

in making any progress, for they felt too exposed in these wide open spaces. In addition there seemed to be an army of farm workers about, driving the very latest and biggest monsters of machinery, and manipulating the very newest gadgets and tools.

The animals all wanted to escape from this world, where they were clearly intruders, as quickly as they could. It was a manufactured world, devoted to human needs and requirements where anything animal or vegetable from the natural world was not only unwelcome, but considered a pest or weed, and treated as such.

So the animals felt it necessary to remain hidden as much as possible during the daytime, and to continue towards their destination in the dark hours when the presence of humans was not such a risk. But, as the days passed, and nothing happened to alarm them seriously, they grew bolder.

Kestrel returned from his morning reconnaissance flight one day to where his friends were sleeping under a discarded tarpaulin. The weather was warm, dull, but very still. Not a breath of wind was blowing.

As usual Kestrel went straight to Fox and gently woke him. 'There's not a soul about,' he whispered. 'Everything's as quiet as Badger's old set out there. If we leave now, we could get away from this unpleasant area today. There are only a few fields for you to cross, and then you'll be just outside the town.'

Fox rubbed both his eyes in turn with his paw, and then scratched thoughtfully. He found Vixen's sleepy eyes watching him.

'Let's go, Fox,' she urged. 'I've hated these last few days. It's been so uncomfortable. Have you noticed how little everyone has been speaking?'

'Yes, I have,' said Fox. 'It must have been the quietest period of the whole journey.'

'It's the influence of this awful district,' Vixen said. 'I've never been anywhere like it before. It's so lifeless. And there's almost nothing to eat.'

'I'll have to wake Badger and Owl, at any rate,' said Fox. 'I won't be a minute.'

Tawny Owl, who had also of late been complaining of the shortage of food, had found himself a sleeping-place in the only tree that could be seen for a mile or more around. Badger was snoring contentedly in a fold of the tarpaulin, quite away from the others. Fox woke him first, and related to him Kestrel's information.

Badger stretched himself while he carefully sniffed the motionless air in every direction. 'Hm!' he grunted. 'It is *remarkably* silent. Can't hear a thing. No humans about. Nothing about, by the sound of it.'

'What do *you* think then?' Fox asked him.

'I think we should get out of this ghastly place at the first opportunity,' he answered. 'Which is, it seems, now.'

They trotted over to Tawny Owl's tree together, and called him. Tawny Owl did not at first reply, and they called again. A muffled sound, something like a hoot, yet more of a sigh, was heard.

'Oh, it's you, Fox,' said the sleepy owl, peering down at him. 'And Badger.'

'Will you come down, Owl?' said Fox. 'We can't see you; you're quite hidden, you know.'

'We've something important to put to you,' added Badger.

'All right,' replied Tawny Owl wearily and, with his wings fully extended, he dropped down between them.

Fox told him of Kestrel's suggestion. 'I suppose we might as well make use of the quietness,' he finished.

'Certainly,' Tawny Owl agreed immediately. 'No time like the present. And perhaps we'll be able to get a square meal tonight.'

The three of them went back to the tarpaulin, and rounded up everyone.

Adder was especially pleased with the early move. 'I can go a good time without food,' he whispered, 'but this place has really been disappointing. There's simply nothing to get one's fangs into.' With a malicious leer at the voles he added, 'I was really beginning to think I might have to look elsewhere for my sustenance.'

'Now, Adder,' Badger remonstrated, 'why will you make remarks like that? See how you've made them quiver. They look quite frightened.'

'Oh, pshaw!' Adder exclaimed contemptuously. 'They should be used to my ways by now.'

'We shall never get used to your unkindness,' said Vole in a hurt tone of voice.

'Come on, now,' Fox broke in. 'That's enough, Adder. Let's get under way. We can all have a good feed tonight. Lead on, Kestrel.'

Following Kestrel's direction, the animals entered the first field – a wide, flat expanse of potato plants. Not a sound could they hear but their own footsteps and breathing. There was no bird-song, no buzzing of insects, and no breeze.

'It's . . . uncanny,' said Mole. 'If we couldn't see the sun, it would be just like being shut in one of my tunnels. Even then I can hear things above me.' Unconsciously he found himself whispering, which increased the feeling of eeriness.

'I don't like it at all,' Fox admitted to Vixen. 'Everything's so unnatural. Look at those plants. They look almost artificial.' He pointed with his head to the potato plant leaves, which indeed had a strange, waxy look about them.

'Yes, they look sort of shiny, don't they?' said Vixen.

'Not at all appetizing in appearance,' said Hare, who was close behind them. 'I wonder what they taste like.'

'Don't do anything silly, Hare,' said his mate sharply. 'Leave them alone. They don't look right at all.'

'I was merely wondering,' said Hare. 'No need to worry.'

'Leverets,' his mate admonished her young ones, 'on no account must you eat anything in these fields. Not so much as a nibble, d'you understand?'

The leverets promised their mother obedience.

The potato field ended, and just a dry strip of dead grass separated it from the next one, which supported sugar-beet.

Keeping Kestrel in sight, they skirted this field and began to cross another, where a crop of cabbages seemed to be flourishing. The rabbits' eyes grew big at the sight of the rows and rows of juicy green vegetables, and their empty stomachs ached for them.

Rabbit called to Fox. 'Can't we stop?' he pleaded. 'We're all so hungry. A few plants wouldn't be missed, after all, and there's simply no one about.'

Fox halted, and the rabbits and young hares, despite their mother's warning, looked at him eagerly.

'It's that very thing that makes me suspicious,' Fox said. 'I don't like this quietness one bit. There's some reason for it, which we don't know. In my opinion we shouldn't risk stopping.'

'Quite right, Fox. Keep going,' said Badger, who felt his friend needed support.

'Fox, *please*,' Rabbit begged him. 'We may not get another chance like this. None of us has eaten properly for days.'

'We hares won't touch anything,' said Hare's mate categorically, and her little ones' faces dropped.

'More fool you,' said Rabbit with contempt. 'There's nothing wrong with those cabbages. They're perfect. Look how fresh they are! You can still see the raindrops on them!'

Fox walked up to a large plant and looked all over it carefully, sniffing each leaf. 'There's certainly some moisture on them,' he agreed. 'The soil underneath is damp too. But it can't be rain. It's been dry for a long time.'

'Is it dew?' Mole piped up. The damp soil made him think of worms.

'I doubt it.' Fox shook his head. 'Not at this time of day.' He sniffed the plant again, more vigorously. 'I'm not sure,' he said slowly, 'but there seems to be a strange smell about them, a sort of mineral smell. Rabbit, you'd know better. Will you have a try?'

Rabbit went to the cabbage, and his nose quivered excitedly. 'No. Nothing different,' he observed, although he *had* detected the mineral smell. He was determined to persuade Fox to give way.

'I still don't like it,' Fox said uneasily. 'I'm not convinced they're safe. And this silence is getting me down. Where are all the insects we usually hear? I'll bet you wouldn't find a single caterpillar on those plants. They look *too* perfect.'

While the animals continued to debate the matter, Mole slipped down from Badger's back. His keen appetite was beginning to master him again. He had been deprived of his usual quota of earthworms for some days, and he had never been without a gnawing feeling of emptiness. The thought that, at last, in this field, there was a good chance of finding a satisfying number of worms proved too much for him.

To his credit, he fought the temptation for at least a few seconds, but Mole, above all creatures, found it difficult to deny the promptings of his stomach. He crept stealthily away from the other animals, until they all had their backs to him. Then he scurried behind a large cabbage plant and began to dig furiously.

'I should . . . be able to . . . catch a few . . . and get back again . . . before they miss me,' he panted as he dug, his whole mind devoted to the thought of plump, pink, wriggling worms. He was soon hidden from sight.

Fox and the rest of the party had not reached a decision.

'I say don't be tempted,' Weasel was saying. 'The plants may be delicious, but surely it's better not to risk anything than to be sorry afterwards?'

'It's all right for you. You don't eat cabbages,' Rabbit said angrily, 'otherwise you wouldn't be so indifferent.'

'Well . . .' Fox began.

'No!' said Badger. 'Fox, don't waver,' he whispered to him. 'Let's get out of this place while the going's good. It's broad daylight. Humans could appear at any moment, and we'd be spotted.'

'I don't like to seem hard on them,' Fox said doubtfully.

'They'll soon forget it, and be glad we went on,' Badger urged. 'I think we . . .' He broke off, as the sound of Whistler's wing made them all look up.

The heron was racing towards them, accompanied by Kestrel and Tawny Owl.

'Come on! Keep going!' they called.

'What is it?' Fox asked, alarmed.

The birds landed together. 'This place is a graveyard,' said Kestrel, and shuddered.

'Poisoned,' said Tawny Owl. 'Nothing's safe.'

'Poisoned?' gasped Rabbit.

'The whole area,' Whistler nodded. 'There's an orchard just ahead. The ground is littered with bodies of bullfinches, chaffinches, blackbirds . . .'

'Then the moisture . . .' began Rabbit.

'POISON!' cried Fox.

'But surely no one has eaten . . .' faltered Kestrel.

'No,' said Fox. He gulped at the danger they had escaped. 'You were in the nick of time.'

'The whole farm has been sprayed with chemicals,' Tawny Owl explained. 'All wild life has fled. Some were too late,' he added.

'For goodness' sake, everyone, let's go,' said Fox.

It was only then that Badger began to look for Mole, who was at that moment emerging from the hole he had dug behind the cabbage.

Badger saw the soil on his friend's fur and feet. 'Oh, Mole!' he wailed. 'What have you done?'

'Worms,' said Adder. 'Infected worms. Mole, you've poisoned yourself.'

Mole looked at them in consternation. 'But I haven't eaten any worms,' he said. 'They're all dead!'

# XXIX

# THE NATURALIST

Fox soon acquainted the wandering Mole with the reason for the death of all the earthworms, and the narrow margin by which Mole himself had escaped being poisoned made the little animal feel as weak as water.

'Now, Mole, let that be a lesson to you,' Badger told his erring young friend. 'No more creeping away with deceitful little plans. You're jolly lucky to be with us still.'

Badger was really as relieved as Mole at his escape, and after lecturing him, smiled with pleasure at the animal's return.

Now the animals' horror of the place lent wings to their feet, and with the ghostly feeling all around them of the silence that meant death, they hurried on.

In the orchard, the pitiful corpses of birds who had

committed no greater crime than that of finding it necessary to eat, sent shudders down the spines of the animals from Farthing Wood.

In another field they saw more lifeless creatures: poisoned fieldmice and beetles, and pretty butterflies which had unavoidably been tainted with the death-dealing spray. Even bees, useful to humans, had ignorantly strayed into this area where only machines and the mathematical minds of men were permitted to hold sway. These innocent makers of honey had perished too.

'I shall feel like a good wash once we're away from here,' Vixen said to Fox.

'We all will,' he answered grimly, as he resolutely led the band onward.

At last they reached the far border of this soulless farmland – a stout hawthorn hedge which ran as straight as a Roman road along its edge.

Fox found a gap for them, and they followed Vixen through into a cool green meadow, where cows were grazing and where golden buttercups grew in such profusion it was as if the sun had settled on the grass.

It was so inviting and refreshing after their recent ordeal that they sank down together in the lush verdure, letting out sighs of contentment. Tawny Owl, Kestrel and Whistler joined in their enjoyment of rest and relief.

'Yes, it's amazing to what lengths humans will go to

preserve their own species,' Tawny Owl said wisely, with a sense of importance.

'How can poisoning help them?' Toad asked.

'It helps them because it doesn't poison *them*, 'said Tawny Owl.

'But how can humans avoid coming into contact with it, when it is they who spray it around?' demanded Weasel.

'None of us could answer that,' Tawny Owl replied, 'as we have never been witnesses to the awful practice. What we all *do* know about, however, is the infinite cunning and cleverness of the human race. This alone is sufficient to tell us that the operation is probably undertaken by some of their lifelike machinery – under their control, of course.'

'But what do they do with all those poisoned cabbages and things?' Rabbit wanted to know.

Tawny Owl began to feel that, on this subject he might have bitten off more than he could chew. But, unfortunately, having once given the impression of being knowledgeable, he was obliged to continue displaying his wisdom.

'All those plants we saw,' he said, 'are eaten by humans.'

'EATEN!' shrieked all the rabbits together. 'THEY'RE POISONOUS!'

Tawny Owl racked his brains for an explanation. To his chagrin, Whistler stole his thunder by answering first.

'It seems extraordinary, doesn't it?' he intoned in his lugubrious voice, 'but it's really quite simple. Although at this moment those crops we saw have enough chemicals on them to poison many of us, there is probably not sufficient strength in the poison to kill a human, although he would certainly suffer to a degree. But, of course, the essence of the matter is that the plants are not going to be eaten *now*. We can only assume that, in their usual efficient way, the humans have rid themselves of any competitors for their food by spraying them with chemicals which will have completely disappeared by the time they are to be eaten. The chemicals are produced to *serve* humans, not the other way about. Therefore they would be quite sure of their own safety in the matter before they ventured to use them.'

'I wonder,' mused Fox. 'Can humans always be right? It must need only a small error for them to put themselves at danger, using such terrifying materials.'

'That we shall never know,' Tawny Owl declared in his wisest tone, hoping to regain his status.

But Adder, as usual, seemed to be able to analyse his motive. With a chuckle as dry as a withered leaf, he said sarcastically, 'Tawny Owl is such a *sage*.'

While they lay talking in the lush grass, a man came into the field through a gate and, avoiding the cows, walked slowly along, looking down at the ground all the time as if he had lost something.

Kestrel noticed him and drew the others' attention to his presence. Normally, they would all have run at once into hiding, but for some reason the appearance of this particular human did not seem to them to pose a threat to their safety.

He was dressed in a duffle-coat and was carrying various instruments, some slung round his neck and others hanging by straps from his shoulders. The animals saw him stop suddenly and, excitedly disencumbering himself of the objects he carried, drop to his knees and look closely at the grass.

The animals looked from one to another in astonishment.

The man, whose excitement seemed to increase, began to write feverishly in a notebook, pausing every now and then to look at the particular spot on the ground that interested him. When he had finished writing, he put all his apparatus on one side and sat down two or three feet from the spot. Then, notebook in hand again, he endeavoured to sketch what he had been so closely examining.

The animals continued to watch with more curiosity, and they were particularly struck by the care and gentleness of the man's actions as he sketched, quite unaware of his audience. He finished his sketch and put away the notebook. Then, taking one of his instruments, he cut into the turf with the utmost delicacy, and removed a small sample of some plant that had obviously been the focus of his attention, and carefully put it into one of his containers. Having written the relevant details on the label, he lifted the container up to the light and began to study his sample from every angle, with a look of profound pleasure.

A total silence had descended on the watching beasts

and birds, and the sound of Toad clearing his throat seemed excessively loud.

'My friends,' he said in an awestruck tone, '*that* is a Naturalist.'

The animals' faces took on an expression of wonder, almost of reverence.

'I have seen such humans before,' Whistler admitted. 'I remember two occasions when the quarry was visited by a human, like this one carrying all sorts of boxes and equipment, who had come to look at the waterfowl.'

'Why do they do that?' asked Squirrel.

'Strange to say, there *are* some humans who are interested in the welfare of wild creatures,' the heron explained.

'It's these very people we have to thank for White Deer Park,' Toad pointed out eagerly. 'It is they who are responsible for the creation of those havens for wild life they call Nature Reserves.'

'It's only when you learn of such kindness and interest in us creatures,' said Badger, 'that you recall that the human race is, after all, a brother species.'

'I shall never consider myself even remotely related to a race who can deliberately arrange to poison every living thing in an area, for reasons that arise solely from their own arrogance and greed,' said the fatalistic Adder.

'Those are strong words, Adder,' said Fox, 'but I'm sure we all take your point. In my view, which may be a selfish one, cruelty of a sort where there is some purpose to it, is not as bad as the senseless cruelty practised by those humans who delight in hunting a wild creature to its death, simply for what they call sport.'

'And don't forget shooting!' said Hare. 'That's *sport* too!'

'But even then, you see,' said Fox, 'it has a purpose, when they afterwards eat what they shoot.'

'It really is extraordinary,' said Vixen, 'that one species can produce specimens who differ so much in their behaviour that they could themselves become enemies. I'm thinking of our Naturalist, and the huntsman. One is so friendly to us, he feels he must lend us his protection; the other sees us merely as something to torment for his own enjoyment.'

'One seeks to preserve, the other to destroy,' Whistler summed up.

'I shall never understand humans,' said Mole.

While they had been talking, the Naturalist had taken a pair of field-glasses and was scanning the sky in an idle moment for something to watch.

'Kestrel, why don't you help him out?' suggested Fox. 'There doesn't seem to be anything for him to look at.'

'Yes, don't let's disappoint the poor creature,' said Adder sarcastically, 'when he's come all the way here to look at nothing.'

Fox could not help smiling. 'Adder, really . . .!' he began. 'Don't you have any sympathies at all?'

'Not for humans,' drawled the snake.

'But surely even you recognize that the Human Race isn't all bad?' persisted Fox.

'Pooh!' said Adder. 'Humans like that one you all seem so fond of are very much in the minority. And don't think he wouldn't change towards us if *his* food supply ran out.'

'You're such a pessimist, Adder,' said Toad.

'I'm merely stating the obvious,' he said. 'Humans always have, and always will consider themselves and their needs first. Oh, there might be a few of your precious Nature Reserves around. But if land should become scarce, and humans find what they've got is not enough, they'll jolly soon forget all about their high ideals of protecting their brother species! They'll take every inch before they remember our existence.'

'There's no need to be so bitter,' said Toad indignantly, feeling in his heart of hearts that Adder was right, but not wanting to admit it.

'You all know as well as I do,' Adder insisted, 'that if it should ever come to a choice between *their* continued existence and *our* continued existence, not one human would hesitate a second before deciding.'

The animals fell silent. Adder seemed to have found an irrefutable argument that was infinitely depressing to them. He looked round at them triumphantly.

'Let us hope, then,' said Vixen, 'for their sake, as well as ours, that situation is never reached.'

'I'm sure it won't be – in our lifetime,' Badger said, in an effort to be comforting. 'Perhaps it never will be.'

For some reason Toad felt himself bound to defend the conception of Nature Reserves. 'I don't know why you bothered to join us,' he said in an aggrieved tone to Adder, 'if you have no faith in White Deer Park.'

'I didn't think my faith was in question,' the snake replied easily. 'The point I was making was what might occur if and when our human friends find they are short of land. I realize it's something that will only occur in the future. Nevertheless, you won't have to look far to find a good illustration of my point. The very reason we are here now is, in case you've forgotten, because land that was once left wild was seized, without compunction, by humans for their own purposes.'

'But Farthing Wood,' argued Toad, 'had not been set aside specifically for the use of wild creatures as a Reserve.'

'Can't we get off this dismal subject?' asked Weasel. 'We can't foretell the future, thank heavens, and I've a suspicion that neither can our clever, all-knowing humans.'

'I agree,' said Fox. 'This sort of argument doesn't help any of us. We're in danger of losing sight of our objective – our only objective – which is to reach White Deer Park.' Despite himself, he found his voice rising as he spoke and he finished up glaring at Adder.

'I'm sorry,' said Adder with a leer that belied his words, 'I meant no offence. I shan't say another word.'

'Good,' said Toad under his breath, but just loud enough to be overheard.

The innocent Naturalist who had prompted the discussion was preparing to leave the meadow, having found nothing else in which to interest himself.

'It seems such a shame when we're all here so close,' said Fox. 'Kestrel, won't you go?'

'Delighted,' said Kestrel, and uttering one of his loudest cries, launched himself upwards with the speed of a rocket.

Against the broad backcloth of sky, he began to undertake a series of acrobatics of the utmost virtuosity: hovering, diving, somersaulting with such breathtaking speed that his friends below felt like cheering.

'Kew, kew,' he called continually as the Naturalist, forgetful of his collection of instruments and paraphernalia, followed his every movement through the field-glasses in spellbound admiration.

It was not long before Whistler decided he, too, had things of interest to show this appreciative human spectator and, after executing a number of preparatory whistles as he flapped his wings, eventually joined Kestrel in the air at a considerably lower height.

There was not much he could do, apart from showing off the majestic motion of his huge wing-beats, but the animals watching the Naturalist's reaction, all felt that he now found the larger bird's appearance of more interest. Kestrel seemed to have the same feeling for, after a little longer in the sky, with a particularly spectacular dive he plummeted to the ground, and rejoined the party.

Fox next tried to persuade Tawny Owl to fly a little.

'No, I shall not make an exhibition of myself,' he answered pompously. 'Besides, I'm sure he's not only interested in bird life.'

'Would he be interested in me?' Mole squeaked excitedly. 'I could show him how quickly I can dig a tunnel!'

Fox laughed. 'Mole, really! How would he see you if you're inside a tunnel?'

'Well, yes, I forgot that,' said the subdued Mole.

'I'll tell you what we'll do,' said Badger. 'He doesn't want to see a lot of animals trying to show him how clever, or agile, or swift-running they can be. He's not at a circus. I'm sure what would interest him more than anything is to see us all simply walking in formation through the field together. I bet *that* would surprise him more than anything. After all, how many humans can have seen a motley collection of wild life such as we are, all strolling amicably in a bunch? Why, he would never forget such a sight to his last day.'

'An excellent idea, Badger,' Tawny Owl was gracious enough to admit. 'I'll join you in that with pleasure.'

The animals waited until Whistler finally returned, and then, automatically taking up their usual travelling positions, they filed slowly and deliberately through the grass, keeping about twenty yards' distance from the Naturalist. Mole and Toad insisted on walking too, and the three birds fluttered along in advance of the column.

Without saying a word, Adder had tagged along behind, and none of the others dared remark on it for fear of upsetting him.

The Naturalist spotted the movements of the birds first, and then the procession on the ground caught his eye. He pressed the field-glasses harder and harder against his face, unable to believe what he saw. But as the movement continued, he realized that what he was witnessing was, in fact, a unique wonder of nature. When the animals reached the far end of the field, he sank to the ground and began to scribble feverishly in his notebook. They watched him then for some time.

'Your idea certainly seemed to create an impression, Badger,' said Fox.

'We've made his day,' Badger chuckled gleefully. 'He'll never forget us.'

'*We* all seem to have forgotten something, though,' said Tawny Owl. 'Our empty stomachs!'

## XXX

# THE CHURCH

The animals spent the remaining few hours before darkness out of sight under the thick hedge. When it was dark enough, they set off singly, or in small groups, to forage and satisfy their ravenous hunger. Fox told them they could have all the time they wanted to accomplish this very necessary and enjoyable task, as they were to have a day's complete rest before continuing their journey through the nearby town. Only Kestrel and Whistler were left in the meadow, intermittently chatting and dozing through the night. Their needs had been satisfied while the daylight held out; Kestrel had hunted from the air, while Whistler had flown a considerable distance before finding a stream where he could indulge his favourite pastime of fishing.

Mole, too, had no need to leave the meadow. He merely

looked for a soft piece of ground, and with a speed greatly accelerated by his hunger, dug himself towards his dinner.

On the animals' return, they went straight to sleep in the thickest part of the hedge and slept the clock round until dusk the following day.

They woke in stages, completely refreshed, and with healthy appetites again. This time Fox told them to eat enough to last them for the next stage of the journey only, and to be as quick as they could about it, as their route now ran through the town, which they could only risk crossing at the dead of night.

When they were ready to leave, the night had become several degrees cooler, and a gusty breeze was blowing. Toad had told them that if they were careful there was not a lot to worry about, as it was quite a small town and had been very quiet when he had passed through it before during the night hours. At his direction Fox avoided the main street, but led the animals along a series of lanes and alleys, each of which was bordered by high brick walls.

The party kept close against these walls, on the darker side of the alleys, and were really quite inconspicuous as the passages were very murky and badly lit. When they came out of the last lane some spots of rain began to fall. This increased very quickly to a heavy shower, but the animals felt it was to their advantage, as the few humans who might be abroad would be looking for shelter.

'The next bit's the worst,' said Toad. 'We have to cross the town square. But don't worry; it should be deserted at this time of night.'

They crossed the road that lay in front of them and entered the square from one corner via an empty shopping colonnade. This square contained an island of flagstones and trees, surrounded on all sides by roads, pavements and shops.

They quickly crossed to the island, and at once froze. Under a pair of lime trees, whose thick foliage afforded excellent shelter from the rain, a group of about a dozen humans, mostly courting couples, was standing.

'No use stopping, Fox,' whispered Toad. 'You must go on. They're not likely to do anything.'

Fox and Vixen broke into a trot, and the other animals followed suit as they passed the lime trees, and made their way to the far end of the island. Luckily the dim lighting in the square and the hard rain combined to screen the column of animals from detection.

They left the square and, turning a corner, found themselves in a market-place. Empty crates and boxes and small heaps of straw, paper and squashed fruit and cabbage-leaves lined the sides of this deserted spot, normally so crowded with eager, jostling shoppers.

'Ugh, what filth these humans make,' growled Adder, as he slithered across the muddy cobbles.

The rain fell harder and harder, and the wind dashed it against their faces in squalls, almost blinding them.

'We can't take much more of this, Fox,' Fieldmouse called from the midst of the soaked, struggling mass of mice.

'It's not much further now,' Toad encouraged them. 'Once we're out of the town we can stop.'

The animals made the best progress they could, and eventually the last shop, the last pavement, the last house was passed. Now that they were able to stop for a rest, they did not at all want to do so. There was absolutely no shelter from the stinging rain. They were surrounded by open playing-fields, devoid of trees or any kind of wind-break.

'This is dreadful,' wailed Squirrel. 'Our fur is so drenched and matted together, we'll all catch our deaths.'

'We came through a storm before,' Hedgehog observed. 'I don't think any casualties were suffered.'

'Nevertheless, it's no less uncomfortable the second time,'

Squirrel insisted.

'What about us?' said Vole. 'We voles, and the fieldmice, will be drowned if we stay here in the open.'

Fox looked all round, his brow furrowed as he strained to make out some object in the vicinity where they could take shelter.

'I can't see *anything*,' he said in despair to Toad.

'I can,' said Vixen. 'It looks like a church. At any rate, it's a big building – on the other side of these fields – look!'

Fox could just make out a dark mass looming in the near distance.

'Come on, my gallant little friends,' he urged. 'One last effort and we're home and dry.'

'Just to be dry would be something,' Squirrel muttered.

'Supposing it's shut?' said the pessimistic Vole.

'If it *is* a church there's sure to be a porch we can shelter under,' said Fox, trying to sound confident.

'Well, don't let's waste time,' said Squirrel, in a weary sort of whine.

Fox started off across the fields, Vixen at his side, with Badger, the hares, Weasel and the rabbits close behind. The squirrels, their usually bushy tails plastered with wet, were a sorry sight as they ran nimbly in their wake. The hedgehogs, whom rain did not bother very much, and the soaked voles and fieldmice were last, save for Adder.

There was a second hazard for the mice, for, because of their size, the heaviness of the drops was an additional hardship. Yet the sight of the church looming nearer and nearer drove them on, with its promise of eventual comfort and shelter.

So the animals arrived beneath the building's towering dark walls, tired, cold, soaked and shivering. The mice were the last to arrive, uttering piteous little cries of misery.

Fox looked at them with a forlorn expression. 'I . . . I'm afraid there's no porch,' he told them hesitantly.

Some of the voles and fieldmice broke down at the news. To have come through all they had, and then to find no relief, was too hard to bear. They huddled together on the muddy ground and sobbed heartbreakingly.

'But just a minute, my little friends,' said Fox, 'perhaps we can get inside. We're not beaten yet. Badger, look after them. I'll have a scout round.' After shaking his saturated coat with a single vigorous movement, Fox began inspecting the walls.

The animals watched him despairingly, while the cruel rain relentlessly lashed down as if it were trying to beat them into the ground. Tawny Owl flew up to the steeple and took up a perch in the belfry, where it was dry. Kestrel joined him, but Whistler remained on the ground standing with his great wings extended as an umbrella over the cowering mice.

Fox disappeared round the other side of the church.

'How much longer will this rain continue?' groaned Rabbit. 'I'm sure we shall all end up being drowned.' He looked with distaste at Toad who, alone amongst the animals, was enjoying every minute of the rainfall, and was busy splashing about in a large puddle.

'Extraordinary habits he has,' Rabbit muttered to Hare.

'Yes,' Hare replied, 'water is certainly a tonic to Toad. Just look how his skin glistens – as if he had put on a new one.'

A shout from Fox made them all prick up their ears.

'Quickly! Round here!' he was calling from round the corner. 'We're in luck!'

In one mass the party of animals scurried round to the other side. Fox proudly indicated a greyish shape that was draped against the brickwork.

'Well, what is it?' Badger asked, almost irritably.

'It's a hole!' said Fox triumphantly.

'There's no hole there,' said Rabbit peevishly. 'What have you . . .?'

'Of course, you can't see the hole,' Fox interrupted him. 'They've covered it with this material' – he indicated the greyish shape which in fact was canvas – 'but we can soon get behind that!'

He at once began to paw an opening, tugging the material away from the wall.

'Ooh, there *is* a hole!' cried one of the fieldmice.

Fox climbed over the broken brickwork that framed the hole and looked back at the animals, all of whom were still watching him, except Vixen who had at once followed him inside.

'What are you waiting for?' Fox asked. 'It's dry in here. It smells strongly of humans, but it's as dark as Badger's set. There's no one about.'

The animals needed no second bidding, and they scrambled together through the hole, Whistler stepping awkwardly after them in his upright gait. Adder was the last to slither between the canvas and the bricks.

'I think Tawny Owl and Kestrel ought to be with us,' Fox said. 'Whistler, will you fetch them?'

The heron cheerfully stepped back into the rain, and soon the three birds appeared together on the threshold.

'Are we complete?' asked Fox, beginning to see through the gloom.

'No,' Adder drawled. 'It seems that Toad finds the rain preferable to our company.'

'Oh, drat the fellow!' exclaimed Fox. 'All right, I'll go this time. Vixen dear, would you help Badger look for a suitable hiding-place? We want somewhere dry and inconscpicuous, and free from draughts.'

'But I can't see anything, Fox,' she protested mildly.

'We could do with your glow-worms now, Badger,' chuckled Weasel.

'Leave it to me,' pleaded Mole. 'Darkness is nothing to me. I'm used to it. I prefer it to sunlight really, you know,' he added, trying to impress. 'Oh yes, the darker the better.'

'No wonder he's as blind as a bat,' said Adder maliciously, under his breath.

'He's just trying to be helpful,' said Badger pointedly, rounding on the snake. 'But, of course, *you* wouldn't understand that.'

Adder remained unabashed.

Mole led the party, at a necessarily slow pace, down one of the side aisles. The animals' feet produced a variety of clipping and padding noises against the worn stone floor, while Adder's scaly body made a dry, swishing rasp as he writhed along behind them. In the almost total darkness the animals had no idea where they were going, and followed the confident Mole quite blindly.

The little velvet-coated animal went forward purposefully, using his instinct to find the darkest corner of a thoroughly dark building. He turned a few corners, and threaded the line of animals between pews, and eventually stopped in the narrow space behind the organ. Here it really was pitch-dark, but in its musty seclusion it was as dry as dust and completely sheltered from any unwelcome draughts.

'Where have you brought us, Mole?' asked Badger.

'I don't know,' Mole replied, 'but it . . . um . . . *seems* all right.'

Fox, in the meantime, had brought Toad into the church, and was sniffing and groping about for a sign of his friends.

'Do you see anything?' Toad asked him.

'No,' he replied, 'but I can smell their damp bodies.'

An unexpected flapping of wings above them made them both jump, but Tawny Owl had appeared to guide them to the hiding-place.

'Good old Owl,' said Fox, trying to mask his momentary fright. 'Well, we should all get a good rest tonight.'

'I'm not so sure I approve of sheltering in a place that seems to have such a magnetic influence over humans,' Tawny Owl remarked. 'But I suppose there is no choice.'

'It's certainly better than being out in the rain,' Fox laughed.

'Personally, I don't like these very dry spots,' Toad said, shaking his head. 'I always wonder if my skin might crack.'

'Nonsense,' Fox told him. 'Anyway, it's only for a day. I should have thought you were tired.'

'I am,' admitted Toad, as Tawny Owl alighted on the back of a pew and then fluttered to the ground.

When all the animals were together, they began to ask Toad in sleepy voices how far away they now were from their destination.

'About a day's travelling, I should think,' he answered. 'However,' he added, as assorted squeals of delight and excitement were heard, 'I can't be absolutely sure, because we've gone a little bit out of the way in our search for shelter. I didn't ever come past this church before, but I do know that, having come through that town, the Park is now very, very close.'

'Do you think we'll have any difficulty in getting back on the correct route?' asked Hedgehog.

'Of course not,' Toad said cheerfully. 'It only needs Kestrel to do a little flying some time tomorrow, provided this rain has stopped. Why, I'm sure he could see the Park from here.'

'As soon as it's light enough . . .' murmured Kestrel, as he tucked his head under his wing.

When he emerged from the building early the next morning, leaving his friends sleeping, Kestrel was pleased to see the countryside looking so clear and fresh. The air was cool and crisp, and the sky blue again, as if washed clean of clouds. The wet grass gleamed and sparkled in the sunlight.

Kestrel flew lazily aloft and stretched his wing muscles. After enjoying a series of swoops and dives, he began to look around him, at the landscape. Sure enough, in one direction, an area of parkland was easily discernible. Kestrel could see stretches of fencing and rolling grassy country, with dark patches that he recognized as bracken, and clusters of trees that were copses or woods. The Edible Frogs' pond was not visible from Kestrel's position, but he decided to fly and have a closer look. There was no longer any doubt as to the park's identity when, as he approached he saw several white blobs moving over the grass, which gradually took form and shape as the very white deer that gave the park its name. As he drew near this

place that the party of animals and birds had been struggling to reach for so long, Kestrel felt that their arrival, which now seemed inevitable, should be suitably memorable, and a plan began to form in his mind.

Back in the church, his friends were not feeling so confident of finally reaching their new home or even of getting safely away from the building, for daylight had brought workmen along to continue their repair work on the broken wall. The sound of human tools banging and chipping at the very place they had expected to use as their exit and, worse still, raucous human voices, awoke and seriously alarmed the animals. In reply to a barrage of questions all more or less encompassing the one demand of what was to be done next, Fox replied grimly that for the present they should sit tight.

'That's all very well,' said Rabbit. 'But what if those men wall us in?'

'There are such things as doors in churches, you know,' Tawny Owl remarked testily.

Rabbit felt foolish, although he tried not to show it. In this he failed dismally. 'Anyway,' he said sullenly, 'there's no knowing when the doors will be opened.'

'Oh, it won't be long.' Fox tried to sound unconcerned. 'Somebody's bound to come sooner or later, with these workmen here.'

'Actually, Rabbit has got a point,' said Hare, surprising his distant cousin by siding with him for once. 'If a human *does* come to open one of the doors, we might well be too slow to get out before it's closed again, and in any case he's hardly likely to hold it open for us while we file through.'

Fox started to think and, as he had begun to do more and more, consulted Vixen.

'It's safer to stay here at the moment,' the animals heard her say to him in a low voice.

Fox looked round at his companions, studying every face. 'Does anyone want to make a dash for it now?' he asked.

No one replied, but there were sounds of shifting feet and one or two coughs.

'Vixen and I are quite ready to accompany any of you who wish to chance it now, rather than finding we might have left it too late,' Fox said.

'We'll probably have a better opportunity later,' said Badger in his soothing voice. 'I think an attempt to leave now might prove to be rather foolhardy.'

The concerted murmurs of the party seemed to express approval of Badger's opinion.

'Then it's decided,' said Fox. 'We wait.'

The noise of the workmen continued unabated, and the animals remained in their hiding-place, listening with sinking hearts to the ceaseless hammering and shouts, and wondering what Kestrel was doing. After some hours, during which time none of them spoke very much, the noise came to an end. Fox looked at each of his companions significantly, as if mentally warning them to be ready.

They waited for the voices of the workmen, who were obviously preparing to leave, to diminish. The light inside the church, filtering through the coloured panes, and striking straight through the clear glass, had moved gradually round the building. A shaft of sunlight, illuminating a thousand dancing motes of dust, now shone obliquely on to the organ pipes, in front of which the crouching animals were all geared for flight.

The rough voices were retreating; there seemed to be only a matter of seconds longer to wait, when a swooping form suddenly alighted in front of them. Kestrel had returned.

'It's no good,' he said immediately. 'Stay where you are. There's a throng of people on the way here, and two of them are just about to open the main door.'

Even as he finished speaking the noises of a handle being turned, followed by creaking hinges, reached their ears. Instinctively they all cowered closer to the floor. New, quieter human voices could be heard.

'What about the wall?' whispered Fox. 'Surely we could still make a dash for it before any more arrive?'

'No, it's hopeless.' Kestrel shook his head. 'They've bricked up the lower part of the hole completely. There's only a small gap left now, about four feet from the ground.'

'Oh no!' Fox groaned. 'We're stuck fast.'

'But we can't remain here,' protested Hedgehog, in an agitated voice. 'It's not dark any more. We'll be discovered in no time.'

'On the contrary,' Fox told him. 'We're as safe as we can be under the circumstances. We're screened all round pretty well, and there is no room for any humans to come close to us. And don't forget, they don't know we're here. They won't come looking for us.'

'I'm sorry I didn't leave with you now, Kestrel,' said Whistler, who always slept well and had not woken as early as the hawk.

'You needn't have come back,' Fox remarked. 'Now you're stuck with us.'

'Kestrel's a good friend,' said Mole.

'Well, I didn't want you to move from here,' the hawk said, smiling in a pleased way. 'I thought I might have been too late

to stop you.'

More voices came through the open door, and more steps echoed on the stone floor. There was a scraping of chairs, and one set of footsteps came nearer and nearer to the animals and then stopped just the other side of the organ which sheltered them. A sound of rustling papers and the varied noises of someone settling himself into a seat were then audible, so that they knew one of the humans was very close.

'Just when we're so close to home,' muttered Toad.

His unconscious use of the word 'home' to describe somewhere none of his companions, except Kestrel, had ever seen, acted as a tonic on the whole party. It reminded them all with a peculiar force that not only was their long journey nearly over, but that in a matter of hours their lives would no longer be governed by the factors of how far they could walk in one day, or how to negotiate some difficult obstacle. They all realized that their escape from the church represented the very last of the obstacles which they had to surmount, before they could begin to enjoy a normal and peaceful life again – something they had almost forgotten how to do. So the thought of that home, and all it meant to each weary creature in his own particular way, produced a resolve, stronger than at any time on their journey, that they would not be stopped now from reaching it by any power, human or otherwise. Each animal sensed this fresh upsurge of moral strength in his companions, and felt his confidence rise.

'We can wait a little longer,' said Weasel philosophically.

'It's only a matter of time,' remarked Mole, who was already feeling pleased at Fox's indirect compliment on the hiding-place he had found them.

'As far as I can see it's a *waste* of time,' whispered Adder. But the party settled down silently, while the echoing footsteps and the low-pitched human voices increased in number.

Finally the shuffling of feet, and the creaking and scraping of pews and chairs, and even the whispering voices subsided, and it seemed as if the church and its people had entered a period of quiet, of expectancy.

The animals had all begun to think that their ordeal might, after all, not be so grim when, with a deafening, blaring shock, the organ pipes behind them suddenly pealed forth.

The noise was so terrifying and sudden that the whole party of animals leapt up, panic-stricken, and scattered all over the church in a sort of zoological eruption.

The birds flew up to the rafters where the terrible sounds of the organ reverberated tremendously, causing them to fly in every direction in their efforts to escape the noise.

Fox and Vixen dashed straight down the nave in blind terror, and more by luck than judgement found themselves at the open door. The voles and fieldmice, the rabbits and hares and the squirrels scurried to every corner, some of them getting under chairs, producing shrieks and screams of alarm from the female congregation. The men, no less astounded, uttered gruff shouts

and exclamations, while the Vicar, who was about to perform a wedding ceremony, dropped his book as Badger lumbered against his legs. Weasel, Mole, Toad and the hedgehogs made for the opposite end of the church, each taking a different and completely motiveless route, their only thought being to get away from that horrifying machine. Only Adder, fortunately for him, was not noticed as he slid his slender body along every hidden crevice and crack he could find to reach the door.

For a few moments pandemonium held sway, but with the ceasing of the wedding music by the astonished organist, the animals' panic was calmed sufficiently, to turn their flight towards the one safe direction.

With the gradual disappearance of the swifter-running animals, the congregation's initial amazement changed to excitement, and soon a general buzz of chatter filled the church.

As Fox and Vixen hurtled forth from the doorway, the bride, with her escorting father, and bridesmaids, were just approaching it. They stopped dead, speechless, only to see, after a short interval, a badger, an assortment of rabbits, squirrels and hares and a weasel gallop out of the door and race off in the direction the two foxes had taken.

The bride looked towards her father, as if silently asking him if this were some sort of omen for her imminent marriage, but his amazement prevented him from forming any words and he merely stammered incoherently. Eventually he seemed to recall their reason for being there, and he began to lead his daughter forward again.

As they were about to enter the church, two birds shot past like bullets, and a third one, of huge proportions, flew directly at their faces, flapping its wings frantically in the confined space, and only veered upward at the last minute, making a rhythmical whistling as it soared higher and higher.

The poor bride shrieked with fright, and four sympathetic echoes came from the bridesmaids. The father's alarm now turned to anger. Telling them to wait on the threshold, he entered the church to discover who was behind the production of what he deemed a very bad effort at a wedding prank. No sooner was he inside than his legs were assailed by a group of scuttling hedgehogs who managed to scramble past him into the open. He began to call out furiously for the member of the congregation whom he thought was responsible for perpetrating such an outrage on his daughter's wedding day. Of course nobody replied, and the Vicar came forward, wringing his hands, and with a soothing voice tried to calm the irate gentleman.

After a minute or two the bride and bridesmaids could no longer bear being kept in ignorance of the matter, and they entered the church in their turn, unaccompanied by the expected strains of the organ.

While the humans stood around and debated, some heatedly and others more calmly, the cause of such an extraordinary occurrence, the smaller animals still inside the building were able, one by one, to make their escape unnoticed. Mole was the last to reach the door, but just outside he found Toad and Adder, trying to look inconspicuous by the wall.

'They went that way,' Toad said, indicating the direction the swifter animals had taken. 'They'll probably wait for us somewhere.'

'I can't see anyone,' said Mole, peering ahead.

'Of course you can't,' said Adder impatiently. 'I'm surprised you could even see your way to the door.'

'Oh, Adder, don't be unkind,' said Mole, badly hurt at the reference to his purblindness. 'Let's . . . let's go on together, shall we?'

'Not much else we can do,' muttered the snake, who felt Mole was to blame for their present position by choosing their hiding-place by the organ pipes.

'I'm sure when they've recovered themselves, Fox will send someone back to help us,' said Toad confidently. 'It'll probably be Kestrel.'

A little further on they caught up with some of the mice, who had been constantly looking back over their shoulders in dire fear of being pursued.

The humans, however, were far too busy arguing and talking inside the church for any of them to think of looking for the cause of the disturbance outside, and pretty soon all the animals had put enough distance behind them for the renewed sounds of the organ not to reach their ears.

# XXXI

# THE FINAL LAP

'It's not like Fox to forget about us,' remarked one of the fieldmice, after they had been walking together for some time through the soaked, glistening grass.

'Don't worry,' said Toad. 'They'll all be waiting for us in a safe spot somewhere. We'll keep going.'

'I'm almost as wet as I was in the storm,' grumbled Vole, who had been one of the last animals to get out of the church. 'This long grass is drenching me.'

'Well, our troubles will be over soon,' said Mole happily. 'I can scarcely believe it, you know,' he added to Toad.

'I shouldn't get carried away just yet,' warned Adder. 'Anything can happen.'

'Pooh, nonsense!' said Toad. 'We're as good as there.

There's no doubt in my mind, at any rate.'

'Will you live in the pond with the Edible Frogs?' Mole asked him.

'Certainly not,' Toad replied. 'I shall visit the pond, of course. But, after the places I've seen, my horizons are wider than the narrow world of mud and weed they cling to.'

Adder's face took on a subtle expression. 'You must introduce me to these friends of yours,' he lisped. 'They sound most interesting.'

Toad looked a little embarrassed, and feigned deafness. But the snake persisted. 'You will, won't you?' he urged. 'I want to meet them.'

Toad coughed awkwardly. 'H'm, well . . . er . . . the trouble is, you see, Adder, it's really a question of . . . er . . . whether they want to meet *you*.'

Adder was not offended. He chuckled drily, and leered at Mole.

Soon after this, Toad's faith in Fox was found to be justified. They heard the unmistakable sound of Whistler's wings, and they called out together to him: 'Here! Here!'

The heron landed and, having greeted them, stepped along with them on his stilt-like legs. As he made no reference to Fox, Toad was forced to prompt him.

'Is it good news or bad news?' he asked unobtrusively.

'Oh, good news,' replied Whistler brightly. 'Very good news.'

He said no more and lapsed into a pensive mood. His companions were puzzled.

'Is . . . is everyone all right?' Mole enquired.

'Yes. They're fine. I'm sorry,' said the heron, rousing himself, 'the nearer we get to our destination the more I find my thoughts turning to . . . er . . . well, to put it delicately, the chance of . . . er . . . perhaps meeting someone of interest in the Park.'

Only Adder divined the meaning behind these words, but as such matters did not interest him in the least, he remained silent. Mole and Toad were completely nonplussed.

'Well, have we *far* to go?' Vole asked the huge bird irritably.

Whistler apologized again. 'I'm so sorry,' he said, 'I've been keeping you in the dark – very wrong of me. They're all waiting for us . . . er . . . under a holly bush, actually. It's not too far now.'

'So the party's complete?' asked Toad.

'Yes, when *we've* arrived,' said Whistler. 'We're very lucky.'

The smaller creatures, who felt they had been quite inconspicuous before, felt considerably ill at ease while Whistler, dwarfing them all, continued to step slowly along at their side. They all felt sure he could not have directed more attention to them if he had been a notice board, but none of them, not even Adder, liked to ask him to go further off, when he had come back specially to look for them.

In fact, Whistler was so absorbed with his thoughts about 'the interesting creature in the Park' that he might meet, that he was not even aware that he was on the ground instead of in the air, and the idea that his noticeable size might attract unwanted attention to the little group completely escaped him.

However, within the half-hour they all arrived safely at the holly bush, and the whole company began to feel very merry, congratulating each other and joking, and beginning to talk about the things they were going to do when they reached the Park.

'I shall eat a huge meal, and then sleep for a week,' declared Tawny Owl, who had had more than his fair share just recently of sleeping and waking at the wrong times.

'I shall look round at once for a suitable spot to construct a new set,' said Badger. He sighed. 'How nice it will be to sleep underground again, without fear of being disturbed – all on my own again, too. How peaceful!'

'Oh, there's nothing like an underground home,' agreed

Mole. 'I shall build the finest network of tunnels any mole has ever dreamed of,' he boasted.

'I'm looking forward to living a normal life up a tree,' said Squirrel. 'Ever since we left Farthing Wood, we squirrels have lived what is for us a completely unnatural existence. We've walked great distances over land, and we've slept at ground level. So just to race up and down some good solid oak trunks, and to enjoy the springy feeling of branches and twigs under our feet will be our reward for all that.'

'To be able to run free, with my family, in any direction, is my dream,' Hare told them.

'To be able to nibble at leisure,' remarked Rabbit.

'To swim when I want to!' cried Toad.

'To go foraging in the moonlight,' said Hedgehog.

'And to feel free from the constant necessity of hiding oneself,' said Weasel.

'To have the time to look for the best berries,' murmured Fieldmouse.

'And seeds,' added Vole.

'To meet someone of one's own kind again,' sighed Whistler, 'er . . . that is, of *particular* interest.'

The animals looked towards Fox. 'What about you?' they asked him.

Fox looked lovingly at Vixen. 'There's my answer,' he smiled.

Vixen smiled back.

'To be, above all,' said Kestrel, 'safe from interfering hands, and to know our home is safe from encroachment.'

'And,' drawled Adder, 'for this everlasting trek to come to an end.'

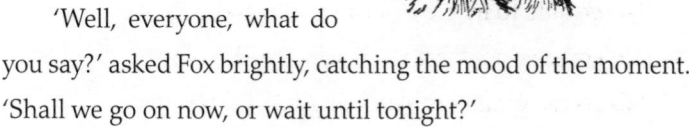

The animals laughed heartily, and as they fell silent, found themselves all beaming at one another afresh.

'Well, everyone, what do you say?' asked Fox brightly, catching the mood of the moment. 'Shall we go on now, or wait until tonight?'

'Now!' cried the majority of the animals immediately.

'Any dissenters?' asked Fox.

'I think I speak for all of the fieldmice, and us voles, when I say we would find it more comfortable to travel later,' Vole announced. But he had miscalculated. A good number of the tiny creatures contradicted him, by declaring themselves as ready as anyone to leave at once.

'Good, that's settled,' said Fox promptly. 'I'm afraid you're very much in the minority, Vole. Everyone is eager to go.'

'And why not?' Kestrel wanted to know. 'The weather is fine and clear; it's the time when most humans are indoors eating; and we can all be inside the Park in an hour or so,' he added persuasively. 'Wouldn't you say so, Fox?'

'Er . . . probably. Toad, what would you say?'

'I should say, now that Kestrel has put us back on the shortest route, two hours at the most,' Toad calculated. 'I can *feel* the nearness of the Park, but we might be just a *little* slower than usual, because . . . well, if you've no objection, I'd rather like to walk the final stretch myself.'

'Yes! Yes! And me!' cried Mole predictably.

'Very commendable of you, Mole,' remarked Badger, raising an eyebrow, 'but are you quite sure? You know . . . er . . . we don't want to be held up at the last minute?'

'I shan't hold anyone up,' Mole said hotly. 'I've just walked all the way from the church, and I'm not a bit tired.'

'Good chap, good chap,' Badger muttered consolingly. 'I'll walk with you.'

'Right.' Fox got up. 'Toad, you must head the column and lead us in.'

'Very appropriate,' Kestrel agreed. 'Just what I'd hoped for.'

This allusion to some arrangement or idea of his own carried no significance for any of the party, and Kestrel's plan retained its secrecy.

Then, with Toad proudly walking in front, his skin glistening with moisture and his beautiful eyes glowing like twin jewels in the sunlight, the animals set off across the rain-spangled ground on the very last stage of their journey.

*

No more than a thousand yards away, the inhabitants of White Deer Park were grouping at an agreed point a short distance from where the heroic band from Farthing Wood were expected to enter the Reserve. At the instigation of Kestrel, who had paid a visit early that morning, the assorted birds and beasts were preparing a jubilant welcome for the creatures whose exploits they were all now familiar with.

Carried for the most part by the winged population of that part of the country, word had spread of the approach of the Farthing Wood community, although precious little had actually been seen of them because of the extreme caution they had exercised all along their route; something that they had gradually developed into a fine art. But sufficient glimpses of one or more members of the party had been caught, particularly during the Hunt and at the motorway, for their expectant hosts at White Deer Park to feel impatient for their arrival as creatures from the real Wild. The fact that the travels and adventures of Fox and Badger, Mole and Toad, Kestrel and Tawny Owl and Adder, and all their other companions, were already something of a legend, served to heighten the impatience of the indigenous fauna of the Nature Reserve.

The Edible Frogs were the inhabitants most inspired by the Farthing Wood odyssey, because they recognized in the animals' guide the very Toad whose acquaintance they had made four seasons ago, and who had spoken to them of the old home to which he must return. They were additionally excited because he alone of the already famous group of animals had made the perilous journey twice, once on his own, and now, retracing his steps in triumph, as the trusted guide of a wonderful brotherhood of wildlife.

So when Kestrel had actually flown into the Park on that morning and spoken to the old White Stag, the doyen of the deer-herd and acknowledged overlord of the Park, news had spread like wildfire of the approaching event that all had been waiting for, friend and foe alike. Natural enmity and rivalry were forgotten as the entire population massed to welcome their new neighbours.

Through his various lieutenants and subjects, the old Stag arranged the various groups of creatures by an ancient oak-stump, a focal point of the Reserve that was known to everyone. There were badgers and foxes and stoats, rabbits, moles, squirrels, hedgehogs, dormice, fieldmice and voles. There were weasels and shrews, toads and frogs, lizards, slow-worms, snakes and newts. There were rooks, crows, jays and jackdaws, pheasants and owls, nuthatches, tits and warblers. There were nightingales and hawks, pigeons, finches and woodpeckers, and there was one very interesting female heron. This magnificent assemblage of Nature spread like a moving tapestry of colour over the glistening grass, and was enhanced by the superb herd of white deer, mustering two hundred head, all of whom stood behind the massive form of the great Stag.

All through the afternoon they waited, every eye turned

on the broken piece of fencing where Kestrel had promised he and his friends would enter their new home. At last the moment came.

The old Stag visibly stiffened as his weaker eyesight made out what the creatures all round him were already talking about. He held himself straight and erect, looking every inch a lord of the wild, as he prepared himself for his welcoming address.

Kestrel had alighted on a fence-post, indicating that the party of travellers was about to appear. Sure enough, a few minutes afterwards, the column of animals came into sight, led by the faithful Toad. As they reached the fence, the animals stopped, looking in bewilderment at the vast array of creatures gathered to welcome them.

'Go on, Toad,' Kestrel said affectionately. 'You ought to go first.'

Kestrel's lack of hesitancy was enough to tell his friends that the welcoming party was no surprise to him. He smiled at their quizzical expressions.

'Don't keep them waiting,' he said. 'They've been expecting you for a long time.'

Toad looked from Kestrel to the reception and back again with some nervousness, but finally, with the urging of the other animals jostling behind him, he gave himself a little shake and passed through the gap.

The old Stag watched them come. Toad, whose speckled

breast began to puff with pride as he advanced, was followed by Fox and Vixen, Weasel, the hares and rabbits; then came the hedgehogs and squirrels, the fieldmice and voles, and after them Mole, Badger and Adder. Finally, in the very rear, the three birds, Tawny Owl, Kestrel and Whistler, actually walked the last few yards.

The old Stag remained motionless until it was clear that the last of the party had entered White Deer Park. Then he lowered his great antlered head, and at once a tumultuous sound of cheers broke over the newcomers. There were shrieks and cackles, roars, squeaks, barks and croaks – in fact, welcoming shouts in every conceivable register of voice.

The old Stag walked forward to meet them and, beginning with the delighted Toad, greeted everyone personally, down to the very smallest and youngest fieldmice.

After this ceremony had been performed, the mass of cheering creatures flocked forward and surrounded the weary heroes, congratulating them anew with the utmost enthusiasm. Then, as if at a signal, they fell back as they divined that the great Stag was about to speak.

'We have all looked forward to this day,' he said, speaking for all the inhabitants of the Park, 'ever since we first heard from our feathered friends of your journey. Nothing I can say can add to the tremendous greeting you have already so deservedly received, except by summarizing everyone's feelings here today. On behalf of *all* the inhabitants of White Deer Park, may I say, quite simply, welcome.'

'Thank you most sincerely,' said Fox, 'for a welcome as heart-warming as it was unexpected. We had no idea our journey was of such interest to you.'

'Oh, my friend, you're all celebrities, you know,' returned the Stag. 'We all want to hear about your adventures, and there's no one more eager than myself. But I know you must be tired, and we've no wish to exhaust you. Fox, if you'll bring your friends this way, we've prepared a spot where you can all rest without fear of disturbance for as long as you wish.'

'What wonderful kindness,' Fox responded on behalf of all.

The animals, after again exchanging many personal greetings with their new neighbours, followed the old Stag and his escort of young hinds to a soft, ferny hollow, surrounded by whispering birch trees, and strewn with dry grass specially cropped by the finest teeth of the herd. None of them was long in availing himself of this luxury. In reply to the Stag's kind enquiry as to when he might return, Fox said that by dusk they would all be completely refreshed, and would welcome his company and that of all his friends.

'What a marvellous reception,' Mole said when they were alone.

'I think I know whom we have to thank for the arrangements,' said Tawny Owl drily. But Kestrel just winked.

When the animals awoke, the ground had dried and the moon was gleaming, pouring its silver light through the leaves of the birch trees. Beyond the trees, it shone on the white coats of the assembled deer, giving them a ghost-like appearance.

Seeing signs of life in the hollow, the deer moved forward, and behind them, around them, above them, and intermingling with them, the other creatures of White Deer Park came to hear the story of the journey from Farthing Wood.

This pleasant duty was, of course, assigned to Badger who had finished composing the song that he had sung to his friends in the quarry.

Just before he began, the old Stag signed for everyone to be silent as, along a makeshift path behind the hollow, stepped a dark human figure.

'It's the warden on his rounds,' explained the deer. 'Nothing to fear from him.'

An excited cry from Vixen arrested every creature's attention. 'It's our Naturalist!' she cried. 'Look!'

And sure enough, now divested of his various accoutrements, the long-travelled band of animals was still able to recognize their friend from the cattle pasture, who had been so enthralled by their appearance.

'A cheerful ending indeed to our journey,' Badger remarked and, smiling happily at his audience, began his song.

# Epilogue
# In the Park

Now that the animals had at last reached their journey's end, they all found themselves so busy for the first week or so, establishing new homes and adapting themselves to a new life, that they scarcely caught a glimpse of each other.

For all of them the wide spaces of the Reserve were theirs to explore, without fear of hindrance or any human intervention. Unaccustomed to such peace, after weeks of stealth and caution on their journey, the animals spent whole days selecting and then rejecting sites for their new abodes, determined to settle only in areas that were the perfection of their individual ideas.

But eventually each animal was content, and then the

bonds of mutual sympathy and comradeship that had been forged during their travels began to tug at every one of them.

There was a day when Mole, who had constructed a network of tunnels close to Badger's new set, dug his way into one of Badger's chambers, just as he had done in Farthing Wood.

As it was only early in the evening, Badger was still dozing. He grunted, and looked up. 'Oh, hullo, Mole,' he said drowsily. 'Well, this is a surprise.'

'A pleasant one, I hope?' Mole asked, a little hesitantly.

'Of course it is,' Badger replied quickly. 'Where have you been hiding yourself?'

'Oh, I've been busy making myself comfortable,' replied the little creature, wiping some stray specks of soil off his nose. 'So have you, no doubt.'

'Yes, indeed,' Badger nodded. 'But it's all done now.' He got up and shook himself. 'I haven't seen any of the others recently, have you? At least, not to talk to.'

'No,' said Mole. 'I only saw Weasel one evening, when I had to surface for a drink. I was thinking how nice it would be to see them all again.'

'Yes,' said Badger. 'We really ought to arrange something. I know where Fox and Vixen have settled. We could go and pay them a visit later on, if you like.'

'That *would* be nice,' agreed Mole.

The two animals continued talking while the evening wore on, exchanging views about their new home and neighbours, and about how quiet everything seemed. When they sensed that it was quite dark outside, Badger led his friend to one of the exits and, after he had thoroughly tested the air for strange scents, they emerged together.

They found Vixen at home who told them Fox was out foraging, but he presently returned, accompanied by Tawny Owl.

All the creatures expressed great delight in seeing each other again, and Fox remarked that the need for companionship seemed to be making itself felt at about the same time in many of the Farthing Wood party, for on the previous day he had encountered Toad and Hare who had both suggested that they all meet in the Hollow.

It appeared, when they began to compare notes, that all of them had seen at least one of their old friends in the last day or two. Tawny Owl had been sought out by Kestrel, and the hawk had also spotted several of the voles and rabbits while he had been flying over the Park. Eventually, it transpired that the only one nobody had seen or, at least, heard of was Adder.

'He was never the most gregarious of fellows,' remarked Tawny Owl.

'Oh, Adder's all right when you get used to his strange ways,' said Badger. 'You've got to learn to take him with a pinch of salt.'

'At any rate we couldn't agree to meet up and leave him out,' said Mole loyally.

'I think I know where I might be able to find him,' said Fox.

The others looked at him, but he would not be drawn.

'Leave Adder to me,' he said. 'I'll get Toad to help me locate him. The rest of you can round up the others tomorrow, and we'll meet in the Hollow the next night.'

His friends agreed enthusiastically with this arrangement, and they parted happily.

The next day Fox found Toad, and mentioned his idea of Adder's whereabouts to him.

'The pond?' echoed Toad. 'Oh yes, he's been there watching the frogs every evening.'

Fox nodded. 'I thought as much,' he said. 'Let's go and see him.'

So Toad and Fox made their way to the pond, and there, by

the water's edge, they found Adder slyly watching the antics of the plump green frogs with a greedy eye. He evinced not the slightest embarrassment at the arrival of the two beasts. 'Good evening,' he said calmly. 'I've been trying for some time to introduce myself to our new neighbours here, the Edible Frogs.'

'I don't know if you'll ever get the chance, as I personally advised them to spend as much of their time as they could in the centre of the pond,' Toad told him with some irony.

Adder again showed no trace of his feelings. He merely slid away from the pond's edge, and asked them to what he owed this unexpected pleasure.

'The whole party is meeting again tomorrow night,' said Fox. 'Will you come?'

'Certainly I'll come,' replied Adder, 'if you're sure my presence will be desired?'

'Of course it will,' Fox assured him. 'I'm sure the animals haven't forgotten that our success in reaching the Park is owed, to a large extent, to a certain action on your part.'

Adder, typically, was not inclined to acknowledge the compliment. 'Where do we meet?' he asked.

'In the Hollow,' answered Fox.

'I shall be there,' said Adder.


Fox and Vixen were the first to enter the Hollow on the next night, and they recalled how it had been the animals' first resting-place after their arrival in White Deer Park.

Their friends arrived at intervals. Tawny Owl came first, and very soon Badger and Mole joined them. The squirrels turned up with Kestrel, whom they had awakened from his roost. He was still yawning.

Then there was a flurry of activity, as most of the animals yet to come arrived together – the voles, the fieldmice, the hedgehogs and the rabbits. While greetings all round were still being exchanged, Weasel, accompanied by the hare family, joined the gathering.

Shortly afterwards, with a slightly bashful air, Whistler stepped carefully into the Hollow, attended by another heron who looked round shyly.

'I hope you don't mind,' Whistler said apologetically as he introduced her to everyone, 'but my young friend here and I have lately become . . . well, almost inseparable.'

'We're delighted,' said Vixen. 'And how attractive she is.'

Whistler beamed, and the female heron coyly murmured something polite.

'A very *interesting* arrangement,' Tawny Owl said sarcastically, parodying Whistler's remarks during the final stages of their journey.

'There you are, Owl. It's not too late for you to follow suit,' Vixen replied with an impish grin, turning the tables on the other bird.

'Humph!' snorted Tawny Owl, ruffling his feathers in a rather disconcerted manner, and trying very hard to appear indifferent.

Fortunately the arrival of Adder diverted the party's attention and Tawny Owl was able to regain his composure.

'You're quite a stranger these days,' Badger remarked to the snake good-humouredly when it was his turn to greet him. 'Can we blame your seclusion on the wiles of a charming young female?'

'There's no need to blame my seclusion on anything except my choice in not visiting anybody,' Adder replied. 'However, if I should happen to come across a creature of the sort you describe, I suppose I shall be seen even less.' His sharp words were belied by a very deliberate grin which caused Badger to broaden his smile.

Some moments elapsed before the animals realized that the only member of the party who had not shown up was Toad.

They all went to look out for him.

'Very strange,' Fox murmured. 'He can't have forgotten?'

'I hope he's all right,' said Mole, looking concerned.

'Oh, he'll be along in a minute, I'm sure,' said Badger. 'Don't worry.'

It was Tawny Owl who spotted Toad's approach first. 'I can see him,' he announced coolly. 'He seems to be taking his time.'

Soon afterwards most of the others could see him too.

'Whatever's he doing?' asked Weasel. 'It doesn't look as if he knows the right direction.'

'He's certainly not coming by a very direct route,' remarked Squirrel. 'He's meandering all over the place.'

They watched the solitary Toad in fascination. He was swerving from left to right and then back again. Then for a while he came steadily on, on a straight course, only to veer away at a tangent quite abruptly, for no apparent reason.

Tawny Owl lost his patience. 'Come on, Toad!' he called irritably. 'We are all waiting for you.'

At the sound of Owl's voice, Toad stopped dead. He seemed to notice the presence of his friends for the first time.

'Hallo!' he called, and followed the salutation by a strange noise – something like a cross between a croak and a hiccup. He then began excitedly hopping towards them, his final hop sending him head-first into the Hollow.

While he righted himself, the animals exchanged puzzled glances.

'How wonderful to see everyone again,' he said in a loud voice. 'I'm sorry I'm late, but I was diverted out of my way. I fell into a puddle! Tee-hee-hee!' Toad collapsed into a fit of giggles, and then hiccupped loudly several times.

'Toad, whatever is the matter with you?' asked Fox.

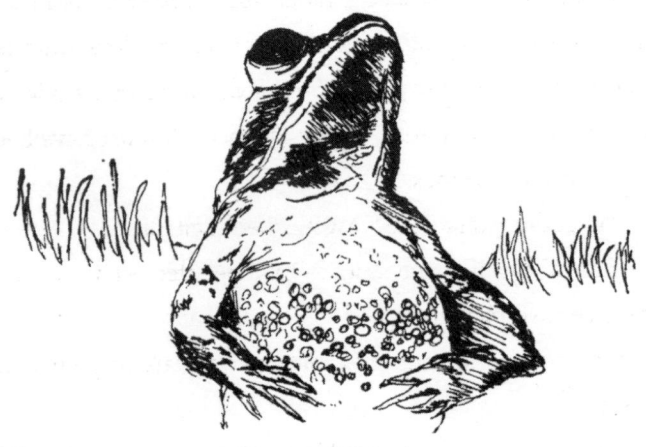

'He's drunk,' drawled Adder. 'I've seen humans act the same way.'

'I *am* drunk,' Toad shouted. 'And it's marvellous!'

'Now calm down and tell us what happened,' said Fox.

'I had been down at the pond, you see,' Toad explained, 'and on my way here I came past the Warden's lodge. I suddenly became aware of a delicious smell – a strong smell: sort of tangy and sour. I was looking round to see if I could find what was making it, and I blundered into a little pool of golden-brown liquid. Immediately the wonderful aroma was all round me, and I couldn't help tasting just a little drop. It was absolutely delicious. I had another drop . . .' Toad paused and looked round with a wide smile for effect.

'The rest of the story is, I think, predictable,' Fox commented wryly.

'Well, really, I only had a mouthful . . . or two,' Toad said mischievously. 'More of the liquid was trickling down into the pool from a big wooden container that was lying on its side just inside the Warden's fence,' Toad explained. 'It must have been seeping through a crack.'

'What did it taste like?' Mole asked excitedly.

'Something like the smell. Only sweeter. And . . . well, almost a musty flavour.'

Mole looked towards Fox, but did not dare ask what was in his mind.

Fox, however, had no trouble in reading his thoughts. 'No, no, Mole, I couldn't allow it,' he said emphatically. 'It wouldn't do.'

Quite unexpectedly, however, Badger for once took an opposite view.

'Oh, I don't know, Fox, really,' he said reasonably. 'The stuff's probably harmless enough. After all, Toad seems to be quite all right.'

Fox divined there was some self-interest behind Badger's attitude. 'Well, it's up to you, Badger.' He shrugged. 'It's your responsibility.'

Immediately all of the party, except Vixen, began to mill around Badger. Toad's face brightened even more, if that were possible.

'We'll just drink each other's health,' Badger said, trying to moderate the animals' excitement. He turned round. 'Well, Toad, will you show us the way?'

'Gladly,' cried Toad.

The little band of animals moved off full of anticipation, Fox and Vixen following in their wake reluctantly.

'Do you think it might be possible for us to move at least part of the way in a straight line?' Adder asked drily, after a while. But Toad did not hear.

Eventually they arrived at the famous puddle and, once Badger was assured that the youngsters in the group were safely under the control of their mothers, he allowed the male animals forward to sample the liquid.

One by one they lowered their muzzles, snouts and beaks to taste. Toad stood on one side, watching for their reactions with immense interest.

It had genuinely been Badger's intention to allow Mole and the other animals to satisfy their curiosity only, but he had not reckoned with the persuasive properties of the brew. He himself was the last to drink, and as he stepped back smacking his lips to get the full benefit of the flavour, he felt a warm glow begin to spread through his body.

He looked at his friends, who were all smiling at each

other, and he smiled himself, knowing they were experiencing the same beneficial feeling as he.

Gradually, in ones and twos, the animals went forward for a second taste of the liquid that made them feel so good.

'Toad was right!' piped up Mole. 'It *is* delicious.'

'Fox, do try some,' said Badger.

'Yes, go on, dearest,' Vixen urged him in a low voice, not wishing that he should be the odd one out. 'I shan't mind,' she added.

Fox walked forward with a distinct lack of enthusiasm. He lowered his head. Then he looked up again at his friends. 'I drink the health of each and every one of you,' he said warmly, and drank from the pool. He raised his head and smiled. 'It *is* very good,' he admitted.

There was now a rush as all the animals scrambled forward to drink Fox's health, and then Vixen's, and then each others'. Even Toad joined in.

'I propose a toast to all the creatures of White Deer Park,' said Toad noisily.

'Particularly one creature,' added Whistler, throwing his head back so that the liquid in his bill ran down his throat, while the young creature in question looked on smilingly.

'Let's drink to all the female animals from Farthing Wood,' said Hare gallantly, thinking affectionately of his own mate.

The animals' heads went down again.

By now the full effect of the warming properties of the

liquid had made itself felt, and the animals began to laugh at each others' glowing faces and sparkling eyes. Fox sensibly rejoined Vixen.

The rabbits gambolled off in sheer high spirits, running rings round each other. This was a spur to Hare, who raced after them and, getting on his hind legs, pretended to box each one of them.

The squirrels shinned up and down the Warden's fence, flicking their tails like quicksilver, while the hedgehogs looped themselves in and out of the palings as if they were trying to knit them together with their prickles.

Tawny Owl went and hung himself upside down by one foot from a tree inside the Warden's garden. Then he swung backwards and forwards, making hooting noises.

Adder, whose capacity for strong drink seemed to exceed everyone else's, continued to imbibe from the pool, completely heedless of the voles and fieldmice who frolicked round him in their new-found courage.

Suddenly, Badger sat down heavily and burst into song, and Mole, recognizing the refrain as the one of Badger's own composition, joined in heartily.

Weasel, who was lying comfortably on his back, took up the tune, and Kestrel, perching on top of the fence, screeched his own unmusical accompaniment. Soon all the animals who knew the words of Badger's song joined in, while those who did not hummed, and Tawny Owl continued to hoot as his contribution.

So the story of their journey from Farthing Wood was retold – not to an audience, but for their own amusement and enjoyment. And as they sang, they relived their adventures, the hazards and the excitement of that long march. Even Adder paused in his drinking and lent his lisping voice to the concert, and the animals found themselves unconsciously drawing together into one group as the priceless feelings of friendship and loyalty entered again, and for ever, into each heart.

The voices reached a crescendo as the song ended with their arrival at their new home and then Fox, without a word, led the column of animals and birds quietly back to the Hollow where they quickly fell into the most peaceful and undisturbed sleep.

So the creatures from Farthing Wood began their new life, and as the months passed their first winter in the park approached.

One day Toad met Adder near the pond. 'Well, it looks as if your waterside vigils will soon have to be curtailed,' he said to the snake. 'My friends the frogs tell me the mud is nice and thick at the bottom of the pond, and it's almost time they settled there.'

Adder's self-possession was, as usual, unaffected. 'There are a few days yet before the ice forms,' he replied enigmatically. 'Those frogs will have the pleasure of my company a little longer.'

But he never did succeed in catching any.

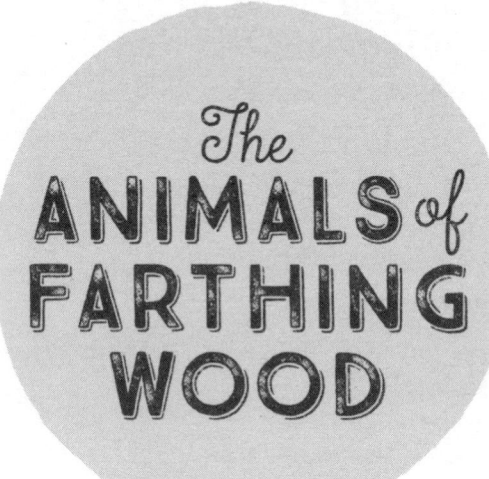

**Turn the page for special bonus material . . .**

# Who's Who in Farthing Wood

*The animals of Farthing Wood are all very different characters,*
*but they must work together to reach White Deer Park.*
*Below is a short glossary of who's who in Farthing Wood.*

### Adder
*He tries to keep his violent impulses in check, but his friends*
*fear that he may be untrustworthy. He thinks of himself before*
*others, and can be cruel and cutting when he speaks.*

### Badger
*Wise and thoughtful, the leader of the group. He is*
*both a planner and a doer, although he can sometir*
*get a little carried away by the sound of his own v*

### Fox
*Clever and quick, he always has an idea in his head, and can*
*get the group out of trouble faster than anyone else. He is*
*willing to brave great danger for the good of his friends.*

### Hare
*He is a good and responsible father who*
*cares for his family.*

### Hedgehog
*Brave and kind but slow. He is quick to act, but lacks spe*
*this may prove fatal.*

### Kestrel
*Sharp and quick, he sometimes struggles to empathise with*
*other, more vulnerable, animals.*

### Mole
*Silly, greedy, slow but good-hearted, Mole is the cause of much concern to his friends, but they love him anyway.*

### Pheasant
*Vain and foolish, he often leads the group into danger with no idea he is doing it.*

### Rabbit
*A nervous, slightly foolish animal with a large family.*

### Tawny Owl
*A very dignified bird, who holds himself rather aloof from the rest of the group, he can nonetheless act quickly to protect his friends when necessary.*

### Toad
*The group's guide, he is brave and tenacious even in the face of great danger.*

### Vixen
*Fast and intelligent, she is free-spirited but her love for Fox makes her decide to become part of the group.*

### Vole
*Highly-strung and liable to panic. He speaks for the smaller animals of the group, the fieldmice, voles and squirrels and hedgehogs.*

### Weasel
*Quick to act, but sometimes lacking in courage – he can panic in dangerous situations.*

### Whistler the Heron
*He joins the group on the way to White Deer Park, and although he is its newest member, he is very caring, always willing to act to save the other animals.*

# Q&A with Colin Dann

### Where did the inspiration for Farthing Wood come from?

Farthing Wood is not based on an actual place, but rather a typical area of woodland and countryside in the South East of England where I've always lived. I was pleased with the name I invented, only to find with surprise in later years that there are indeed places called Farthing Down, Farthing Pond and so on.

### Talk about the writing process – how did the book change between first idea and final draft?

This was my first attempt to write an animal story. I did plenty of research on British wildlife in order to supplement my own amateur enthusiasm for the subject. Then I chose the characters I wanted to write about and fleshed out the adventures they'd be likely to meet on their long journey. I wrote the whole story in pencil, something I've always done, before (in those days) turning to my typewriter. I find it the easiest way to make alterations and corrections as I proceed. By the time I had a finished manuscript I'd spent the best part of a year composing the story.

### Was *The Animals of Farthing Wood* inspired by any of your own experiences?

No, not by my own experiences, but by my concern for the plight of wildlife in this country, particularly the South East, the most developed part, where so many species have suffered a decline in numbers due to habitat loss.

### Is wildlife preservation something you felt passionately about at the time? Is this still the case?

Yes, I did and still do. As time has gone on, the need for wildlife preservation has become ever more urgent.

### How difficult was it to get into the mindset of your animal characters?

It wasn't difficult. The animals I wrote about have their own particular lifestyles and preferences which seemed to me could be used to develop their characters regarding each other and also in the face of the dominance of the human race.

### Do you think that animals can be people?

No. But they have their own characteristics which are well known - the resourcefulness of a fox, the timidity of a rabbit, the determination of a toad to return to his place of birth to breed, and so on, which can be expanded into believable methods of behaviour, almost along human lines as it were.

**A lot has changed since you wrote the book in 1979. Do people still have the same concerns about conservation as they did then? Could the book still be written today – or, if it was, what would you keep the same, and what would you change?**

Concerns about conservation now are hardly ever out of the news. Back in 1979 there were certainly concerns but not on such a level. This just illustrates how much more vital it is now to take action to preserve species before it really becomes too late to do so. If I were writing the book today I wouldn't make any changes, but maybe the emphasis on the real threat of extinction to some creatures would ned to be reinforced. For instance the butcher bird (the red-backed shrike) has all but disappeared from the British countryside since the book was originally written. Hares are rarer and in the South East there has been a massive drop in hedgehog numbers.

**What other books would you nominate to become modern classics?**

*The Incredible Journey* by Sheila Burnford, *Life on Earth* by David Attenborough, *The Secret Diary of Adrian Mole aged 13 and 3/4* by Sue Townsend, *War Horse* by Michael Morpurgo and *Sold for a Farthing* by Clare Kipps are all classics in my book!

# Activity: Create your own nature reserve

*'A Nature Reserve is a piece of land – or water – of exceptional value and interest because of the rare animals or plants – or both – in it.'*

*'It sounds wonderful,' said Hare's mate. 'Peace and security all the time. No hiding. No running away. No guns!'*

Animal refuges are incredibly important – as Fox, Badger and the rest of their friends know, sometimes they can be the difference between life and death. Not everyone has a garden, but there is always something you can do to help out the animals that live around you.

• If you do have a patch of ground near you, try to make sure that you let at least part of it become overgrown. Grubs and minibeasts can live in it, providing food for birds and small animals just like Mole and the mice and voles.

• Try to persuade the adults you live with to let you build a small pond. It's important that it has different depths – birds will drink and bathe in the shallows, while deeper areas house insects and newts.

• If you are lucky enough to have a pool or a water feature near you, make sure there is always an easy way out. You don't want to end up trapping animals, as happens to the friends in the swimming pool in Chapter 6!

• Pile up old leaves in the corner of any outside space – this provides a safe habitat for frogs and toads.

• Don't just feed birds bread! Make sure your feeders are somewhere cats can't easily get to, and put out cheese, porridge oats, apple slices, bacon rind or even bits of baked potato.

• If you live near a busy motorway or road, see if you can persuade the adults around you to build a tunnel underneath it, to help animals cross safely – just as the hedgehogs do in Chapter 26, animals can very easily become confused when faced with cars.

# Could you survive to White Deer Park?

The animals of Farthing Wood know that they must reach White Deer Park – even though they may not all survive the journey. But could you make it all the way? Take this test to find out.

1. You come to a river. It's been raining, and the water is high and running very fast. You know you need to cross - so what do you do?
a) Jump in on your own and try to swim across.
b) Jump in with your friends – you can support each other, so long as you all keep your heads.
c) Keep on walking until you find a shallower place to use as a ford, or a small bridge – that water is dangerous!

2. You go into a field and discover some very shiny and un-nibbled lettuces. They smell a little strange, but you're hungry. What do you do?
a) Eat them!
b) Try a leaf or two and then wait for an hour or so to see if you're affected.
c) Leave them. There could be something wrong with them.

4. The farmer has spotted you – and he's not happy! He thinks that you've been stealing food from his fields. He's got his dog, and a gun – what do you do?
a) Sit tight. You're so cute that he's bound to forgive you.
b) Try to outwit the dog. It's used to taking orders, after all, and you're a free-spirited wild animal.
c) Run! Let's hope you're faster than the dog or the gun.

5. You come to a road. The traffic is moving fast, and you're frightened. How do you get across?
a) Run as fast as you can, and hope you slip between the oncoming cars.
b) Go slow. Caution is important!
c) Watch the traffic carefully. Is there a pattern you can spot? Maybe if you wait for night to fall, the cars will get less frequent.

6. Fire! It's cutting off the route you wanted to take, and it's moving fast. What do you do?
a) Run at it – try to break through quickly.
b) Stay still and see what happens.
c) Turn around and run away as fast as you can – the most important thing is to stay alive.

# So, how did you do?

Mostly As: You wouldn't last a day in the wild! You need to become much more cautious to survive.

Mostly Bs: You're on the right track, but you're still making some worrying decisions. You need to be careful if you want to reach White Deer Park.

Mostly Cs: You're a natural survivor. You're guaranteed to reach your goal – and to bring as many of your friends with you as possible.